A TALE OF TWO CRUSHES

CORI COOPER

Apeiron

Copyright © 2025 by Cori Cooper

Coristories.com

Book Cover by Cori Cooper

ISBN: 9781953491862 (Paperback)

ASIN: B0FS4VGZND (Kindle)

To: Grandma and Grandpa Turley
For reading my very first stories

Chapter One

"A multitude of people, and yet a solitude."
A Tale of Two Cities

My old Dodge pickup shuddered to a stop in the parking space between a convertible and a lifted truck. I kept my hands on the steering wheel, gripping it so tightly that my knuckles turned interesting shades of white and pink. I leaned forward to stare through the windshield at the massive, sprawling building that was Prescott High School.

Home of the Badgers.

What was I supposed to do now?

I didn't know how to be a new student. I've never been a new student before. I went to the same schools with the same people for my entire life. I didn't even know where the front of the building was.

I should have made a better plan. I mean, we moved to Arizona almost a week ago, and since going to school is kind of the law, I knew somewhere deep down that I would have to be a new student eventually. It's just that the last couple of months had been a complete whirlwind. It wasn't until I pulled into the school parking lot just now that it really hit me that I wasn't in Durango anymore.

This must have been how Dorothy felt when her house landed on the Wicked Witch of the West.

I rested my forehead on the steering wheel so that I wouldn't catch the eye of any passing students who knew where they were going and what they were supposed to do next. It was starting to wig me out.

My phone twitched with a text, and since I wasn't doing anything besides questioning my parents' life choices, I picked it up.

> *Happy First Day Of School!!!! Go Knock Them Dead!! I Love You!! You Got This!!!!*

Oh, Alicia! Thank goodness! I really needed her capital letters and ridiculous number of exclamation marks right now. I missed her so badly it was like someone just put my soul through a paper shredder.

I shot back a quick text that sounded way more confident than I felt, then pulled my reluctant booty out of the vehicle, along with my backpack and phone. As soon as I shut the door of my truck, the bell echoed through the parking lot.

It was fine.

I already knew I'd end up walking into class late today. Dad had a deadline and Mom was helping Grandma, which meant I had to take the twins to the middle school. So, it was inevitable. They got to school on time, and I was late. I had mentally prepared myself to awkwardly walk into my first class and have everyone stare at the new girl, but it still made my heart skitter into my throat to think about it.

I stepped onto the curb, somehow misjudging where it was, and stumbled onto the sidewalk quite gracefully.

Not.

My cheeks burned all the way around to the back of my neck as I righted myself. I don't care what Embarrassment told me to do; I refused to see if anyone noticed. I swung my backpack onto my shoulders and started walking like I knew where I was going.

First stop was the front office. Dad and I tried to complete all my class registration online before we left Durango, but the system was finicky. We weren't able to upload my personal documents or do anything other than submit my name and previous school information. I had a folder in my backpack with all the stuff they needed to complete my registration, including my transcript.

Now all I had to do was find that front office.

It would be nice if high schools were like malls—for a lot of reasons—but specifically, I'd appreciate one of those big map things that showed you where everything was. All color-coded and bold-lettered. That would be awesome. I'd like to order one of those, please.

"Hey."

I didn't turn around at first because there was no one in this state or city that knew me well enough to 'hey' me.

When the word came a second time and then a third, my brain finally caught on that someone was, in fact, trying to get my attention. Shame wondered if whoever this was wanted to comment on my spectacular tripping back there, then told me to keep on trekking. Curiosity wondered why anyone would need to talk to me badly enough to call out three times.

Curiosity won out in the end. It usually did, I just couldn't stand suspense.

I turned around. A guy jogged the rest of the way to where I stood. His brown hair looked highlighted with honey gold streaks, which created quite the contrast with the grubby tennis shoes and plain blue t-shirt he wore. Most guys I knew that spent time coloring their hair also spent money on designer clothes. So, just guessing here, it was probably his natural color.

Nature had been kind to him.

When he got close enough for me to see his eyes, their clear blue color made my breath stall in my throat. It was like his eyes had crawled out of the ocean on a summer day.

Cynicism piped up again.

Why in the world did he want to talk to me?

Every single high school movie I'd ever seen came back to haunt me. Guys didn't usually talk to nerdy new girls unless they had something nefarious planned. He was probably jogging over to mock my Target jeans, or fake ask me to prom and then throw raw eggs at me from the sunroof of the limo.

"Hey!" He paused to catch his breath. "Is this your first day?"

Oh no. Was it that obvious?

Now Paranoia joined the party. Did I look so out of place, so abnormal, so bizarre that everyone was going to know I came from a totally different state? The rest of high school stretched out before me in an instant: a lunch table for a party of one, Friday nights playing solitaire, prom night teaching myself to knit washrags while I watched reruns of *I Love Lucy*.

I shook myself to get out of my head and said yes in a way that sounded like I had a slow leak and had also suddenly morphed into a snake.

The guy's smile never wavered. "Awesome! Welcome to Prescott! My name is Asher."

And then he stuck out his hand.

Wait, I was confused. Was he really trying to shake hands with me? That was what my parents did. Shouldn't we be high-fiving or fist-bumping or something…I don't know…cooler than a handshake?

Insecurity really needed to take a hike. It was kind of driving me bonkers.

I took his hand and gave him a solid two shakes. "Hi, Asher. I just moved here from Colorado. My name is Holland."

"Holly?"

I slipped my hand away from his and pushed a lock of hair behind my ear. "No, actually, it's Holland. Like the country."

I loved my name with a fiery passion, but it always did take some explaining.

"No kidding? That's lit! I wish my parents thought of something like that for me. I could be Africa or, like, Germany." His voice deepened and added a ton more aggression. "Nice to meet you. My name's Germany, ja."

I stepped back with a fake shiver. "It's probably good they didn't. I'm not sure if you're about to mug me or hug me."

"Hug you, for sure." He laughed, then his eyes met mine and a zip went down my back like someone just doused me with cold water. At first I thought it was just me, but Asher cleared his throat and looked away so quickly that I had to think he felt it too.

"So, anyway. Holland, who moved here from Colorado, do you know where the office is? I can help you get there if you need some help. I'm happy to help." He winced. "And now I'm going to stop saying the word *help*."

"Curious." I tipped my head to the side. "Does Prescott have its very own high school welcome wagon?"

I was teasing, but also serious. I don't think my school in Durango had any kind of new student outreach program, so maybe this was an Arizona thing? Or a Prescott thing? Basically, I needed to know if talking to me was something Asher was assigned to do or something he wanted to do.

"Yes ma'am." He tipped an imaginary cowboy hat and hooked his thumbs through the belt loops. "We Prescottonians have a long-standing tradition of high school hospitality 'round these parts." Then he fake spit into the bushes next to me.

I stared at him.

Wait, really?

He laughed. "Actually, I saw you pull up just now. You looked stressed."

That was way more believable, and also super embarrassing.

"Hey, it's fine." He smacked the side of my arm, grimaced, then shoved his hand in his pocket. "Seriously though, don't worry about it. No one else noticed; I'm just a highly observant guy." The tips of his ears were slowly turning red.

He looked so uncomfortable. I wanted to help put him at ease, but the only problem was, um, me. Alicia gave me a shirt for my birthday last year that said, 'Keeping it real awkward', and that pretty much summed me up right there.

"Did I say *Prescott* wrong?" I blurted.

Asher looked up and smiled. "You can say it however you want to say it."

"Yeah, no." That's not how anything worked in this world. There's a right way, and there's a wrong way. I didn't want to start this new chapter the wrong way. "How do you say it?"

"Prescott."

Yeah, I thought so. When he'd said Prescottonians, it sounded like Press-kit. I'd been saying it like Press-scott. I'm so glad I caught that before I really embarrassed myself.

"You can say it however you want, really," Asher continued. "I promise there's nothing in the state legislature about city name pronunciation, and no masked ninjas are going to drop from the sky to take you away if you do it a different way than someone else."

Even though it was incredibly weird, I could stand there and watch his lips say the word *legislature* for the rest of my life. "Are you sure? That ninja thing is totally believable."

"Right?" Asher glanced over his shoulder. "And yes, I'm sure. My dad's a senator, so I know the state legislature inside and out. You know how some kids get fairy tales at bedtime?"

I nodded.

"Yeah, well, me and my siblings got state legislature."

I couldn't tell if he was messing with me or not, and I didn't get a chance to ask. Another bell rang, reminding me there was something in this world besides Asher's sea-blue eyes.

"Oh no, that's the tardy bell. Is that the tardy bell? You're going to be late." I pulled my phone out of my back pocket and shoved it in the front pouch of my backpack. I didn't want to forget and sit on it once I got to class. "You should go."

"But you need help finding the office, right?" he said, totally calm in the face of a tardy. "And probably your first class."

I don't know why I was trying to convince him to leave me when I really did need help.

"Correct answer? Yes, actually, that would be great if you could show me where the office is."

"I'll walk you there." He jerked his head toward the school. "It's on my way."

"Really?" I skipped to catch up and struggled to keep up with his long strides. He noticed my frantic hop-walking and slowed down to a more comfortable pace.

So thoughtful.

Asher grinned. "I'm an office aide first period."

Well, that was convenient.

Even though the walk was short, Asher covered a lot of ground. He pointed out a landmark to help me find the parking lot where my truck was waiting, the cafeteria where mostly lower classmen ate lunch, and the football field where his brother was apparently the star quarterback.

Other than the landmark to get back to my truck, I barely heard any of the words he said. I was too caught up in the *way* he said them. He had a slight drawl on some of his syllables that was just delicious, and there was a dimple in his left cheek that peek-a-booed every once in a while. I was too busy watching for it to make another appearance, I didn't notice when Asher turned toward a set of double doors. I caught myself just before I plunged head-first into some hearty yellow bushes.

Asher held the door open for me and stood back so I could go first.

"Thanks," I said as I scooted through. My eyes stayed glued to the shiny floor as Embarrassment took over. I really hoped Asher couldn't tell that I was checking him out. I was probably so obvious. In fact, I'm sure I was. It's just that I'd never felt this way before. I'd only daydreamed about it, and Mr. Darcy, a lot.

Asher was too good to be true.

There had to be something wrong with him.

I surveyed him from the corner of my eye, trying to find a flaw. His hair really was fantastic, but his eyes were kind of close together, and his nose threatened to turn beaky as he got older.

Those were some mighty fine straws I was grasping at. Who was I kidding? Asher was, like, the perfect guy. It was bonkers to fall for him already; I'd just met him. What was happening?

I tried to distract myself by focusing on the floor, which was not thrilling, then the trophy case display. A basketball on the top shelf caught my eye.

1999 Champions Whittaker, Mackay, Hernandez.

A game ball, I think, and those were probably the star players. Under that was an obviously old picture of a football team autographed by Linus Whittaker, whoever that was, and a big 'Can Do' sign in blue and gold.

That's all I got to before Asher led us into the office.

"Hey, Mrs. Goddard." Asher saluted with two fingers. "This is Holland, um..."

"Morriss."

"Holland Morriss." He shot me a killer grin punctuated with that dimple. "She just moved here from Colorado."

Mrs. Goddard looked like she stepped right out of an Austen or Dickens novel. Her puffed pompadour and high-neck blouse secured with a cameo brooch were at least a hundred years behind the now.

A pair of glasses hung around her neck by a golden chain, which she lifted to secure the glasses on the end of her nose. She swiveled in her chair to face a computer screen and started moving the mouse through a bunch of screens.

It totally messed with my mind. A piece of parchment with a quill would have been a better fit, or, with a bit of a stretch, a typewriter might work too.

"Holland Morriss. There you are. I thought I remembered you." She looked over the top of her glasses and smiled at me. "Great name, by the way."

"Thanks," I said, even though my parents really deserved the credit.

"Perfect. It looks like everything is here." She glanced at me when I let out an astonished breath of air. "I know, the system is a bear. Luckily it was working correctly long enough for me to contact your previous high school, so I think I have everything I need as far as your transcript goes. Let's go through it together, though, to be sure. Do you have your documentation with you?"

I pulled the folder out of my backpack and pushed it across the desk. She took it and opened it primly. "I'll need to make copies, of course."

"Of course," I murmured.

Asher held out his hand. "I'll do it while you guys figure out her schedule."

Mrs. Goddard smiled in gratitude and turned back to the computer. "Let's see. Obviously we have the core classes... No, hmmm..." She took off her glasses and let one side dangle as she squinted at the screen. I shifted from one foot to the other until her eyes found me. "You're doing concurrent enrollment with BYU-Idaho?"

I nodded.

Originally, the plan was for Alicia and me to graduate from high school with our CNA certification from Colorado State University, then room together while I finished nursing school and she went on to medical school.

That was before Grandma got sick and my parents decided we were needed in Arizona. BYU-Idaho had a great concurrent enrollment program that I could finish up online. It was the best option now that my future was as clear as scrambled eggs.

"So..." Mrs. Goddard peered at the screen a moment longer, then looked at me again. "You're just here for electives, is that right?"

Actually, I was hoping to take a full class load at school and also do college classes at night so I could graduate a year early. I didn't anticipate having much of a social life in a new city with zero friends.

But that was before I met Asher.

He walked back into the office, my folder in one hand and the copies in the other. When he handed me the folder, my fingers brushed his hand, sending sparklers up my arm.

"Thank you, sir." Mrs. Goddard smiled at Asher briefly as she took the copies from him.

While she flipped through my papers, I kept glancing over at Asher. He was just so hard to ignore. My eyes loved him as much as they loved an old bookstore with shelves of leather-bound classics.

Which was a lot. Old bookstores with shelves of leather-bound classics were practically my most favorite thing to stare at until today.

Asher watched Mrs. Goddard make notes on the screen, his forehead divided into a bunch of lines. He didn't seem to notice that I couldn't stop looking at him.

That was a win, I think.

Wait, what had Mrs. Goddard asked me? There was a weird tingle in the air like a question left unanswered. Something, something, something about...oh yeah, electives! I closed my eyes to focus in on the words I needed to say next instead of the words, 'yes Asher, I'll marry you even though we're seventeen and I only met you some minutes ago'.

Dang, this crush was a doozy. It hit me hard and from out of nowhere. I needed to get a grip before it morphed me into a creepy, obsessed stalker.

I opened my eyes and snapped my attention onto Mrs. Goddard. "That's right. I'm just here for the electives."

"Well, then, you have a choice of Spanish, French, or German for your language. You can do P.E. or play a sport, and you'll need to choose something artsy from this list." Her hand hovered over the printer next to her desk until a paper finally emerged. She flourished it across the desk and set it where I could read the options.

Asher coughed.

And it sounded like the word *Spanish*.

I turned my head slightly, my eyebrow raised.

Asher coughed again. *Spanish* was much more obvious this time.

"Spanish?"

Asher nodded with a grin.

"Spanish it is," Mrs. Goddard said without looking up. "There's only one class for juniors, so that will be second period. Let's try and get your classes to line up so you can come late and leave early. You'll want that extra time at home to work on college classes."

I wasn't so sure I did anymore, but okay.

Maybe I should just stop pretending and ask Asher what his schedule was, then copy that.

And after that, maybe I could stamp the word *DESPERATE* on my forehead in permanent ink.

Come on, Holland. Focus. Get a grip.

"Yes, this will work." Mrs. Goddard turned the computer screen. "First period is at home. Second period, Spanish. Third period, girls P.E.—I believe they start with a yoga unit, so that's nice. Fourth period, lunch. Then fifth period you can choose between theater, art, and creative writing. Sixth and seventh periods, you will spend at home."

Asher didn't cough in with an opinion, and I was getting a grip anyway, so I asked for creative writing. I wasn't very good at drawing, and I hated being in front of people, but I loved to read, so that seemed like the best option. I waited for Mrs. Goddard to enter it in and print my schedule.

"Since you have this period free, you may sit in the office, or Asher can show you around the school."

"I'd love to see the library," I blurted before she'd finished talking. I adored libraries almost as much as bookstores. Plus, then I'd be able to spend some more time with Asher instead of sitting in the office like I'd gotten in trouble. That was a no brainer really.

Mrs. Goddard handed over my schedule and nodded to Asher. "Thanks, dear. You have a wonderful first day."

"Thank you." I folded the paper and tucked it into my back pocket. "It was nice to meet you, Mrs. Goddard." I did a little accent on her last name so that I almost sounded like Emma in the BBC movie.

The thought made me smile.

Chapter Two

•❤•❤•❤•❤•❤•

"No one who can read, ever looks at a book, even unopened on a shelf, like one who cannot."
Our Mutual Friend

Asher peppered me with questions the whole walk through the winding halls. As soon as I answered one, he was ready with three more. I felt like a supreme narcissist by the time we reached the library.

I was all prepared with a barrage of questions for him, except that when we walked through the door, I got walloped by the scent of a billion old books crammed together. I stopped for a second to shut out the world and breathe it all in. When I opened my eyes, Asher smiled at me.

"What?" I pushed hair away from my face, then didn't know what to do with my hands, so I let them sort of float back down to my sides.

"Let me guess, you really love to read?"

I was as transparent as one of those windows lined up behind the librarian's desk. "Correct answer: yes. I really do."

That was easy to admit; what was hard was sending the question back to him. What if he hated reading? What if he thought *David Copperfield* was a magician and *Oliver Twist* was a dance move? Those would be deal breakers, and I wasn't quite ready to let go of my instantaneous and completely irrational crush on him just yet.

This had never happened to me before. I mean, sure, I got the occasional crush on some of the guys in Durango, but since I knew most of them since I was a baby, it was more of a maybe-I-like-you-now-that-you-don't-eat-crayons-anymore kind of thing.

Alicia told me once that there was something magical about falling for a guy you barely knew. That was after one of her visits to the university library where she pretended she was already a college freshman to flirt with the hotties. I thought she was all kinds of crazy for doing that, but now I kind of got the reasoning. Since I didn't have any information on Asher—other than the fact that his dad was a senator—he could be whoever I wanted him to be.

At least until reality checked in.

But that was easy to ignore. I could let myself believe he was practically perfect in every way for at least a week before reality caught up to me. Two weeks if reality was sluggish.

It could be blissful and exciting because the possibilities were endless.

I just hoped Alicia wouldn't rub it in for the rest of forever when I told her.

Forever is a very long time.

"Holland?"

I blinked rapidly as I adjusted from my thoughts to Asher's face. "Yeah?"

He laughed as we wove through tables toward the back corner of the library. "Never mind."

"No, what were you going to ask?"

Asher moved his hair out of his eyes. "It's stupid. I just noticed you say 'correct answer' a lot when you're answering questions."

Did I? I tried to think. Maybe I did. Was that weird?

It was weird.

I was weird.

Asher went on. "I've never heard someone say that before; it's awesome! I want to start doing it too. Would you be totally offended if I copied you?" His smile was a teensy bit teasing and a lot a bit sincere.

So, wait.

He liked it?

Really?

"I don't know…" I stopped walking so I could pretend to think extra hard. "You have to be really exceptionally awesome to incorporate 'correct answer' into your vocabulary. You *might* have what it takes. I don't know; it's too soon to tell for sure."

He nodded seriously. "I'll practice and we'll see if I can pull it off, yeah?"

"Yeah."

We smiled at each other for what felt like a lot of minutes. I could hear them ticking away on the clock somewhere behind me. It should have been awkward to stare at each other that way, but it just felt awesome.

"So," Asher cleared his throat and started walking again. "What's your favorite book?"

My favorite book? What was that line from *Ever After*? "I could no sooner choose a favorite star in the heavens"? Something like that. Whatever it was, it was so true. All the books I'd read and loved were my friends.

"I can't pick just one."

"Top three, then."

That was a little easier. "*A Tale of Two Cities, Gone with the Wind*, and *Sense and Sensibility*."

"*Sense and Sensibility*?" His forehead scrunched into a billion lines that I proceeded to read between.

He didn't know what that book was, which meant he probably only read comic books or the dialogue between characters on his video games. I tried not to let Disappointment crush me, but it has a really fat butt.

Asher went on. "That's interesting you like *that* Jane Austen book and not *Pride and Prejudice*."

Wait.

Wait, wait, wait, wait.

He knew *Sense and Sensibility* was a Jane Austen novel without me explaining three times?

No way!

He had to be a reader. He had to be! Could I be that lucky? I needed more information, like, yesterday. I turned my head to see him more clearly and tried to be smooth like butter. "So, uh, why is that interesting?"

Asher ran his hand along a cart of books as we passed by. "I've never heard anyone say they loved an Austen book that wasn't *Pride and Preju-dice*, and usually they only love that one because they have a huge crush on Colin Firth or Matthew MacFayden."

I was officially taken aback. It took a second to get words to come out of my mouth. "I've never heard a guy my age rattle off Mr. Darcy actors like he'd watched them a million times." My lips twitched. "Explain your-self. Really, I have to know more."

Asher gestured to a table near a fake potted tree. "You've been car-rying that bag forever. Want to put it down?"

I slipped the backpack off my shoulders and set it on the table. It wasn't heavy at all; the only things in it were my lunch, some stuff to decorate my locker, gel pens, and that file of all my personal stuff. "Don't you have to get back to the office?"

"Eventually," Asher smiled. "There are twelve other office aides. It's essentially a free period. In retrospect, I should have just taken a free period, except I wanted the extra credits so I can graduate early."

"Yeah?" Was it too much to hope that he wanted to go to college in Colorado like me?

"Yeah," he shrugged. "I thought it might be good to get out of here sooner."

"Sooner than what?"

"Sooner...than, you know, graduation." Asher slipped into the plas-tic chair with a Sharpie heart in the center of the back and tapped his finger. "Isn't that what you're doing? With your concurrent enroll-ment?"

"Yeah." I sat across from him and folded my hands on the table. "Me and Alicia— she's my best friend back home, I mean, back in Durango—we had this whole plan to graduate from high school with our associate's degrees and then go to Colorado State together while we intern as nurses. But then my family moved." It was hard to feel as sad about it as I did before I met Asher.

He made moving to Prescott look really good.

"Why Prescott?"

I squinted one eye. "Are you trying to get rid of me? I've only been here, like, seventy-two hours."

Asher laughed a lot louder than my dorky comment deserved. "No, please stay forever. I was just wondering why, of all the places in the world, your family chose to move to Prescott, Arizona."

"Yeah, still sounds like you're trying to get rid of me."

Asher shook his head all flustered, and I took pity on him.

"Correct answer: because my grandma lives here and she fell a few months ago. She broke her ankle. It was pretty bad; she needed surgery and everything. Her recovery is super slow, and my dad is her only child. Since he can work anywhere, he and my mom decided it was stupid to live so far away."

"That's nice your dad can work from anywhere." Asher stretched his arms over his head, making his biceps look extremely mesmerizing.

"Mmm hmm." I tried not to stare, but I had this thing for biceps. It was weird, I knew it, but what's a girl to do?

Luckily, Asher distracted me from massive oogling with a question.

"Who's your grandmother?"

"Shawna Morriss."

Asher's arms fell from behind his head and hit the table with a loud smack. "You're kidding. I do yard work for Mrs. Morriss. She lives down the street from my grandparents."

Was he just messing with me? Prescott was way bigger than Durango; the chance that he really knew my grandma wasn't that high. "On Juniper Drive?"

"Yeah, she's great! I went over when she got home from the hospital and raked pine needles. I tried to take out the trash and vacuum too, but she wouldn't tell me where the stuff was. She was too worried that the cupboards and closets were messy."

"Oh my gosh, that's totally my grandma!" I laughed and caught Asher's eye. My neck went insta-hot like I just got an impossibly bad sunburn. "That was so nice of you to help her."

"Yeah." Asher was suddenly fascinated with a ding on the table. "Well, she makes really good cookies."

Didn't I know it. Her chocolate chip cookies were magic, and the snickerdoodles? Well, there are no words. One of my earliest memories is of Grams waking me up at five o'clock on a Saturday morning during one of our summer visits to make snickerdoodles and eat all of them for breakfast. My mom was so ticked, but it was seriously the best.

My trip down memory lane stretched too long. Now there was the most awkward silence in the history of awkward silences hanging over us. I hurriedly went through everything we'd talked about since we came to the library, trying to find something that I could resurrect as a topic. But my brain was being bonkers; all it wanted to do was revel in the thought that me and Asher were meant to be.

Oh, wait!

"So, you never did explain how you know that Jane Austen wrote both *Sense and Sensibility* and *Pride and Prejudice.*"

Asher coughed. "Didn't I?"

"No," I said, shaking my head. I was not about to let him off the hook. "You didn't."

"And I guess there's no way you're going to forget I said that?"

"No way."

"Well then." Asher straightened his shoulders and twisted from one side to the other. "The reason is I have a mom and two older sisters who are obsessed."

That didn't explain anything. I was obsessed with books, and my brothers thought reading was something you had to do as a punishment when you went over your screen time.

My skeptical look did not go unnoticed.

"Yeah, okay. Well, my family is tight, and my sisters are bossy. Until they both moved out, they made us listen to the audio books for *Pride and Prejudice, Sense and Sensibility*, and *Mansfield Park* on all the family road trips."

"*Mansfield Park*?" That wasn't usually a favorite. "And what did you think of that?"

"I think my sisters chose that one to torture my brother because he hated it so much."

I laughed. "Yeah, it's kind of the worst. I'm an Austen fan, and I can barely get through it. Fanny Price is just so..."

"Spineless, right? I want to reach through the audiobook and smack her."

And I wanted to reach across the table and smack Asher. But not the kind he was talking about.

This was crazy!

I'd met this guy, like, forty minutes ago, and I wanted to kiss his face off. I was not that kind of girl. He was either a wizard and put a spell on me, or there was something in the Prescott City water that completely zapped my senses.

And wizards aren't real.

So...

Asher went on. "Yeah, the worst. I don't mind *Northanger Abbey*, though. I mean, I only watched the movie, the one with the chick from *Rogue One*, but I liked it. It's funny how her imagination makes everything all dramatic. Actually, I think that's where Isla gets it from."

"Isla?"

"My oldest sister. She's married and has two kids now, but she is still the queen of drama queens."

"I bet that makes life interesting."

"Yeah, her husband is a saint."

I noticed a loose string on the hem of my jacket and twirled it around my finger. "Have you seen, listened to, or read *Emma*?"

"You ask me that after everything I just told you?" Asher tipped his chin down in a very grumpy-old-man impersonation that told me he *had* seen, listened to, or read *Emma*, but that gave me absolutely no information about what he thought of it.

"Did you like it?" I tugged the string and rolled it into a ball between my thumb and forefinger.

"Do *you* like it?" Asher threw the question back so fast that it took me a moment to respond.

"I asked you first."

"I asked you second."

My forehead furrowed so that I could see my eyebrows crawl together. "Why are you avoiding the question?"

"Why do you think I'm avoiding the question?"

"Asher!"

"Holland!" He laughed but wouldn't give in.

"You are seriously acting like my little brothers." I held up a hand. "Twelve, that's how old. Do you really want to act like a twelve-year-old?"

Asher gave me a mischievous smile that pretty much turned my stomach into gelatinous goo. "Sometimes I do. It's way less pressure."

I narrowed my eyes, trying to pin him with steel. I have mastered this look on my brothers; they crumble in its wake. Sometimes it even works on adults. It's that powerful.

And Asher was no exception.

He held up his hands in surrender. "Okay, you got me. I give. I'm avoiding your question because I can't talk about Jane Austen anymore. My man card is evaporating, I can feel it. I had to distract you."

"And you went with middle schooler?"

Asher shrugged. "There are worse things."

I seriously couldn't think of any.

But maybe it was better that he did. I've never talked to a guy about my love of Jane Austen or any of the classic novels from that time period. Once, I brought up Charles Dickens on a date with a guy in Durango, and he started talking about chickens. It was so weird. No one else, not even Alicia, got my love of classic literature.

Which was why it was so totally thrilling to sit across from Asher and hear him say Jane Austen's name like he knew who she was, instead of like something that made him want to throw up.

I seriously wanted to marry him.

Was that even legal?

I had to stop gawking and say something before it got even more awkward.

Awkwarder?

Awkwardly?

Anyway, words. I needed words.

"Okay, I'll let you change the subject without protest if you answer this one last question about Jane Austen."

Asher spread his hand out. "That's fair."

"Do you *like* her books?"

Asher slumped forward. "Holland, my man card."

Which meant he did. He wouldn't be concerned about the stupid man card—whatever that was—if he didn't like them. It wouldn't matter.

Okay, it was official

I loved him.

"Fine, you don't have to answer anymore girly questions. No more Jane. So, then, what is your thing?"

"Whew," Asher let out an exaggerated breath that sounded very drama-queenish to me. "Like, in general? Or book wise?"

"Let's start with books, since we're on the subject and are kind of surrounded by them."

Asher glanced around at the library shelves, then focused back on my face. "Correct answer..." He paused and gave me a smile that melted my bones. "Did I do that right?"

I pretended to consider. "I'll allow it. Favorite books?"

"Correct answer: I like sci-fi and fantasy. *The Lord of the Rings*, *Dune*, stuff like that." He tapped the table with one finger. "Have you, uh, read any of those?"

Had I read them? Oh, please. He was looking at the girl who saved up for two years to buy the Easton Press leather-bound illustrated edition of *The Lord of the Rings* with *The Hobbit* included. It sat on my shelf with no purpose other than looking stinking awesome.

And it did a very good job of that.

"Are you kidding me right now? I love *The Lord of the Rings*. Best. Books. Ever."

His finger froze in mid-tap. "Wait, you've read them? You didn't just watch the movies?"

"Actually," I said, tossing my head, "I've read them multiple times, and I refuse to watch the movies."

Asher stared at me for so long that my leg started to jiggle under the table. Paranoia barged back in to wonder if I had an enormous booger dangling from my nose or something. Why else would he stare at me like that?

I turned my head to the side to rub my nose as discreetly as I could.

"Wow," Asher said finally.

Great, there really was a booger, and it really was enormous. Wow-worthy enormous. I bent over, pretending to look for something in my backpack so I could clear both nostrils with the end of one of my sleeves.

Nothing showed up, so no booger.

Then, what was he wowing about?

I sat upright and jabbed a stick of lip balm in the air. "It's so dry here." I opened it up, swiped it across both lips, and then mushed them together.

"Is it?" he asked absently.

I dropped the lip balm back in my bag without thinking, which meant it was gone forever in the deep crevasses of the main pocket.

Asher placed his hand, palm down, between us and leaned forward. "You've really never seen the movies?"

It took me a minute to realize he was still talking about *The Lord of the Rings*. I'd had a thousand thoughts since then. Thoughts about boogers and lip balm; they sort of drove away everything else.

"Really, really," I answered and winced. That's what my brothers said all the time. Middle schoolers. I was quoting middle schoolers. "I mean, I really haven't."

"And you refuse to?"

I couldn't tell if he was impressed or disgusted. Until this moment, I didn't know there was such a fine line between the two.

"Correct answer: yes."

"Wow."

I felt the need to explain, even though he didn't ask to know the whys and what fors. "Most of the time, books into movies are so disappointing that it kind of ruins the books for me. I didn't want that to happen to Frodo and Sam. After all they've been through, they deserve better."

Asher shook his head slowly. "I completely agree. This is freaking me out. Everyone I know likes the movies better. My best friends, my family... My brother thinks the books are insanely boring. He snored through most of it the last time we drove to California. He can't stand Tom Bombadil."

"I love Tom Bombadil!"

"Me too," Asher said, and then started back up with that staring thing again. "Wow. Holland, I know I just met you and this is crazy, but I have to ask. Do you..."

A shrill bell rang through the super quiet library. The contrast was so ridiculous that it made me jump out of my seat. Asher rose quickly but way smoother than I did. "First period is over."

"Yeah." I bent down for my backpack strap and swung it over my shoulder.

"So, second period is Spanish. Are you ready?" Asher asked.

I nodded.

He jabbed a fist in the air. "Vamos!" Then he looked around, his ears turning pink. "That was really weird, I'm sorry. I meant that I'll show you the way there if you're ready."

"Sure, I'm ready." A smile tickled the corner of my mouth. I placed a fist on one hip and the other in the air. "Vamos!"

Asher doubled over, laughing too hard to stand up straight. I kept the pose until he got a hold of himself. He tried to talk twice but stopped himself both times to gulp for air.

My arm in the air was starting to fall asleep.

"What? Did I say it wrong?"

"No, it's not that." Asher finally got the words out. "I guess I didn't realize how incredibly dorky I looked until I saw you do it. Remind me to never do that again."

I lowered my fist to slap his arm. "Actually, I think you're just jealous you couldn't pull it off as well as I did."

"Yeah, something like that." His eyes warmed my skin everywhere they landed.

I looked away, pretending the strap on my backpack was in desperate need of adjusting.

"Hey, Holland?"

"Yep?" I glanced up.

"Are you going to stick around for lunch?"

I stopped fiddling as I tried to think through the mush that had become my brain. Was I going to stick around for lunch? I couldn't think what that meant. I brought a lunch. I was going to eat it. But the sticking part? Yeah that wasn't computing at the moment.

Why did such a simple question sound so complicated?

"I'm just asking because it'd be cool if you sat with me and my friends. I didn't know if you planned on going home or off-campus or whatever, but if you aren't, you can eat with me, with us, in the commons. We always sit in the corner by the drinking fountain. And now I'm babbling. Just tell me to shut up already and put me out of my misery."

Okay, now I understood what he was asking. I tried not to grin like a fool. "How about I tell you yes instead?"

Asher looked up, his ears now a deep shade of red. "Yeah?"

"Yes, I'd love to. Thank you."

A slow grin took over his face. "Yeah, you know, I just felt sorry for you. New kid, eating all alone in a room full of people who are laughing and talking. It would be so pathetic." He let out a long breath and crossed his arms over his chest. "I don't want to have to look at that."

"For reals?" I tipped my head to the side. The look on my face must have been borderline lethal because Asher took a few long steps away to put some distance between us.

His laugh, though, boiled over and came back for me as if it couldn't and wouldn't leave me behind.

That had to mean something.

Like, maybe he was kind of, sort of, a little bit into me too.

Chapter Three

"It is a pleasant world we live in, sir, a very pleasant world."
The Old Curiosity Shop

Asher waited for me outside the gym when I emerged triumphant from P.E. Mrs. Goddard was right about the yoga unit; we spent the whole class period in Sukhasana—basically crisscross applesauce—while the teacher led us through some breathing exercises and guided meditations. I breathed and meditated with half my mind while the other half replayed every single thing Asher said to me since we met in the parking lot. I also spent an alarming amount of time recreating the way he looked while he said all of it.

So, yeah. P.E. was pretty awesome.

"Holland!" Asher lifted a hand so I could see him in the crowd.

Like I could miss him.

"Hey!" I waved back, ignoring the stares from some of my P.E. mates as I hurried to where Asher waited. No doubt some of them liked the guy. How could they not? My major crush developed after about five minutes of talking to him. Just imagine what it would feel like if I'd known him for years.

Yeah, I would probably sit around all day, every day, doodling his name and daydreaming about prom. It was a very good thing I hadn't known him my whole life. I would get nothing done.

"How was P.E.?" Asher smiled at a girl who called hi as she went by. Even if I wanted to feel jealous about that, I couldn't. His eyes never left my face while he talked to me.

"Awesome!"

"Really?" His smile dropped into an exaggerated frown. "Are you one of those girls who lives for competitive sports? Are you going to challenge me to an arm wrestling contest in the middle of the lunch room and beat me so badly that my man card never recovers?" He tilted his head down the hall and started walking in what I assumed was the direction of the cafeteria.

I fell into step beside him. "You're really worried about that man card."

"Actually," he said as he stopped mid-stride as someone cut him off, then started walking again, "if it were up to me, I wouldn't care at all, but my brother is constantly questioning my man card, and now I have a complex."

I shot a smile his way. "That is a very sad story."

"You have no idea. My brother has a water-proof, titanium-clad man card the size of one of those clearance signs they twirl on street corners when a store is going out of business."

I giggled. "There's a visual."

"Well, it's true. Ask anyone, and they will give you a five-minute mono-logue on how perfect my brother is. You need proof? Here's proof. Every girl I've ever liked meets him and decides they like him better." Asher glanced at me. "So, basically, you are never going to meet my family. I hope you're okay with that."

It was suddenly extremely hard to breathe.

Did he just tell me he likes me?

My heart began beating double time, and it had absolutely nothing to do with dodging other students while trying to keep pace with Asher. Thoughts swirled around my head like soft serve, each one too slippery to hold on to or examine.

"Oh no." Asher slowed down but didn't stop walking. We'd just round-ed a corner and were in full sight of the commons.

"What's wrong?"

"Tenley has that look." Asher grimaced.

Almost all of the wh- questions jumbled to the tip of my tongue, which of course meant there was no room for any of them to come out.

Who is Tenley?

What look?

Where is she?

Why is that look a problem?

Asher stopped walking completely now, causing a slight traffic jam behind us. People figured it out and went around; it was barely an inconvenience, but we still were on the receiving end of a couple of dirty looks.

That is, until Asher grabbed my arm and pulled me over to the side of the hall. When that happened, everything else faded into oblivion. I didn't even notice there were people around anymore, much less anything about their looks. Because Asher was touching my arm.

I never knew I could be this pathetic about a guy.

And I kind of loved it.

"I should probably warn you about Tenley. We call her Commander Controversy. She's always in the middle of advocating for something or the other."

It took me a second to answer because I was still reeling from his hand on my arm. Every sense was hyper-focused on that one little area. I had no idea there were so many nerve endings on my forearm.

I took a deep breath. "That doesn't sound like a bad thing."

"It's not bad, exactly. Just super intense. Tenley is suuuuuuper intense."

"Asher!" Tenley's hands were on her hips as she stalked across the commons toward us.

Asher fixed a smile on his face and let go of my arm.

Sadness.

"Hey, Ten. What's up?"

She stopped right in front of him. Even though she was at least a foot shorter, it was like she towered over Asher. "Don't you dare 'what's up' me. Did you talk to the faculty?"

Asher sighed. "Can I eat lunch before we start this? I'm starving."

She glared at him for a moment, said, "Fine," then whipped around and stomped back to the corner by the drinking fountain.

"Wow," I said. For that one brief moment, it was like all the oxygen was sucked out of the room.

"Right? She's really great, just intense." Asher started toward his friends. "Come on. If I put this off too long, it will be like Mount Vesuvius up in here. And I really am starving."

It wasn't until I got to the corner of the commons, clutching my backpack with my lunch bag nestled inside and looking down at Asher's friends, that I started to feel incredibly awkward. There were two girls and three guys lounging on the carpet or propped against the wall. Five pairs of eyes fixed on me like the Tower of Sauron as Asher introduced me to the group.

"Holland? Like the country?" one of the guys asked. His fingers flicked the pages of a thick book in his lap. I couldn't tell what book it was, but I'd be willing to bet it was *World of Warcraft* secrets or a *Dungeons and Dragons* guide. Every person I ever met who was into one of those things wore a black shirt with a silver dragon sprawled across the front.

Like this guy.

"That's right." I followed Asher's example and dropped to a seated position on the floor. That was a good idea; now we were all at eye level instead of everyone checking out my nostrils.

"So, Holland," Asher pulled a lunch bag out of his backpack and used it to point at the dragon shirt guy. "That's Bryan. Next to him is Ethan."

A preppy-looking guy with Ken-doll blond hair and hipster glasses smiled in my direction.

"Then Ryker."

He was tall and thin with not one but two lunch trays on his lap and knees. Both were filled to capacity with a variety of food.

"Dara."

She was wearing a headband with black cat ears and a printed t-shirt that looked like the Cat Woman costume. Also, she had whiskers drawn from her nose to her cheeks, probably with black eyeliner. My mom helped me put together a similar costume when I was in the first grade. It was a little weird that this girl was wearing a cat costume to high school and it wasn't even close to Halloween.

Dara looked up with a super bright smile and gave an enthusiastic wave, and my first impression was instantly bamboozled.

She reminded me so much of Alicia.

I guess weird doesn't look so weird when it's accompanied by friendliness. Wow, that was deep stuff. Someone should cross stitch that onto a pillowcase.

"And, that's Tenley. You met her already…sort of. Well, you saw her anyway. When we were in the hall earlier." Asher took a big bite of a turkey sandwich.

"Hello." Tenley smiled warmly as she leaned forward. "Holland, what is your opinion on the growing trend of teenage vaping?"

"Wow, Ten, give her two seconds to breathe before you do that." Ethan took a bite of an apple, waving it around to punctuate his words. "Normal people don't start conversations that way."

"Normal?" Tenley's voice cracked on the high note. "Excuse me? Normal isn't even a thing."

"You know what I mean," Ethan said, rolling his eyes.

Tenley sat up, ramrod straight. "I'm sorry, but I think it's important to find out right away if someone's views align with mine. Then I don't waste precious time trying to be their friend if it is really not going to work out."

"Savage," Dara growled, and then licked the top of her hand.

Ryker threw a wrapper at her. "Don't do that while I'm eating."

She blinked in surprise. "What?"

"That licking thing. It makes me think of cats."

"Thank you," Dara bowed her head.

"No, you didn't let me finish. Because then I think of cats licking, which makes me think of what they lick, and then it grosses me out, and I can't eat. I have practice after school. Eating is necessary."

Dara stared at him a minute, then hissed.

And she did look exactly like a cat when she did it.

"Come on, Ryker," Asher extended a hand. "You know Dara likes to stay in character. Cats lick. It's what they do."

Dara licked her hand really slow, watching Ryker the whole time. He tried to glare, then gave up and grinned. "You're obnoxious."

"Thank you." She smiled, and even that looked catty.

Bryan glanced up from his book, which I could now see the cover of.

It was a *Dungeons and Dragons* manual.

Nailed it.

"Tenley, I don't know if you noticed, but none of us in this corner agree with all of each other's views, and yet, here we are."

"That's different," Tenley sniffed. "We've been friends for so long that we don't really have a choice anymore."

"I'm for sure rethinking my choice of friends," said Ethan. He shot Tenley a look and tossed his apple core in a nearby trash can. When it thunked into the metal interior, he elbowed Ryker and raised his hands in the air.

"Score!" Ryker said through a mouth full of food.

Asher leaned closer to me like he was getting something from his bag, but instead he whispered, "I'm so sorry."

I just smiled.

This was not the weirdest group of people I'd ever encountered, believe it or not. And actually, I kind of loved their banter. It reminded me of Alicia and my friends back home. I mean, back in Durango.

Just one big, weird, dysfunctional family.

My stomach chose that moment to let out a horrifying roar. "Oh!" I pulled out my lunch bag and used all my concentration to unroll the top so that I didn't have to look at any of their faces. I could hear the sniggering, and that was humiliating enough.

Ryker said, "See what happens? Eating is necessary."

"What'd you bring?" Asher peered into my bag.

I'm sure he was thinking that would take the attention off my very vocal stomach, but it just made it worse as I pulled out two bento boxes and stacked them on the floor in front of me.

Everyone stopped what they were doing to watch.

If my stomach wasn't going berserk and telling everyone all about it, I would have left my lunch in my backpack and eaten it in the bathroom before my next class. Just to avoid the questions. I took a deep breath and started opening the lids of my bentos.

"What the..." Bryan tipped his head to the side. "I can't actually identify anything in those containers."

I set the lids on the floor and tried to explain. "My mom is super into health."

"So am I," Ethan said, wrinkling his nose. "But I don't know what I'm looking at."

"What's that?" Ryker poked a tentative finger at the homemade cheesy cashew dip my mom made with nutritional yeast. "And that?"

"Cashew dip and kale chips."

"What and what?" Tenley looked alarmed.

"And this," I held up a baby carrot to stop the gawking, "is a carrot stick."

Dara snorted, then covered her mouth.

"Seriously, you guys. You act like you've never seen food before." Asher shook his head and took another bite of his sandwich.

"Is that food?" Ryker pointed to my lunch.

Asher just rolled his eyes.

"Wait, wait!" Tenley's eyes lit up. "Are you vegan to prevent animal cruelty?"

"Come on, Tenley!" Ethan shook his head. "It's too soon."

She opened her mouth like she was about to unleash all of Hades on Ethan's head, so I felt like it was my duty to interrupt. Not only would that keep Tenley from thrashing Ethan with her words, but then I could explain my lunch. I'd rather just tell the story instead of becoming some mysterious enigma.

"Actually, my mom's parents both died really young, one of cancer and the other of heart failure, so she is crazy healthy. We don't eat anything packaged unless it has five ingredients or less, and we can recognize all of them. She makes everything at home, even this cheese." I held up a mozzarella ball before I popped it in my mouth. Once I chewed and swallowed, I concluded with, "It's not bad. Plus, I want to be a nurse, so I think it's good to practice being healthy."

"So, you don't eat pizza?" Ryker held up a slice.

"Sure I do, but it's homemade and usually has a cauliflower crust 'cause my mom likes to throw vegetables into everything."

Ryker wrinkled his nose, which made the blaring lack of vegetables on both of his trays all the more obvious.

"I think that's cool." Asher put down the cookie in his hand. "Good for your mom."

"Thanks." I shrugged, not sure if that was the best way to respond. It wasn't really my decision how my family ate, but I guess I was saying thanks in lieu of my parents. Maybe that made sense.

"I would totally sneak junk food into my room. I'd have a whole stash under my bed," Bryan said as he flipped the page of his book without looking up.

"Seriously," Tenley put a hand over her heart. "I might die without barbeque potato chips."

I didn't really know what to say to that. No big deal. It was fine. They were just wigged out because of the anomaly. If I kept sitting with these guys, they would get used to my weird lunches in a couple of weeks. I could deal with the gawking until then.

Asher watched me for a minute, then turned to Bryan. "Hey, Bryan, do you still have that D&D tournament this weekend?"

And off the conversation went without me. Asher was my hero.

I finished eating everything in the box with dip, carrots, and kale chips then set it aside. My stomach was appeased, but I really loved my mom's mozzarella balls with basil, so I ate those too and tried to keep up with the conversation.

Tenley zipped up her lunch bag with flourish and stuffed it in her backpack. "Are you done eating, Asher?" She stared at the cookie sitting forlornly on top of his bag.

He leaned back and stretched his legs out in front of him. "Yes."

"Can I have your cookie?" Ryker asked.

Asher pushed it toward him.

"Thanks."

"Okay, enough messing around. Let's do this." Tenley scooted closer to where Asher and I sat, pulling a notebook along with her. She opened it to a page filled with scribbles and pressed the page into Asher's face.

His eyes crossed as he tried to read.

"What do you think?" Tenley's foot twitched, bouncing the notebook.

Asher took it out of her hands, set it in his lap, and bent over.

"Asher?"

"I'm reading."

Tenley blew out a huge gust of air. It ruffled her bangs, giving her a disheveled appearance.

I wanted to help Asher out, like he'd helped me earlier, so I tried to think of a way to distract Tenley while he read. I finished chewing the last of my caprese salad and swallowed hard. I had to take a couple drinks out of my water bottle before I could talk around it.

"So, what's this for?" I gestured to the notebook.

"Oh!" Tenley said. "Thanks for asking. The school just announced on their Facebook page that they are no longer going to sponsor Runway Careers. They can't fit it into the budget." She said those last words like they were covered in vinegar and lies.

"Wait, what?" Dara sat up straight, forgetting her purry cat voice. "Are you serious?"

"As malnutrition," Tenley said in a grim voice.

"But, they've done Runway Careers for, like..." Ryker stared at the ceiling as his words slowly vanished.

"Since my grandpa went to school here," Asher said without looking up from Tenley's notebook. "He started Runway Careers. Him and my grandma."

I felt like a nerd, but I could no longer put off the inevitable. "What is Runway Careers?"

Dara answered, her face all lit up. "It is the coolest tradition in the world! People in the community sign up, then they come to Runway Careers, dressed like they would for work. You know, police officers in uniform and so on. If you can talk a member of your family into doing it, then you get to announce them as they walk the runway. And *then*, there's a meet and greet where you get to talk to the person who actually has the career you want and find out more! It is so cool. My favorite part is that we also get to dress up like the profession *we* want. Cause dressing up is my jam, right? It used to be pretty low key, but now it's a huge deal. We rent out the country club, and there's this insane catered dinner and strobe lights and a DJ... Crazy. Anyway, freshman year, one of the seniors had an aunt staying with them who was a real actress from California. That's how I found my life calling." She paused, like she just realized she wasn't in character anymore. The cat woman voice returned. "It's amazing. They can't cancel it. It would be a cat-astrophe."

Ethan groaned.

Okay, I still didn't get it.

Tenley must have noticed the confused look on my face because she put a hand on my knee, and her voice softened. "It's basically a fashion show for careers."

"That's what I just said." Dara lifted a hand.

Tenley ignored her. "It's an important part of our decision-making process. Without Runway Careers, we'd all end up playing dorky games in our mother's basement for the rest of our lives."

"Hey!" Bryan's head shot up. "*Dungeons and Dragons* takes skill. And math. Lots of math. You'd know that if you'd ever played it."

Tenley tossed her head. "I don't have time, Bryan. I'm too busy saving the world. You're welcome."

Bryan glared for a minute, then went back to his book, grumbling to himself.

"D&D is pretty complicated," I said because Bryan looked so forlorn and because he was the only one who didn't make a big deal about my lunch. Even if that was because he was absorbed in his game book, I still owed him one. "It takes lots of skill."

The grateful look Bryan gave me was its own reward. "You play?"

"I have played. Once. My friend Candice had a tournament last New Year's Eve. It was super fun. I was a gnome librarian named Nim."

Tenley stared at me in disbelief.

"I've never seen a librarian character before." Bryan flipped the pages of his book, scanning the paragraphs. "Did you mean a barbarian?"

"No," I shook my head. "I was a librarian. Candice made it up for me, with powers and everything, because I'm such a bookworm."

"A bookworm?" Tenley jabbed her finger in the air. "And which side do you take in the great controversy of electronic versus paper books?"

Ethan stood up. "I'm out."

"Where are you going?" Dara clawed the air in front of Ethan.

"Anywhere but here. My Commander Controversy Meter just maxed out. You with me?" He appealed to each person around the circle, except for Tenley.

"I gotta put some stuff in my cross-country locker, anyway." Ryker stacked his trays and stood up too.

"Perfect, let's go do that. Bryan?"

"Sure, I'll come." He closed the book and stashed it in his backpack.

Dara watched him closely, rising to her feet when he did. "I'll come too."

Tenley's face was expressionless until all of them were out of sight, then impatience took over every one of her facial features. "Are you done reading yet? Seriously, Asher? I could have read it three times by now."

"We all know you're amazing, Ten; you don't have to brag." He set the notebook down, smiling at her look of disgust. "I'm done."

"And?" she leaned forward so far forward that her chin was only inches from the ground.

"And the faculty isn't going to go for it. They weren't happy about losing Runway Careers either; it's a longstanding tradition. But there isn't any money in the budget for it this year. They had to get rid of the tailgate party and pep rally and move prom to the gym. It's tough all around. I think we have to let this go."

"How can you say that?" Tenley bounced upright. "I thought you, of all people, would have my back."

"I do, of all people, have your back, Ten. I just don't know how to make this work."

I'd been half listening as I packed away my containers and empty water bottle. Their conversation didn't really have anything to do with me; I was too new. Plus it didn't apply to me anyway. Alicia and I have had our career path paved since sixth grade. But maybe it was because I *was* new and not invested yet that something clicked into place.

"I might have an idea for you guys."

Tenley was too huffy to look at me, but Asher gave me his full attention.

"I better make sure I understand what's happening first. Are you saying the school has to cut Runway Careers because of budget issues?"

"Yep."

"And that's it?"

Asher tipped his head to the side. "What do you mean?"

"Just, there's not another reason? Like, it's not culturally offensive or violates an amendment or something?"

"No," Asher smiled. "Just budget issues."

"So, I'm not sure how things work here, but back home—I mean, in Durango—when someone wanted to do something, they could start a club. Anyone could do it."

"Okay." Asher's expression encouraged me to go on, but Tenley's did the opposite.

"What are you getting at?" she clipped the words in frustration.

I knew she wasn't frustrated at me, so I let it roll and kept my voice light. "For example, if you want to do Runway Careers and there isn't any money in the school budget for it, you can start a club. You can do your own fundraisers to get the money and put the show on yourselves. At least, that's something students could do in Durango. Is that how you do things here?"

I was afraid to look at either one of them. It was a dumb idea.

"I mean," I fiddled with the zipper on my lunch bag, "it was just a thought."

Tenley jumped to her feet and snatched the notebook out of Asher's hand. "Oh, my gosh. You are brilliant! That is the best idea I have ever heard! I have to go talk to Mrs. Weinzinger. I'll see you guys later."

And just like that, after a whirl of words and notebook pages, she was gone.

I was left feeling a little dazed. "Was that okay?" I asked Asher. "I didn't mean to butt in."

Asher's lips curled into a smile. "Are you kidding? I think you just found your new best friend. Tenley is going to love you forever after this."

CHAPTER FOUR

"It is the most miserable thing to feel ashamed."
Great Expectations

There were only a few minutes left of the lunch period, so Asher and I threw away our trash and headed towards the locker hall. I hadn't had a chance to find mine yet, so he offered to help me.

We walked in silence, him thinking whatever it was teenage boys thought after they ate lunch, and me basking in the look on Asher's face when I told him and Tenley my idea.

It was like he thought I was something special.

So, maybe he *was* into me?

Oh!

I just remembered!

While we were in the library, Asher was about to ask me a question when the bell rang. I had to know what he was going to ask me. I wouldn't be able to concentrate on anything else until I knew.

"Hey," I began super eloquently.

"Yeah?"

"Um..."

Wow, that was even better than the first attempt. I rolled my eyes at myself and tried again. Third time's the charm, right?

"Remember when we were in the library and you were going to ask me something? And remember when you didn't because the bell rang?"

What was I thinking? There was no way he would have a clue what I was talking about. Uncertainty took my hand and swung it as we walked down the hall.

"Anyway, I was just thinking about that and started wondering what you were going to ask me," I said in a rush, the words all squished together, making it practically impossible to pull them apart.

I was such a nerd.

Asher cleared his throat. "I didn't think you heard me. I mean, I was hoping you forgot. Just because I don't want you to think I'm a stalker..." He ran a hand through his hair. "I'm not making any sense, am I?"

"You're not not not making sense."

He stopped walking, "Did you just passively-aggressively agree with me?"

"I'm not not agreeing with you."

Asher laughed. "Your locker is right here, by the way." He took a step forward and slapped the front of locker 119. "Do you have your combination?"

"Yes." I swung my bag around to pull out my schedule. Mrs. Goddard had written my locker and combo at the top. I moved closer to the combination and gave it a couple of good spins to undo whatever the last person did to it. "Are you trying to distract me so I'll forget to ask you what you were going to ask me earlier?"

Asher paused for a moment. "Yes?"

"I thought so." I glanced at the paper and turned the dial to the right, then the left, then the right again, and pulled up on the lever.

Nothing happened.

"Sometimes they jam. Let me try." Asher held out his hand for my schedule.

I paused before I gave it to him.

"I'm not going to hack your locker." He grinned and twirled the dial.

"I didn't think you would."

"Sure you didn't. And you didn't pause to consider it either." He pulled the lever. The locker shuddered, stuck, and then opened.

"Yikes," I said, stepping back. "Is the door going to fly off?"

He shut the locker. "It's just sticky. You try."

I took his place in front of the locker and tried again.

Nothing.

The third time, I did a little jig while I twirled the lock. My dad is a firm believer that dancing a jig and holding your mouth right will fix most problems. It must have worked because the door flew open just fine. Either that, or third times a charm really is a thing for me.

"Awesome!" Asher lifted his hand for a high five. "You did it. And, also, I committed your combo to memory so I can open your locker whenever I want."

I shook my head as I put up a magnetic mirror on the door and arranged some extra folders on the one crooked shelf. When I was done, I shut the door, then turned around and leaned on it.

"So, about that question."

Asher's face went super blank. "What question?"

"Nope." I jabbed a finger in his face. It almost hit his nose. "Neither one of us is leaving until you ask me what you were going to ask me."

"Don't you want to get to class? It's always good to be early."

Yeah, that was true. What was also true was that I wouldn't even be able to concentrate on class if he didn't spill his guts. I would spend the whole period obsessing.

I increased the intensity of my glare.

"Alright, alright, alright!" He lifted both hands. "I was just going to ask for your phone number. See, it's creepy. I'm a super stalker. I haven't even known you for twenty-four hours."

I held out my hand.

Asher stared at it.

I laughed. "Give me your phone, and I'll enter my number."

And then he squirmed. "I don't have my phone today."

"Okay." My hand dropped. "I'll write my number down for you, no biggie. Let me find a pen."

"Wait, don't do that. It will be too easy for me to misplace it, and someone will find it." Red blotches made their way along his cheeks. "How about I put my number in your phone, and you can call me? I know it's weird, but that will work, yeah?"

"Sure," I searched my bag for my phone, unlocked it, and held it out for him.

His hand shook slightly when he reached for it. He bent over the screen, his thumbs moving all over the keyboard. After a minute, he looked up with a sheepish grin. "Sorry to make it awkward. I just—"

"No, it's fine." I took the phone from him and checked that he put something in the contact line. He did, just his first name. A burst of confidence took hold of my tongue. "I'm really glad to have your number. Maybe you could show me the town? I've only visited Prescott a few times; I don't know my way around very well."

A slow smile spread across his face. "Absolutely."

"Great." I tucked my phone away. "I'll call you and we'll do something, then."

"Perfect."

"Fantastic."

"Awesome."

Before I could think of another adjective, the bell rang.

Asher pointed down the hall. "Creative writing is that way." Then he pointed down the opposite hall. "And I'm this way. I guess I'll talk to you soon?"

"Soon," I nodded.

"I'm really glad I met you, Holland."

"Me too, Asher. But, about you." I cringed. So awkward! "I mean I'm really glad I met you, too, Asher. Anyway, I'm going now."

Asher's laugh followed me as I turned in the direction he pointed and started walking. When I reached a bend in the hall, I glanced over my shoulder. Asher was still standing by my locker, watching me walk away with a huge smile on his face.

As soon as the bell rang at the end of creative writing, I whipped out my phone and texted Asher. I'd spent almost the entire class period devising what I wanted to say. Eventually, I found the perfect mixture of casual and interested.

I sent it and stashed my phone away again.

Then Uncertainty started a parade in my brain. It was so loud and full of flaming-baton-twirling chimpanzees that I had to stop walking in the middle of the crowded hall to search for my phone again.

Maybe it was stupid to text him so soon. I don't know. I reread the text to Asher while people jostled my elbows. One guy got me so good that I almost dropped my phone. It slipped out of my hands and would have come down to a stampede of tennis shoes if I didn't have such amazing hand-eye coordination. I snatched it out of the air and gripped it tightly, my heart racing. Not because of the near-death-of-my-phone experience, but because my text was soooooooo dorky.

Needy.

Borderline pathetic.

And it was too late to do anything about it. I already sent it. With all the technology happening in the world, I wish someone would invent a text eraser. People should be able to send a text but then edit or delete it after it's sent, like the way we can edit our Instagram posts.

I had to fix it.

So, I texted again while I walked to my truck.

I text-walked.

I'm not proud.

I pushed send and then felt like an idiot.

I should have just left it alone. I mean, it wasn't great before, but now it was like I'd made myself the spokesperson for the definition of *wishy-washy*.

Ugh!

I pushed the doors out of the school harder than I meant to. My palms stung a little, but the fresh air felt amazing on my flushed face. I took a couple of really good, deep breaths and headed towards the parking lot, trying to think of a text I could send that would fix my stupidity.

By the time I reached the driver's door, I had it figured out.

> *So, Asher, apparently I'm a nerd. I just wanted you to know that I'm grateful for your help today, and I'm glad you gave me your number so we can hang out. That is, if you want to hang out with me after reading all my nonsense. Thanks for understanding. Talk to you soon!*

This time I reread it before I sent. It would have to do. I couldn't think of another way to undo what I had done. It was better to just admit I was awkward. Hopefully he would understand.

I tucked my phone away for the last time and headed home to work on my college courses before dinner. Regret followed me the whole way. I just hoped I'd be able to concentrate; I was pretty sure my entire brain would be connected to my phone, waiting for the ding of a text until there actually was one.

Mom was gone when I got home, probably at the gym. Grandma's door was closed, and Dad had a sign on his office that very nicely reminded everyone not to disturb him. He was either on a call or in the middle of an intense project. Either way, I was on my own. I dropped my stuff by the door and went to the kitchen for an apple.

All those dealings with Uncertainty really worked up an appetite.

There was a note on the fridge from Mom that confirmed her whereabouts and asked me to put the eggplant lasagna into the oven at four. She was going to pick up the twins after their first day of middle school, because…middle school, and she was going to stop by the store on her way home.

We went through a lot of lettuce at our house.

I grabbed an apple out of the fridge, washed it off, and took a big bite. Mmmm, Honeycrisp. It was perfect. Exactly what I needed to forget that I might possibly have ruined everything with the guy of my dreams.

Cause of death: abundance of dorky texts.

It was tragic, really.

I checked my phone on the way to my bedroom, even though I told myself I wouldn't, and felt a drop in my stomach when there were no notifications.

Of course there were no notifications.

I'd only texted Asher ten minutes ago. And he was in class by now. He said he didn't have his phone with him, which could mean he left it in his locker or in his car. Phones weren't allowed in class, so that made sense. If it was in his locker, he might check it at the end of this hour. If it was in his car, he probably wouldn't see my text until after school. That meant I had one to two hours to stop obsessing about the whole thing and try to get some work done.

So, that's exactly what I did.

Time flies when you're having fun, and also when you're doing college courses online. In what felt like only a few minutes, the front door opened and Mom called for me to come help unload groceries.

"How was your first day?" She gave me a one-armed hug. The other arm was laden with bags.

I hugged her back, then went to the trunk. When I reached for some bags, Brett bumped me hard, sending me into Rhett, who bumped me back into Brett. I was a human ping-pong.

"Seriously?" I caught my balance enough to skip backwards, breaking the rhythm. "You guys are the worst!"

Brett laughed uproariously, his mouth full of what used to be carrot sticks and was now orange goo. He bumped my elbow again as he walked into the house.

"It was funny." Rhett emerged from the trunk carrying multiple bags. "Admit it."

I would do no such thing. Not yet, anyway. I tossed my head and grabbed the last two bags. My brothers might be heathens, but at least they did their part. I slammed the trunk closed and followed them into the house.

Mom looked up when I entered the kitchen. "Holland? Did you put the lasagna in the oven, sweetie?"

Oh, shoot.

"I totally forgot, Mom. I'm so sorry!" I dropped the bags on the counter and hurried to the fridge to pull it out.

"Don't worry about it; it's fine." Mom closed a cupboard and stopped to tap her forehead a few times. "We'll just have to come up with something else for tonight. The lasagna will keep one more day."

"I'm really sorry, Mom. I got in the zone and—"

She smiled a real smile, not a pained one. "It's really okay, Holland. Help me think. What can we do that's quick?"

"Pizza!" the twins shouted together.

"I don't have any cauliflower." Mom pursed her lips.

I patted her shoulder. "They want you to order it, Mom."

She shuddered. "Enriched flour, fake tomato sauce with high fructose corn syrup, and nitrates in the meat? Never!"

"Maybe we can find a place that does organic pizza?" We'd done that before in a pinch, and it really wasn't bad.

"No, no, no." My mom looked around the kitchen. "We are all smart, capable, creative people. We don't need to rely on fast food and delivery to feed ourselves. Look, I bought some chicken. Let's see if Dad got the grill set up. We can make chicken salad."

The twins' faces fell.

"I'll roast some potatoes," I said. "I'll get them in right now, and they'll be way done by the time the chicken is ready."

That perked the boys up, like I knew it would. They were suckers for some good roasted potatoes. Because who wasn't?

Mom shot me a grateful look on her way to Dad's office, which was all the encouragement I needed. I emptied the rest of the grocery bags at record speed until I found a bag of baby potatoes.

Even better. I wouldn't have to cut them.

I turned the oven dial to 425 and dumped the potatoes into a colander to rinse them. Then I had the twins pat them dry while I searched for the roasting pan. Brett salted and Rhett peppered. They poured the potatoes into the pan, and I put them in the oven.

Thirty minutes to taste-bud heaven.

Dad and Mom were in the backyard chatting while the grill heated up. I used tongs to put the chicken on a cookie sheet, had the boys season it, then took it out to my dad.

That should make up for my dinner blunder. I was so caught up in my work—and to be honest, Asher's pending text—that I practically let my family down.

That was it. I wasn't allowed to check my phone again until the next morning. That was my penance for making my family almost starve.

Chapter Five

"Ask no questions and you'll be told no lies."
Great Expectations

So what if the first thing I did when I got up in the morning was check my phone? I think that's perfectly understandable considering how much I tossed and turned all night, replaying each ridiculous letter of my texts. Of course I wanted to see what Asher said in reply. It made a ton of sense.

But the joke was on me because there were no texts from him. Not even to tell me I was a nerd bomber. Alicia texted a few times to ask how my first day of school went and then to tell me about her day. If I wasn't so hung up on Asher ignoring me, I would have been majorly homesick.

I texted Alicia back real quick so she wouldn't feel ignored, then I jumped out of bed and ran to the bathroom before Criticism could start broadcasting thoughts of how idiotic I was. When I turned on the shower full blast and sang a couple of Faouzia songs at the top of my lungs. I almost drowned out all the mental chatter.

Almost.

Mom sat at the kitchen table with a mug of something steamy and one of her fitness magazines spread open in front of her. I avoided looking at the page as I walked by; I was so not in the mood to see someone sweating attractively as they demonstrated how to do the perfect squat. I pulled a carton of eggs from the fridge and grabbed a cast iron pan out of the cupboard on my way to the stove.

"What kind of eggs are you making?" Mom asked without looking up from her magazine.

"Scrambled." I knew the twins would want some eggs too, and that was their favorite way to eat them.

"Whole egg or whites?" She picked up her cup and peeked at me over the top.

"I was going to do whole. Do you want me to scramble some whites for you? I can make some for Grandma too. Is she up?"

Mom shook her head. "She's sleeping in; she had a rough night. And I already ate, but thank you. There are some diced vegetables in the fridge if you want to add them to your scramble."

"Thanks." I went back to the fridge and found the glass container. There was no way the twins would want vegetables, but I could scramble plain eggs, then sauté some vegetables for mine.

Criticism was really noisy while I cracked eggs and whipped them with a fork. It didn't even help when I repeated the alphabet backwards and recited nursery rhymes. That usually made those negative thoughts run for the hills. I poured the egg mixture into the hot skillet and sighed.

"You okay?"

I was too busy with my mental war to notice Mom beside me at the sink, rinsing out her cup.

"Sure." I tried to smile brightly, but it sagged somewhere in the middle.

"Yeah?" Mom leaned on the edge of the sink and folded her arms.

She wasn't going anywhere.

"No," I said. The whole story came bursting out of my mouth like someone lit the fuse on a handful of fireworks. After I finished telling her all about yesterday, I sighed deeply. "He hasn't texted back, Mom. I think I blew it. I should have waited longer to text. Or maybe not done it at all. For sure not done it a second time or a third. I don't even want to go to school today. He's going to think I'm some kind of freak."

When I looked up, Mom's smile disappeared. Her face was all sympathy. "I think you're too hard on yourself, Hols."

I stirred the eggs with one hand and pulled my phone out of my back pocket with the other. It was easy to find my text thread with Asher; I thrust the phone in front of Mom's face. Her eyes crossed slightly as she took it from me. My free hand tapped the counter while I waited for Mom to read it through.

"Oh."

"Yeah," I sighed again. "I am such an idiot."

Criticism was rapidly morphing into Shame.

Mom set the phone on the counter next to me and shook her head. "It was a little awkward, sure, but that's not a big deal. Everyone is awkward sometimes."

"You're not."

My mom was like Mary Poppins, practically perfect in every way.

She snorted. "I'm flattered you think so. Let me tell you what I did just yesterday. I was in the locker room at the club, changing for a class, and I happened to glance over at the lady next to me. I noticed she had a bra with those cooling gel inserts, and I've been wanting to try one, so I told her I've been wanting to try out her bra."

"Like, you said those exact words? 'I want to try on your bra'?"

Mom nodded, her mouth twitching into a smile. "Those exact words. You should have seen the look on her face; she was totally horrified."

No kidding. I felt horrified and I wasn't even in that moment. "What did you do?"

"I laughed and explained that I meant I've been wanting to try out that kind of bra, then I asked her how she liked it, and we had a good conversation. It wasn't a big deal, Hols, and neither is this." She swung her hand over my phone. "You'll work it out, I'm positive."

Well, I wasn't. But somehow, knowing that my mom had confidence in me helped. Maybe it would work out alright.

Maybe it wasn't a big deal.

Maybe it was fine.

I got two plates out of the cupboard and dished plain eggs for each of my brothers, then added some of the vegetables to the skillet with my eggs. They just needed to warm, so after a couple of good stirs, I turned the heat off and moved the whole skillet to one of the cold burners.

"You good?" Mom asked.

"Yeah," I nodded. "I am. Thanks, Mom."

"That's my girl. I'll go get your brothers." Mom tweaked my nose and walked out of the kitchen.

It'll be fine.

It'll be fine.
It'll be fine.

I pulled into the parking lot at school just a few minutes before Spanish class was supposed to start. I sat in my truck for a moment, turning my phone around and around in my hands. I'd played through all kinds of scenarios and concluded that my best bet was to pretend that nothing cringe-worthy had happened at all.

I opened the text thread with Asher and typed.

> *Hope you have a good morning. See you at lunch!*

That felt better. It was a totally normal thing to text someone. I texted those same words to Alicia all the time.

Except that I just now realized I would actually see Asher before lunch. Duh. We had Spanish together. I'd see him in about two minutes.

I groaned and dropped my head to the steering wheel. There was no getting around it; I was just going to feel like an idiot no matter what I did.

Ugh, ugh, ugh, ugh.

Well, no use putting off the inevitable. If he was going to publicly declare, in Spanish, that I was a loony, then I would face it like a champ. Languages weren't my strength, so I probably wouldn't even understand him.

Yeah, that was better. I could face the day now. I tucked my phone away and got out of the car. I even smiled at people I passed as if nothing in the world was pear-shaped.

The extra few minutes in the truck meant I didn't have time to go to my locker, but since all my class books were digital and I had a spare notebook in my bag for notes, that wasn't a big deal. I scooted into Spanish just as the bell rang. The teacher, Señor Herrera, stood up to welcome everyone to the exciting world of Español, and I took that opportunity to scan the classroom for Asher.

My desk, the only spare desk in the class, was in the back corner, so I had a perfect view of everyone present. Asher was three rows over, four desks up with his head bent over his lap. I couldn't see what he was looking at, but whatever it was completely held his attention.

I kept glancing from Señor Herrera to Asher until my eyeballs felt like ping-pong balls. It was giving me a serious headache. I squeezed my eyes shut to alleviate some of the pressure, and when I opened them, Señor Herrera was standing at Asher's desk with his hands on his hips.

Asher didn't look up.

Señor Herrera cleared his throat loudly. A group of girls behind Asher to burst into giggles.

Now Asher noticed. "Buenos dias, Señor," he said in a jaunty voice. His right hand covered the middle of his desk, then moved to his jacket pocket as if he was trying to hide something. It must have been something incriminating because he went nuts with the Spanish, like he was trying to distract Señor Herrera with a barrage of words, most of which did not make any sense at all. "Yo quiero jugar la nevera ahora. Tienes el gato en su abrigo los martes?"

I wasn't amazing at Spanish, but I was pretty sure that translated to "I want to play the refrigerator now" and "Did you have the cat in your coat on Tuesday?" If Asher's intention was to jumble Señor's brain, then mission accomplished. Señor Herrera looked like someone had slapped him in the face with a tamale.

It took a few moments for Señor to gather his wits enough to respond. He opened his mouth just as the speaker above his desk erupted with a series of cackles.

"Señor Herrera, please send Asher—*cackle cackle*—to the office immediately— *cackle cackle*."

Señor pursed his lips as he looked down at Asher. "Sounds like you're needed at the office."

"Yeah, uh, lo siento. Disculpe, perdon. Yo, uh, no te vive mas tarde." He stood up, gathering his things with fumbling fingers. I watched and puzzled. Did he just say "I live more later"? Or "I'll live you later"?

Either way, it didn't make any sense.

As Asher bent over to grab the strap of his backpack, his cell phone fell out of his pocket.

His cell phone.

My breath stalled in my chest. He'd been looking at his cell phone, which meant he'd read my texts. Which meant...

What?

Asher reached for his phone, but it was a stretch, and the tips of his fingers flipped the phone further away. Right onto Señor Herrera's shoe, actually, who picked it up and held it with his finger and thumb.

"Asher?"

"Si?" Asher blew his hair out of his eyes, straightening to face Señor Herrera.

"Next time I see your cell phone out after I've started class, it's mine forever. Comprende?" He dropped the phone into Asher's outstretched hand.

"Yes, comprendo. Sorry-o." Asher tucked his chin into his chest and zipped out of the classroom without looking at anyone.

My stomach curdled.

Suddenly I wasn't so sure everything was going to be okay. If he didn't think my texts were the stupidest texts of all time, he would have looked at me at some point this morning. He knew where my desk was; he'd helped me find it yesterday. So either he thought I was a world-class weirdy or he didn't really care where I was or what I was doing.

Both of those were the worst thoughts ever.

One of them had to be true though. If he was interested in me, he would have looked for me this morning. Or, I don't know, answered my texts already.

I dropped my head to my desk and stifled a groan. This new girl thing was the pits. I ached for my group of friends in Durango who knew I was a weirdy and loved me anyway. I don't think people can accomplish that kind of acceptance without large amounts of time. The next two years of high school wouldn't be enough. Which meant I was destined to spend the remainder of my life here as a social outcast, eating with the lunch ladies and making friends with teachers.

Despair settled on the back of my neck like a clinging monkey. I was too busy drowning to shake it off, and I certainly didn't hear a word of Spanish for the rest of the period. Despair has a knack for filling my head with buzzing and my feet with lead. I dragged myself to P.E. and would have possibly died there if it wasn't for Ms. Adrian's obsession with Downward Dog.

At some point, with my head almost touching the mat and my butt in the air, Despair fell off my back and Optimism took that opportunity to jump into place. And since Optimism has a much better grip, it stuck around.

Thank goodness.

No worries, I would figure this out. It would totally be okay. Once I got to lunch, I'd have a chance to talk to Asher, and everything would get sorted. I could explain myself; he might understand. Everyone says and does dumb things sometimes. No worries.

I could always count on Optimism to make the best of things.

When we were released to the locker room, I changed quickly and hurried through the halls. If I could make it to lunch before Asher did, I would have a few extra minutes to gather my thoughts. That was a good idea, since my thoughts were like Cirque du Soleil today.

My feet stalled for a moment when I saw Tenley, Ryker, and Ethan already sitting in the commons corner. I didn't really know them very well. Was it weird if I showed up without Asher?

Actually, come to think of it, I didn't really know Asher that well, so…

Fake it 'til you make it.

I picked up the pace, taking long, confident strides. Tenley looked up when I was just a few steps away.

"Holland!" She jumped to her feet and grabbed my arm. "Come, sit. I have to tell you what happened!"

I did what she said, shifting to find a semi-comfortable spot on the hard floor. "What happened?"

Tenley's arms waved through the air, punctuating her words. "Yesterday at lunch I went to talk to the Vice Principal about your idea to form a club, and guess what?" She didn't wait for me to respond. She just took a deep breath and plunged right in. "We can do it!"

The waving arms and hyper speed of her speech distracted me enough for the words to take a few moments to sink it. I was still stuck on responding to her apparently rhetorical question until I realized the 'it' she was talking about was forming a club.

To fundraise.

For Runway Careers.

Okay, I was back online.

"That's fantastic!" I clapped for her. "I'm so glad that worked."

"Me too!" Tenley pulled open a bag of popcorn. "So, we have to start planning. They are giving us until Christmas break to make enough money to cover Runway Careers, or it's a no-go."

'We' and 'us'?

I guess that made sense. I sort of stepped in it yesterday. If I didn't want to be part of Tenley's project, I should have kept my mouth shut.

And really, I wanted to help. It would be fun to be part of something. Not only would it lessen the probability of spending the rest of my high school career volunteering to help the janitors, but it would be fun. I've never heard of something like Runway Careers before; I wanted to watch it unfold.

"Awesome. What do we do first?" I asked.

Tenley shot Ethan a look. "See, some people are supportive when their friends need help with something. Some people are ready to help, no questions asked."

"Yeah," Ethan snorted, "and some people haven't been roped into random projects since they were in kindergarten. Burnout is real, Ten."

She rolled her eyes.

Ryker swallowed an enormous bite of one of his burgers. "You know us, Tenley. We'll give you a hard time and whine and complain, then we got your back. Just like always."

"Really?" She gave Ethan a skeptical look.

Ethan shoved a handful of chips in his mouth and slumped against the wall. "Yeah, fine, what he said, sure."

"Yay!" Tenley shoved her lunch aside and set a notebook in the middle of the circle.

"Hold up, let's wait for everyone else before you go nuts." Ethan said. "Then you only have to say the spiel and make the assignments and drive everyone crazy one time."

"Oh, good idea, actually." Tenley straightened. "I should eat too. I forgot to finish my lunch yesterday, and I was dying by last period."

I took that as a cue to pull out my own lunch. Just as I figured, the novelty of my chicken salad with freeze-dried peach slices and quinoa bites was way less today. No one even glanced twice. Dara joined us halfway through my salad, and I almost didn't recognize her. Thankfully, Tenley said Dara's name when she sat down or I would have introduced myself all over again. Instead of all black and cat ears, Dara wore a black and red shirt, put her hair in pigtails, and had outlined her big blue eyes all around with black eyeliner.

I had no idea what that meant.

"Harley Quinn," Tenley said, catching my confused look. "That's the character of the day."

So, did that mean Dara dressed up like a different character every day? That's, like, three hundred and sixty-five costumes. Less if she only did school days, but still, way more than the average person. I was suddenly aching to see the inside of her closet.

Bryan showed up a few minutes later wearing a gray tee with a purple dragon today. His D&D book was tucked under his arm.

"Where's Asher?" Tenley's leg jiggled impatiently.

"Oh, right." Bryan settled into place near the drinking fountain and put his book on the ground next to him. He leaned to one side to pull his phone out of his back pocket. "He texted me right after third hour. He has an NHS meeting, so he won't be at lunch today."

He won't be at lunch.

I was fifty percent relieved and fifty percent disappointed.

And also ten percent confused.

Yeah, that didn't add up.

"He texted you?" I asked slowly. "Is, um, Asher a big texter?"

It was a weird question, I knew, but no one looked at me strangely, for which I was very grateful.

"He is when he has his phone," Bryan said, tucking his own phone away and reaching for his lunch bag.

"So, um, he answers his texts right away, usually?"

Ethan rolled his eyes. "Yeah, like, instantly. It's super annoying, actually."

"You think everything is super annoying." Tenley shook her head. "Okay, we'll just have to fill Asher in later. In fact, Dara, can you record this? I don't want him to miss the first official meeting of the Runway Careers Club."

"The what?" Ethan looked stricken.

While Tenley filled us in on the specifics, I let my mind loose. It was itching to overthink and overanalyze, so I gave myself permission. Just this once. With boundaries so I didn't go completely bananas.

The conclusion was dismal.

If Asher answered his texts right away, and I knew for sure he had his phone...

Oh man, I blew it with him.

That's all there was to it. If that wasn't the case, he would have responded by now.

So, that was that.

The end of me and Asher.

It was over.

Over before it started.

I let those awesome thoughts carry me through the rest of the day.

CHAPTER SIX

•❤•❤•❤•❤•❤•

"We need never be ashamed of our tears."
Great Expectations

Did I cry?

No, I did not!

Okay, fine, maybe a little. I could totally pass it off as allergies. And it wasn't in front of anyone. I held it in until the end of creative writing when I was on my way to my locker to stash my junk until tomorrow.

With a pathetic little sniff, I twirled the combination on my locker, then pulled up on the handle.

Nothing happened.

Of course nothing happened.

I looked to the right and noticed all the happy people with their lockers open, no problem. Then I looked to the left with the same results.

How nice for them.

I flipped the combination a few times and tried again.

Nothing.

Third times a charm, that's my trend.

Except for not today.

The locker door was determined to stay closed. It was one with the metal. I stared at it for a minute, hoping that I had somehow developed super mind powers that could make a stubborn locker move.

No such luck.

"Open, you," I whispered and then tried the lock again.

Still stuck.

Frustration took over my hand and slapped the locker. "Open!" I hissed.

It didn't.

I hit it with the side of my fist two or three times—who's counting—and tried again.

Nope.

That's when the slapping and slamming went nuts all over the front of the locker. I never claimed that Frustration was logical. Obviously I knew it wasn't going to make my locker open, but it felt pretty dang awesome to beat the junk out of it anyway.

"Hey?"

The voice was loud enough for me to hear over my locker-door rampage. Just like that, Frustration abandoned me, and Embarrassment now sat on my head.

Was I really attacking my locker with extreme prejudice in a crowded hallway?

Yes.

Yes, I was.

I turned around slowly.

And came face to face with my greatest nightmare.

The most gorgeous guy of all time stood in front of me. His blond hair glistened with sun-bleached highlights and flopped across his forehead in a way that was just asking to be touched. His green eyes were unreal: bright and clear and totally fake looking. His face was tanned, perfectly proportioned, and wrinkled in confusion. His mouth was...

Yummy.

That was the only word for it.

And this is the guy watching me lose it.

Fantabulous.

Why couldn't he come around when I was strolling through the hall with perfect hair, waving to all my friends, and looking way hot?

Oh, yeah. Probably because that never happened to me.

I pressed my lips into a pained smile. "Hello."

"Do you..." The side of his mouth quirked upwards. I tried not to stare at it too hard because it was doing weird things to my insides. "...need some help with that?"

"Oh, no. I'm good."

"Yeah?"

"Sure, great. Perfect, even. I'm just having a heart-to-heart with my locker. It's fine."

He let out a chuckle that rattled me to the bones.

What in the world was wrong with me? My heart was pounding like the percussion section of a symphony orchestra.

It was a little alarming, not gonna lie.

"It looks more like assault than a heart-to-heart, just so you know." He leaned a shoulder on the locker next to me, like he was preparing to stay awhile.

Yes, please.

"I can't get it open." I held out one empty hand to prove how helpless I was. "I tried, like, six times."

"Mind if I give it a go?"

I shook my head and moved over so he could reach the lock. But I didn't move far enough away. The spicy, manly scent of his cologne kicked up in the air around us when he moved. I breathed deeply, then held my breath to savor it.

"What's your combination?"

I gave it to him, trying not to think about Asher. This was seriously hard because just yesterday I stood in this same place, giving those same numbers to Asher so he could open my locker. I banished him from my brain by bringing up lyrics to multiple songs until something stuck. I couldn't think about Asher; I just couldn't. It made my stomach curl in an uncomfortable way.

The guy finished the last number and pulled up on the handle. The locker door stuck for just a minute, then swung open.

"How did you do that?" I glared at the offensive door. "I seriously did exactly what you just did, and it wouldn't open."

He grinned a heart-throbby grin and stepped out of my way. "It's just like anything else; you have to show it who's boss."

"Well, I see where I went wrong." I looked at my locker, trying to decide. Should I just empty it out and spare myself the drama of trying to open a sticky locker later? It was probably safe to assume that I couldn't rely on a beautiful stranger to happen by every time I needed to get something out of here.

I reached for the magnetic mirror on the door.

"Are you giving up?" Wow, even smirking looked good on this guy.

"I think so, unless you want to come by my locker every morning and afternoon and open it for me just in case it's feeling cranky that day."

He let out a short laugh. "Did you know you talk about your locker like it's alive?"

"Wait." I widened my eyes until they stung. "You mean it's not? Stop!"

His short laugh turned into a long, belly laugh. Oh, my goodness; it was so delicious. And over way too soon.

Mr. Hotness grabbed the door of my locker and leaned closer. "By the way, my name is Chandler. What's yours?"

"Chandler," I repeated. The name fit him perfectly. His face shifted into a furrowed forehead and scrunched eyebrows. Okay, he was confused now. Why? I thought back over what he'd just said and then got it. "I mean, my name isn't Chandler, obviously. I was repeating your name so I wouldn't forget it. Not that I would forget it. It would just be weird to have to ask you your name again. I mean, if we run into each other again. I mean, not that we're going to run into each other again. Hey, could you do me a favor?"

He was laughing too hard to answer.

"Could you just shove me in my locker and close the door? I would be so grateful."

He took a deep breath so that his words came out steady. "I don't think so."

"Really?" I sighed, "because I think it would be best for all of us, actually."

"No way," he shook his head. "I haven't been this entertained in, like, a month. I want to see what you do next. FYI, if it's lame, *then* I'll stuff you in the locker."

He wasn't serious. People's eyes don't twinkle like that when they're serious. Which was really too bad because apparently, I was a walking disaster. How was I supposed to function in life as a well-adjusted adult if I couldn't even have a conversation with an attractive guy without putting my foot in my mouth.

Not just my foot. My whole dang leg.

"Here." Chandler pumped his shoulders a couple of times. "You're going to conquer the locker today. We have about two minutes before we have to get to our next classes. That's tons of time to master it. Yeah?"

I shook my head. "Not really. Plus, I'm pretty sure you have something better to do than watch the new girl try to open and close her locker a billion times."

"I do," Chandler said, shrugging one shoulder. "But it can wait. Come on, give it a try."

He was serious.

For reals, he was going to stand there and watch me practice opening my locker until I could do it on my own.

I didn't know if that was adorable or ridiculous.

How do I get myself into these situations?

I let my backpack drop to the floor and closed the locker with a clang. The bell rang for the last period just as the noise faded away.

"Okay, really. You're going to be late for class."

"And so are you."

"No," I shook my head. "I'm headed home. I'm only here for part of the day. Really, Chandler, this is ridiculous. I'm sorry you had to see me and my locker duking it out. I'm sure we'll come to terms eventually. This really isn't your problem."

"You're right," he smiled. "It's not a problem."

"Chandler—"

He held up one hand to interrupt. "I have weight training this period. I can be late. Coach gives us a break if we're diligent, and I spend a butt ton of time in the weight room."

That's right he did. Those muscles didn't build themselves.

"So, I have time. I'm going to stay here until you get this."

"Why?"

His very distracting shoulders rocked back and forth. "Because you need help and because I want you to tell everyone you meet from now until forever that Chandler Whittaker is the nicest guy in Prescott."

"Oh, really?" I couldn't stop smiling.

"Yeah," he said. "Obviously."

I stared at him a moment longer—because he was very stare-able—and then turned to my locker. "Okay, let's do this." My fingers trembled as I twirled the combination until I told them to knock it off. It was no good letting Chandler see how much he was affecting me. Or that I was borderline pathetic.

I tugged the handle up, holding my breath to see if it was going to open.

It didn't.

I turned to Chandler with my lips pressed together tightly. Mostly so I didn't shout an alternative cuss word like *shishkabob*. I'd already done enough weird emoting for one day. "It didn't work."

He jerked his chin at a guy passing by, then leaned closer. "Try again. I'll watch really closely this time. Maybe I can figure out what's happening."

What was happening was his cologne was turning my insides into mashed potatoes.

"Okay." I kept my voice steady with Herculean effort and tried again. Still didn't work.

"My locker hates me," I sighed.

"No, I think I know what the problem is. When you lift up on the latch, you kind of tug it like you're begging it to open."

"I am."

"Well, you gotta tell it, not ask it. You're the boss of the locker. Watch." He twirled the combination, then looked at me to make sure I was watching before he jerked the handle upwards.

The locker popped open.

"See? Try again. This time, open it like you mean it."

I totally meant it every other time I tried, but I was willing to follow his instructions. When it was time to lift, I stood on my tip toes and leaned into the locker, yanking upwards.

The door opened with a clang.

And I almost fell on my behind. I wasn't expecting it to do anything, so the opening motion threw me off balance. I fell into Chandler's shoulder and had to grip his arm to get my feet under me again.

"You're the boss!" He steadied me with one hand on my elbow.

Yeah, I sort of felt like one.

I closed the locker door and tried one more time to make sure the first time wasn't a fluke.

It wasn't.

My locker opened right up, and this time I kept my balance.

Unfortunately.

I put some of the heavier textbooks from my backpack inside. Confidence assured me that I would in fact see them again now that the locker was my friend. Then I closed the door for the day. "Thanks, Chandler. You're my hero, really."

"All in a day's work."

We stared at each other for a very long time.

It was very awesome.

And also very confusing.

I enjoyed staring at him, fact, but not when I had no idea what he was thinking. Boys were weird that way. He could be contemplating how to ask me out or reliving an epic moment in sports history.

My eyes flicked to the exit sign down the hall. "Well, um, thanks again. I guess I'll go?"

"Wait." He reached out a hand that didn't quite touch my arm. "You didn't ever tell me your name."

"Oh, it's Holland," I said, then braced myself for the questions and comments on how weird or different or creative my name was.

They didn't come.

"Cool. I'm meeting some friends after football practice to go to a movie and stuff. Do you want to come?"

Wow, I did, but I also sort of felt like throwing up.

"Um..."

He watched me and waited while my thoughts flew all over the place. I knew my mom would love it if I hung out with people, which was good. But she would also want to meet them first, which was bad. And as much as I loved the thought of getting to know Chandler better, I wasn't all that keen on hanging out with a group of people I'd never met. That was kind of overwhelming.

Yeah, that was the one. Overwhelm was dancing the rumba all over my thoughts.

"What?" Chandler asked when the silence stretched way past the point of comfort.

What indeed? What should I say?

"Um..."

Yes, even better the second time. Come on, Holland, you can do this.

"So, my mom..."

"Sure, yeah, you can totally bring her," Chandler said.

My head jerked to the side. "No, I mean, that's not what I was saying. My mom worries; she'll want to meet you before we go out. I mean, not that we're going out. Before I go out with your friends, she'll want to know who I'm with." I took a deep breath, my cheeks warmer than jalapeños. "And I have some assignments due. I'm not sure how long it will take, soooooo...."

Chandler nodded. "I get it. That's cool." He shrugged one shoulder and looked away.

Wait, what did he get? Did he think I was coming up with excuses not to hang out with him? Confusion began searching through the things I'd said, trying to figure out what was going on right now.

"Um," I put a hand on his arm before I could talk myself out of it. "I'd love to hang out with you and your friends. Really. I didn't mean to sound like I didn't want to."

"You sure?" He raised one skeptical eyebrow.

"Absolutely. Yes, I'm sure."

"Then how about we do this, Holly..."

My mind stuck on the word *Holly*. Did he think that was my name? I had the weirdest sensation that he was talking to someone else. And I couldn't correct him, not when he was in the middle of talking.

"... after football, I'll come by your house and meet your mom. Then we go. Does that work?"

Wait, was he for real? He was going to come by my house and meet my mom? He didn't look like he was joking, but my heart started to sink into the dark recesses of my belly, waking up Paranoia.

There was no way he was serious.

Why would he go to all that trouble to hang out with me?

Paranoia was right. Really, I wasn't that cool.

"Sure, okay." I nodded, turning towards the door. It would be easier for him to make his getaway if I wasn't looking at him, and this way I felt like it was my choice to let him go.

Chandler grabbed my bag strap and tugged, causing me to stumble backwards a few steps. Almost into his arms. As dreamy as that would have been, Paranoia had a way of making romance practically impossible.

"Where are you going?" Chandler asked.

"Oh..." I glanced at the exit again. "Home?"

"I'm great at a lot of things," he laughed, "but I can't read your mind. You're going to have to tell me where you live, Holly."

Shoot, Holly again. He really did think that was my name. I was going to have to correct him, but I couldn't right now, not with Paranoia all up in my grill.

Whatever, I guess it wasn't the worst thing in the world if he thought that Holly was my name. It wasn't a bad name; it just wasn't mine.

"Holly?" He waved a hand in front of my face.

"Sorry." I laughed awkwardly. "You want to know where I live?"

"So I can come by later...and meet your mom?"

Wait, so, he *was* serious about that.

Chandler laughed as he zipped open my backpack and pulled out a notebook. He ripped out a page, then grabbed a pen from his back pocket. With a pen poised over lined paper, Chandler looked at me expectantly.

I rattled off my address before Paranoia could stop me. If he was serious enough to pull me back and write down my information in pen and ink, I was not going to question it.

Well, not anymore.

"Cool." He folded the paper and stuck it in his pocket. "I'll see you in a couple of hours, Holly."

"Yeah," I waved. "See you then."

As I walked away, my mind raced like it was headed for a clearance sale at Bath and Body Works. Was he really going to show up at my house? Why? There were probably a billion girls at this school who would have loved going out with him and his friends. A billion girls prettier, smarter, more coordinated and way less awkward than me.

Why did he ask me?

Was I just a novelty? Like, he'd already dated all the girls he was interested in dating and I was new, so that made me the obvious next choice?

Well, that wasn't a pleasant thought at all.

I pushed that one away, along with the rest of the negative chatter, and let myself believe, just for a moment, that he wanted to get to know me better because he could tell right off that I was something special.

It could go either way, right? So, why not my way?

Chapter Seven

• ♥ • ♥ • ♥ • ♥ • ♥ •

"It was the best of times, it was the worst of times."
A Tale of Two Cities

There was no way I was getting any homework done with Chandler coming over to my house. It didn't matter how many hours separated me from that moment. I was already a distracted wreck and all I'd done was drive home. It was asking too much to solve equations and conjugate verbs.

As soon as I got home, I stashed my stuff in my room, got a snack, and went on a wild cleaning spree. As I picked up paper, crayons, charging cords, books, and my brothers' mini tank toys, I understood my mom so much better. She always went nuts cleaning when people were coming over. She even cleaned the insides of cupboards and places the guests would never see. At this moment, I was obsessively thinking about vacuuming the crawl space under the stairs.

Mom came home an hour and a half later while I was fluffing pillows in the front room. "Hey, hon! Can you help me bring in... Whoa!"

I straightened. Was that a good whoa or a bad whoa?

"The house is so clean! It looks fabulous! To what do I owe this surprise?" Her eyebrows dropped. "Did you wreck the car or eat an Oreo or something?"

I laughed as I set the *Faith* pillow back into place and went to work on the *Blessed* one. "No way. Never would I ever. Just cleaning."

"And, why are we cleaning exactly? Whoa, did you dust the fan?"

Here was the part where I needed to tell my mom what was coming so she could prepare herself to not embarrass me when Chandler showed up. I took a deep breath.

"I met a guy today; he's coming over after school. He invited me to a movie with some friends. I can go, right?"

When I glanced up, Mom looked stricken, but she covered it up so smoothly that I almost thought I imagined the look. "Sure, that's great. What's his name?"

"Chandler."

"Chandler. Is that a city?"

"And Holland is a country," I reminded her. My parents didn't really have the high ground when it came to judging names.

"Right, well, that's great. What's he like?"

I decided to leave out the part where he was hot enough to melt an icicle. My mom would probably not enjoy that comparison. "He helped me open my locker when it got stuck."

I hoped that was enough to sell her. I didn't really have any other proof that he wasn't Jack the Ripper's great-great-grandson.

"Oh, that's so nice. I made protein bites. Have him come in for some, okay?"

Mom's baking was dismal and her cooking wasn't exactly mainstream, but her peanut butter protein bites were delicious. I was glad she suggested those and not her quinoa spinach puffs. Alicia got gaggy just from thinking about those things.

I finished my whirlwind clean up job and then went upstairs to figure out what to do with myself. I had on one of my favorite shirts—a denim button-down with roses embroidered on one side—and a pair of black leggings. Cute and comfortable. Thankfully, I'd stayed clean while I was cleaning so I didn't need to change my clothes. That was good because Chandler would probably notice and think I was trying to impress him.

I wasn't trying to impress him.

Okay, I was.

But he didn't need to know that. I could be subtle. I put on some lip gloss and reapplied mascara, then tried to get my hair to do something other than lay there like a slug, but it was uncooperative. I stuck a headband on and then stuck my tongue out at my reflection.

It made me feel a little better, even if it didn't help the hair situation.

The doorbell rang as I walked down the stairs. I gripped the banister and tried to remember how to breathe. That wasn't something I usually gave much thought to; I just did it automatically. Except for right now. My breath kept getting stuck somewhere in my chest.

Maybe this was a terrible idea.

Maybe I wasn't the kind of girl who could go places with exceptionally hot guys.

Maybe this was going to be a disaster.

My mom's voice sounded loud and clear, welcoming people into our home. I steadied myself at the bottom of the stairs and then plunged into the living room before I could talk myself out of it.

"Hey, Chandler."

He stood by the front door with two other guys. My mom was nowhere to be seen.

"Dude, you were right. She's totally hot," said the guy to Chandler's left. A classy fellow, obviously.

Chandler smacked him on the back of the head and then gave me an apologetic smile. "Sorry about John. He forgot to put his filter in this morning."

The other guy, a tall red-head, snorted. "What filter?"

"Bruh," John slapped Chandler's arm away, then glared at the other guy. "You were thinking it too."

They all gave each other massive stink eyes while I tried to find a closet to disappear into. The only one in this part of the house was the one where I shoved all the random stuff I picked up while cleaning. If I opened it, I would get crushed by an avalanche of junk.

Which, actually might be better than listening to them rib each other and comment on my looks like I wasn't standing right there.

Hm, choices, choices.

I was about to dive for the closet when my mom came back in, holding a tray of protein balls. "Oh, Holland, there you are! I already met your friends, Chandler, John, and Dillan."

Well, she was one step ahead of me. Though, I would have been totally okay un-meeting John. Now he was checking out my mom while she extended the tray to each of them.

So gross.

"Well, what are the three of you going to do today?" Mom asked. Her timing wasn't awesome; all three guys had just popped a protein ball into their mouths. With all that peanut butter, we had at least a minute of watching them chew before they could answer.

Chandler swallowed hard, his eyes watering, but he answered without sounding strangled, which was impressive. "We were going to go to a movie at Harkins, but there's nothing playing, so we're going to Dillan's house to watch *The Princess Bride*. His mom will be there the whole time, and we're meeting two other girls, Mylee and Janis. Dillan lives pretty close. I can give you the address if you want."

My mom blinked a few times, then glanced at me as a smile spread over her face.

He was good.

"Yes, please. I'll get a notepad. That all sounds lovely. What time will you bring Holland home?"

"Is ten alright? At the latest."

"That's just fine." Mom left the room for a moment and returned with a sticky note pad and pen. Chandler took it, scribbled the address down, then gave it back.

Mom was practically gushing, which meant I had to get us out of there fast or she was going to forget herself and bring out my baby pictures. And that wasn't the only reason. I also wanted to leave so John would stop ogling my mother. It was really starting to creep me out.

I stepped forward, herding the guys toward the front door. "Thanks, Mom. See you later."

"Have a good time!" She followed us onto the front porch and waved. She kept waving as Chandler opened the passenger door for me. I buckled myself in—so grateful I didn't have to sit in the back by John—and when I glanced up, my mom was still standing there with her arm swinging in the air.

Didn't that hurt?

What was I thinking? She could go on for hours. She probably considered it part of her workout for the day. Chandler noticed me staring at the house and chuckled. He started the car up and honked as he drove down the street.

Well, I'm glad he was amused.

It took less than ten minutes to drive to Dillan's house, a fancy two-story thing near the country club in a gated community. The house was ginormous and painted beige with stone halfway up the front.

Kind of artsy.

"What do your parents do?" I asked, trying to cut through the silence in the car. It was probably because of me. Guys didn't normally sit around in cars totally silently, did they?

"Golf, mostly," Dillan snorted. "Well, my dad does. My mom is a professional online shopper."

Was that a thing?

I didn't want to ask and risk looking stupid. We got out of Chandler's car and followed Dillan into the house. The scent of peach potpourri smacked me in the face as soon as I walked through the door.

"Shoes off!" A woman's voice traveled whatever great lengths it had to reach us. I get why people want shoes off, but I am always so embarrassed when I have to do it. Feet always smell, and socks randomly get holes.

I slipped my shoes off, checking my sock seams while pretending to arrange my shoes against the wall. No holes; that was good. I couldn't tell about the stench though. Sometimes it is so difficult to catch a whiff of your own B.O.

"Dillan, come here, please."

"You guys go to the TV room. I'll meet you there." Dillan rolled his eyes and headed through a door to the right. I trailed after John and Chandler, taking in the perfectness of the house.

No scuffs on the walls. No crooked or unprofessional photos. Everything was glamorous and pristine, like someone arranged it and then stuck it in place with Gorilla Glue. The further we went down the hall, the more convinced I was that either no one actually lived in that house. Either that, or they were all robots.

John opened a door to the right and Chandler stepped aside so I could go first. I went down a couple of steps and found myself in a home theater, complete with reclining leather chairs arranged stadium style and a huge projector screen attached to the wall.

As big as the wall.

I stumbled forward and caught myself on the back of one of the chairs.

"Sit there," Chandler gestured, then he brushed by me to get to his seat. "I'll take the one next to you."

"Oh, ho, ho." John waggled his eyebrows.

Chandler ignored him as he settled into the chair, adjusting the back so he was slightly reclined. He hooked one arm behind his head, the picture of chill.

I, on the other hand, sat ramrod straight, trying to figure out what to do with my hands. "Do we need to help with anything?"

"Nah." John plopped into a seat a few rows over. He propped his feet on the seat in front of him and grabbed a remote. "Dillan has people for that kind of thing."

People?

I didn't get much time to contemplate what that meant before the sound of chatter wafted in from the hall.

"I know, right? And then I showed her my Coach, and she was so green!"

"No way?"

"Well, yeah. She was so proud of her Target purse or whatever that I had to do it."

And suddenly, I got the sickest feeling in the pit of my stomach. I could picture both girls before they entered the TV room. Blonde or brunette with highlights. Professionally applied make-up from actual make-up artists. Brand name clothes and perfectly proportioned everything.

Too bad they were blocking the exit. I would have flown out of the room and made my excuses to Chandler later. This was my worst nightmare come true.

Swank girls.

Hot girls.

Popular girls.

Obviously there were girls like that in Durango. Tons of them. They were the ones who treated everyone else like downgraded, second-hand rejects. But they were easier to ignore when I had my people all around me. Here, I felt so exposed as they walked into the room.

Exactly as I envisioned them.

Blonde, not brunette. They stopped short when they saw me sitting next to Chandler.

He tipped his head back to see them. "Hey Janis, Mylee. This is Holly. She's new here."

"Holland," I whispered.

"Oh," one of them sniffed. "I didn't know there would be...other people here too."

She made "other people" sound like a disease.

The girl who hadn't said anything gave me the kind of smile people do when they find out they just sat in gum.

The two of them linked arms and strode to the seats next to John, then bent their heads together and started whispering. Every so often, one of them would lift her chin and eyeball me for a minute then go back to whispering. From this angle, I honestly couldn't tell them apart. They were both blonde, highlighted, and tanned.

Were they twins?

"Hey, Chandler?" I leaned close so I could whisper without the others hearing me.

He peeked open one eye and raised the other eyebrow. "Yeah?"

"I think, um, maybe—"

I didn't get to finish.

Dillan chose that moment to stroll in, followed by an entourage of uniformed people carrying trays of food. They set everything down on a long table against the wall, arranged plates, napkins, and utensils, then left.

"Thank you," I said as the last person left. I didn't know if they were siblings, staff, or Dillan's crazy aunts and uncles. Whoever they were, it was really nice of them to set that all up for us.

An eruption of giggles followed my words.

I looked down at my hands, my stomach curdling. The aromas wafting from the platters were magnificent, but I knew I wouldn't be able to eat a single thing.

"Let's go," Chandler said.

At first, I thought he'd noticed his friends were buttheads and wanted to leave entirely. To which I almost said yes, please. Then I noticed that he jerked his head towards the food.

Oh, he meant 'let's go get some food'.

I followed him because it was easier to do that than to explain in great detail how his friends made me want to throw up.

Chandler grabbed a plate and started piling it high. I took one too, but I held it in my hands uncertainly. Smorgasbords were so awkward for me. I'd never seen one that wasn't an excuse for people to load up on junkie food. But this was a fancy house, and rich people were healthy, right? Surely there was something there that wasn't overly processed. I wasn't nearly as strict as my mom was about eating, but junk food really gave me a belly ache. The last thing I needed right now was more reasons for my stomach to hurt.

I leaned over the table to take it all in.

Stuffed mushrooms? No thank you. I hated mushrooms, no matter what they were stuffed with. Same for the deviled eggs. Sometimes I liked them, but these had suspicious chunks in them that gave me the willies. Pass on the mini eggrolls and pizza bites. Carrot sticks I could do. Ditto for celery and broccoli. I filled my plate with those, then examined the dip. Maybe hummus? That might be okay. I put a spoonful on my plate, added some air-popped popcorn and a few apple slices, then went back to my seat with Chandler.

I'm glad I hadn't noticed Mylee and Janis standing behind me in line or I might not have been able to pick up a thing. Now I had a clear view of them hovering over the food, making comments about how this or that thing was fattening and full of carbs. Now they were talking even louder about how some girl they knew only ate vegetables and popcorn because she *obviously* needed to lose some weight.

Insecurity popped up.

Wait, were they talking about me?

"Hurry it up so we can start the movie already!" Dillan glared at them and yanked the remote out of John's hand.

"Hey!"

"My house, my remote."

John gave his opinion with a word that burned my ears. My stomach was flipping and flopping all over the place. Would it be weird if I just stood up and ran out of the room?

When the lights dimmed and the movie appeared on the screen, I seriously considered army crawling across the floor and letting myself out. I had my cell phone; I could call my mom for a ride. Or even walk. I think the map app gave directions for walking too, although I'd never used that particular function.

My hands clutched my untouched plate of food. One eye watched Buttercup torture her farm boy and the other eye drifted to the door.

Should I?

Shouldn't I?

Should I?

Shouldn't I?

Shame said that Mylee and Janis might track me down at school tomorrow and goad me if I left early. No to mention they'd probably tell everyone they knew about the weird new girl who snuck out of movie night via army crawl, ditching Chandler and offending Dillan for life.

I couldn't do that.

I might not care for Chandler's choice in friends, but I really did like *him*. He was nice and helpful and, who was I kidding, he was super hot. And, even more amazing, he seemed to like me.

John laughed at something on the screen and turned to Mylee. "Buttercup is a babe."

"Pig." She flicked a piece of popcorn at him.

Okay, at least we could agree on that.

I set my plate on the floor next to my chair and leaned closer to Chandler. My intention was to be near enough to whisper that I needed to go home. Because, uh, I forgot about a super important thing that I needed to do right away. Super urgent. Way important. Totally can't ignore it.

As I shifted, my hand moved and brushed against Chandler's.

The lighting from the movie was just enough that I could see the lazy smile that spread across his lips. He reached over, his fingers intertwining with mine. Our palms touched and a zing went up my arm.

"Better?" he asked.

Oh, he had no idea.

Chapter Eight

"One always begins to forgive a place as soon as it's left behind."
Little Dorrit

Chandler held my hand through the whole movie. That was the only thing in the world that kept me in that TV room. Especially once Mylee and Janis started up their commentary. If they weren't criticizing the costume choices, they were rating each actor's hotness factor.

Which was just ironic when, not long ago, one of them called John a pig for saying practically the same thing.

It was really hard to watch and enjoy the movie with all that snarky in the air, so I didn't even try. I watched and enjoyed Chandler instead.

If someone told me he used to be a piece of marble that a master artist chiseled into humanity, I would believe them. Chandler was so perfect that it was almost painful to look at him, and yet, I didn't want to stop.

His profile in the dim light was magical.

When the movie ended, John stole the remote and pulled up a Marvel movie.

And that was my cue.

"I should probably get home," I whispered to Chandler.

He checked his watch. "It's early."

"Yeah." I wiggled my head, trying to think of an excuse. The wiggling must have worked because I remembered the assignments I hadn't done when I chose to clean the house freakishly fast instead. "I have some school work I still need to do."

"Dedicated," he said.

I couldn't tell if he meant that in a good way or a bad way.

"Nerd," John said behind his hand.

Mylee and Janis thought that was just hilarious.

"No worries. I'll take you home." Chandler squeezed my hand and stood up. "I'm going to take Holly home, guys. I'll be back in a bit."

"Oh, ho, ho!" John called. "Kiss her once for me, bruh."

Chandler picked up a throw pillow that rested on one of the chairs and tossed it at John's head.

John saw it coming and tried to duck out of the way. He wasn't fast enough. "Ouch! Dude! That had a button on it!"

Chandler smirked. "See ya." Then he led me out of the room.

Once we got into the hall, I could finally breathe again. I had no idea how squished I felt in there until now. It was like my lungs were expanding for the very first time.

"Have you seen that movie before?" Chandler swung our arms as we walked down the hall.

"*The Princess Bride*?" I asked. "Of course. I think it's a life requirement or something. A right of passage."

"Yeah."

"It's a good movie, but I really love musicals. Like, *The Phantom of the Opera* is pretty good." I liked that one, but it wasn't my favorite. I just named it because it had some fighting and action. That usually made a musical more palatable for people who weren't freakish about them like I was. I also named it because... "My favorite song in the world is *All I Ask of You* from that musical."

Silence.

So, that was probably more information than he cared about. Way to overshare, Holland. Embarrassment creeped up on me, making me squirmy. I needed the silence to go away. All I could think to do was ask him something, anything, to get rid of all the awkward in the air.

I couldn't ask the same question, though, because duh, of course he'd seen *The Princess Bride* before. We just watched it together.

What else, what else, what else?

"What's your favorite movie?"

There, that wasn't so hard.

Brava, Holland.

Chandler sucked in his cheeks, his lips puckered just enough to start giving me ideas.

Whoa.

Okay, maybe we were holding hands and maybe he gave me some smoldering glances during the movie, but kissing? That was fast.

Way fast.

This whole thing was moving fast actually. I didn't know anything about this guy except his last name and that he had impeccable taste in cologne. I didn't even know what his favorite movie was.

"Do you mean favorite, like the best I've ever seen? Or favorite, like the one I can watch over and over."

"Either," I said.

His eyes drew up to the ceiling. "I watch *Rocky* with my dad every weekend he's in town. That's about it. I don't really watch movies, honestly; I watch sports."

Sports.

I didn't know anything about sports. Better to change the subject.

"What about reading? What's your favorite book?"

He pushed the heavy front door open. I was so happy to be out of that place that I had to rein in the desire to fling my arms out to the side and spin in a circle. That house had a vice grip on my soul. When I'd recovered enough to remember I asked Chandler a question—one he hadn't answered yet—I went ahead and asked it again in case he was also so caught up in euphoria to hear me the first time.

"Book?" He glanced at me.

"Yes, you've heard of them?" I squeezed his hand. "Folded pages with writing on them. Lots of writing, actually. Enough to tell a whole story."

Chandler grinned. "Sassy. Here, let me get that for you." He opened the car door and waited until I slid in all the way before he closed it. In the three seconds I had to myself while he walked around to his side of the car, I wondered what I would do if he didn't like to read. That'd always been kind of a deal breaker for me.

Chandler slid into the seat next to me, his cologne muddying my senses. I guess we could find other things to talk about. Books weren't the most important thing in the world, were they?

And to make what was jumbled even jumblier, Chandler's arm came around the back of my seat as he twisted to back out of the driveway.

Then it stayed there.

My thoughts were popping like kernels in hot oil. I didn't know what this meant. Was Chandler the kind of guy who held hands with a lot of girls, so it didn't mean much to him? That might be the case because he was really casual about it. Or was holding hands the start of something big?

I willed it to mean something.

Something more than that he was just a touchy-feely guy.

Was he into me?

I peeked over at Chandler to see if maybe Drama also had a grip on him too. It didn't appear to be the case. He had one arm draped on the steering wheel, the other resting on the back of my seat. His shoulders were relaxed and every once in a while, he'd mouth along to the lyrics of whatever song was playing.

Must be nice. I wish I could be that chilled out. I didn't even know the title of the song coming out of the speakers, much less the words. Plus, I could barely hear it over the chatter in my brain.

Chandler turned the corner onto my street. He hadn't said a single solitary word to me since we got in the car and I had to know why. Did I offend him with my affiliation for musicals? Or because I made him leave before the rest of his friends? Or because my shirt was the wrong color?

What was it? Why didn't he talk?

Oh, ugh. There it was. Overthinking came stomping back into my mind, and if I didn't do something, it was going to keep me up all night mouthing off all the reasons why Chandler was silent. None of them would be helpful or uplifting, and then I'd have a migraine all weekend. That wasn't going to work for me. I had big plans to Facetime with Alicia; finish unpacking my room; and take a long, luxurious bubble bath.

"So, what *do* you like?" I blurted, and then pursed my lips. That sounded so cringe. It would be nice if I could suck those words back in and lock them up tight.

"I'll tell you what I don't like." He guided the steering wheel to turn onto my street.

Uh-oh.

"Okay, sounds good," I said, kneading my hands together in my lap.

"Everything from the eighties, sappy poetry, old books, vegetables, history, and girls that only talk about themselves."

Chandler pulled into the driveway of my house and put the car in park. He moved both hands to the steering wheel as he stared out the windshield, his brow furrowing in obvious deep thought. It was like he forgot I was even there.

Should I just…go?

I reached for the door handle. The metal felt cold against my palm. I didn't pull it, though. I couldn't. If I left like this, I was going to go bananas. What did he mean by telling me things he didn't like? Was that a hint? I looked down at my outfit. Maybe it was kind of eighties. There were tons of pictures in the attic of my mom in leggings when she was a kid, but eighties leggings were different; they were looser and had stirrups. I for sure didn't spout any poetry tonight, did I? Though I did put a ton of vegetables on my plate.

I was in so much turmoil that I couldn't remember anything I'd talked about, much less if it was all about me.

I better cut my losses and go.

"Thanks for inviting me to hang out with you," I said, making my voice bright and chirpy. I couldn't say "thanks for introducing me to his friends" because I wasn't really grateful for that. I'm sure they were lovely people—maybe they were having an off night—but I would not be sad if I never had to hang out with them again.

"Yeah, of course."

He didn't look at me.

The muscles in my belly tightened. Did I do something to offend him? Did he hate me now? Or did he regret holding my hand? Maybe he did it out of habit and then was sorry. There could be something about my palm that repulsed him.

Apparently, Paranoia was back.

Just lovely.

"Well, um, good night, then."

Chandler swung his head in my direction. "Oh, are you going in?"

"Um, yes?" I wasn't sure what I was doing anymore. Maybe my brain detached from my cranium because everything looked sort of fuzzy all of a sudden. "This is my house."

Then I tried to laugh. It was a valiant effort but really didn't work. A goose honk, donkey bray was the result.

Super attractive.

"Yeah." His hands dropped onto his thighs. "Look, you're a cool girl, Holly..."

And why did he keep calling me Holly? It was insufferable, especially right now.

Hey, yeah, Chandler, it sounds like you're about to give me a supreme brush-off, but when you do it, could you use my real name? It's Holland, not Holly. Just so I know it's actually me you're talking to when you crush me. Thanks so much. Super appreciate it.

"...and I want to get to know you better."

Wait, what?

He wanted to get to know me better?

Did I hear that right?

"Man, this is weird." He ran a hand through his hair, mussing it in just the right way to make him look even more devastatingly handsome. "I just broke up with Mylee a few days ago."

Well, that explained some things.

"She was the worst girlfriend. Like, clingy. Super self-centered. I didn't notice at first, but she is not always a nice person. And now, she can't let it go. It's super awkward that we're still hanging out. You probably noticed." Chandler let out a long breath, then met my eyes. "I bet you're wondering why I'm telling you this."

Yeah, actually.

I nodded.

"I'm just sick of all the games people play when they're dating. It's stupid." His hand slid across the space between us so smoothly that I almost missed the moment when he took my hand. "You don't seem like a game-playing girl. You're real, you know? Like when you yelled at your locker earlier? That was awesome. Most people care too much what everyone thinks to do something like that." He took a deep breath. "Are you busy tomorrow?"

I saw his mouth moving and heard the words coming out, but I still couldn't wrap my head around the meaning.

Could it be that my talent for doing supremely embarrassing things in front of others made me attractive?

That did not seem right.

But I wasn't about to argue.

"I don't think I'm busy. I'll have to check with my parents. What do you have in mind?"

Chandler's face lit up with a dazzling smile. "Cool. We're having a picnic at the lake tomorrow; my family is. And my parents love it when we bring people. Do you want to come?"

Okay, that *had* to mean something.

"I'd love it," I smiled. "I'll check with my parents and text you."

Except I just realized I didn't have his number.

"Yeah, I won't have my phone until tomorrow. How about I get your number and check in with you in the morning? If you can come, I'll pick you up."

"That sounds great! Do you have paper and a pen or something?"

Chandler patted his chest like a pen and notebook might be hiding there—lucky things if they were—and then looked through the middle console. "Hang on." He leaned way over so that his head was practically in my lap, and opened the glove compartment.

Holy guac, he smelled good.

All kinds of interesting junk fluttered to the floor. Chandler ignored all of it and reached for an old receipt. It was so faded that the typing wasn't visible anymore on either side.

"This will work."

"I have a pen." I waited for him to right himself—though it was sad when he moved away—and unzipped my purse. A pink gel pen was the closest, so that is what I was going to use. I took the receipt from his hand and scribbled my number. Gel ink smeared super easy, especially on the glossy receipt paper, so I waved it in the air a few times to help it dry before I handed it over to him.

He folded it up and put it in his back pocket. "Cool. I'll talk to you in the morning. Like at nine?"

So, I take it he wasn't an early bird. Good to know. I would add that to the Chandler file in my brain that was slowly filling up with important information.

Likes sports, sleeps in, helps people open super stuck lockers, hates eighties stuff and mean girls.

I wished the list was longer.

"Sounds great. Are you sure your parents won't mind if I crash your family party?" I flipped the zipper of my purse through my fingers.

"Are you kidding? They invented the saying, 'the more the merrier'. They seriously love company."

I sat up straighter. "Okay. Can I bring anything?"

"Just you."

Well that was easy. Me went everywhere with me.

"Cool," I said, sounding way more like Chandler than was normal. "I mean, that's easy. I'll talk to you tomorrow, then." I pushed the door open and stepped around the car. Before I headed up the front walk, I turned to wave a final time.

Chandler stuck his head out the window. "See ya, Holly."

My parents had no problem saying yes. Dad was so excited I was going on a date that it was almost insulting. Weren't dads supposed to clean shotguns and threaten potential suitors with evil eyeballs? Apparently, my dad was the type to toss me to the highest bidder.

When I told him this, he just laughed and said it wasn't like that at all. He had such a fun time in high school dating and stuff that he wanted me to have the same experiences. That was all.

I decided to let it go, but I still wondered.

True to his word, Chandler texted me at precisely nine-o-clock the next morning. I responded that it was a go, and he sent a very un-emoji-ed 'cool'. He would be at my house at eleven to pick me up.

That gave me half an hour to get ready and ninety minutes to disappear into *Great Expectations* so that I didn't have to spend any more time listening to the opinions of Overthinking or Paranoia.

I was so thoroughly invested in the shenanigans of Ms. Havisham that I didn't even hear the doorbell ring.

"Holland!" Mom's voice floated up the stairs.

"Coming!" I tossed my book on the bed and gathered my things with rapid speed. The less time Dad had to shoot the breeze with Chandler, the better.

When I went to the front door, Dad was nowhere to be seen. Neither were the twins. Thank goodness. It was just Mom chatting with Chandler, and no baby books were in sight. Maybe my parents weren't as embarrassing as I thought they were. Maybe they were growing out of that phase.

"Did you pack sunscreen, honey? Chandler says the sun beats down at the lake. We don't want you to burn like you did that time at the beach." She winked at Chandler. "Lobster red."

Okay, I take back what I just said about being embarrassing.

That time at the beach wasn't my fault. How was I supposed to know that clouds don't actually protect a person from the sun? It seemed logical that it would be safe to frolic on the beach without sunscreen or hats when it's overcast.

"I'll get the sunscreen," I grumbled as I went to the hall closet. As soon as I opened it, I realized my mistake. Everything I'd shoved in there the day before came tumbling out with a vengeance.

"Whoa." Chandler, who had been lounging on the couch, jumped to his feet.

"I'm fine." I kicked at the pile to get it back in the closet. "I'm fine." The sunscreen was still on the shelf above the chaos, so I grabbed that and skipped over everything else to get back to stable ground. "I have the sunscreen!" I held it up for my mom to see like a trophy.

She stared at the mess, her face arraigned in wrinkles. "Want to tell me about this?" Her hand waved over the mound of random stuff.

"Um."

"Never mind." She placed a hand on her forehead. "Just please clean it up before you go."

"Sure, no problem." I set my purse on the coffee table and did my best impersonation of a snow shovel to pile everything back into the closet. It was a little sticky when I tried closing the door, but a good heave with my shoulder got the door to click. I swished my hands together. "All clean."

Mom closed her eyes. "I'm going to pretend I didn't see that."

"I'll clean it for real when I get home." I slid my purse onto my shoulder, tucking the sunscreen in deep so it didn't fall out. Despite my grumbling, the last thing I wanted was to be lobster red for the next two weeks.

Mom still hadn't opened her eyes when I leaned in to kiss her cheek. The touch made her peek one eye open and sigh. "Bye."

"Love you, Mom. See you later this afternoon."

She nodded and waved, then left the room as soon as possible. Probably so she wouldn't be tempted to organize the closest herself before I had a chance to do it. The cleaning bug was strong with my mom.

"Ready?" I smiled at Chandler, then opened the front door.

He hurried to the door and grabbed a spot just above my head. "I got that."

"I can open a door," I smirked. "I'm a big, tough girl."

He grinned. "Yeah, but you shouldn't have to. That's what my mom says anyway. She'll ask you if I opened doors and complimented your appearance, so make sure you tell her I did both."

He hadn't actually said anything about my appearance, but that was okay. Compliments were kind of embarrassing anyway.

Chandler pulled the front door closed behind us, then grabbed my hand to keep me from walking to his car. A small tug got me so close to him I was breathing in his exhales. "Have I told you how hot you look?" His eyes smoldered.

I take back all the mean and hurtful things I said about compliments. He could look at me like that and say those words all day every day until graduation and beyond.

Whew, was it getting warm out here?

"You just did," I said flippantly so I didn't for reals swoon right there on the sidewalk. I tried to be flippant, anyway, but it didn't really work for me. My voice was all breathy and my heart pounded in my ears.

"Cool. Make sure you tell my mom that Chandler Whittaker is the nicest guy in Prescott." Chandler stepped away, but kept hold of my hand. "You really do look hot, by the way."

Was he telling the truth? Insecurity didn't think so. I hadn't looked hot, like, ever in my entire life. I was more of a cute kind of girl. Or adorable. I got that one a lot, actually. Holland is just soooooooo adorable. That red hair and all those freckles. Soooooooo adorable.

True to form, Chandler opened the car door for me then took the driver's seat and started it up. "Sorry I was late. I forgot it's not my day for the car, so I had to do a deal with my brother to come pick you up even though he's not using the car today because we're all going to the same place. Still had to make a deal." Chandler let out a loud breath and twisted the steering wheel way too hard. He had to scramble to correct it so we didn't end up on the neighbor's lawn. That made him let out another breath, louder and way more annoyed.

It was best to ignore that part and go back to his family. The more I knew, the better prepared I could be. "You have a brother?"

"Yeah. A twin, actually."

"Really?" That was kind of a big deal, actually, another guy who looked like Chandler walking around this world. It sort of boggled my mind. Maybe I should introduce him to Alicia. We always joked about marrying brothers. Twins would be even better.

Whoa, slow down, Holland.

I hadn't even known Chandler for twenty-four hours yet. How about I just concentrate on getting to know Chandler better instead of planning our double wedding with Alicia and his brother.

Great plan.

"Yeah. I also have two older sisters—they won't be at the picnic, though—and one younger brother. He'll be there, too."

"So, there's your twin brother, your younger brother, and your parents?" That was good to know. The butterflies in my belly calmed. I could totally handle twins, younger siblings, and parents.

"That's right. Easy, yeah?"

"Yeah, my little brothers are twins," I said. "Do you like being a twin?"

Chandler hesitated, then shrugged. "Sometimes, I guess. It was cooler when we were kids, but now it's kind of annoying."

"Really? My little brothers love being twins. They're obsessed with it, actually."

"How old are they?"

"Twelve."

"Yeah, well, talk to them when they're seventeen and they have to share cars and phones and video game controllers."

I laughed.

"We're almost there. Look." Chandler pointed out the windshield. I leaned forward, waiting for the lake to appear. I'd been trying to squash the desire to see water for over a week. We had a stream that ran through our property in Colorado. I named it Mr. Gurgles when I was a kid and still called it that in my head where no one could hear me. It was embarrassing, but I missed falling asleep to the sound of Mr. Gurgles almost as much as I missed Alicia.

Almost.

The lake came into view.

"Pretty," I said.

"Yeah, we love it." Chandler pulled into a parking spot next to a boat trailer and cut the motor. "Dad brought the boat and Mom made sure he didn't forget the canoes, so it should be a blast. Are you ready to meet my family?"

"As ready as I'll ever be, I guess."

We both got out of the car. Chandler reached out his hand, waiting patiently while I scooted around the front to grab it.

"They're not scary. Like I said, they love people." Chandler swung our arms and talked about his dad's boat while we made our way to the picnic area. His mom and dad were watching for us. They came running up as soon as we got close.

"Holly! I'm so glad you came! We love to meet Chandler's friends! Are you hungry? Lunch is just about ready." His mom enveloped me into her arms and expensive perfume. I could tell it was expensive because it wafted off her like it was her natural scent. Only high-quality stuff can pull that off.

His dad shook my hand and introduced himself as Linus Whittaker, Junior. His name sounded really familiar, but I couldn't think of where I would have heard it before.

Kathy, Chandler's mom, linked my arm through hers and walked me to the gazebo where linen tablecloths covered the gross picnic benches. "Come meet our other boys. This is Zack."

A younger version of Chandler, but with brown hair instead of blond, waved from his place at the table. He was obviously doing an in-depth quality control on the chips because he couldn't stop shoveling to even say hi.

"Where's...oh, there he is! Of course he's on the boulders." Kathy waved at the other brother, beckoning him to come where we were. I looked around for Chandler. He was talking to his dad, but when he saw his brother coming, he stepped closer and took my hand.

I don't know why I felt so nervous. His family was great.

"Holly," Kathy stepped closer as the brother came into view. "This is Chandler's twin brother, Asher."

Chapter Nine

"Chandler's twin brother is Asher, Alicia. Asher!"

"Wait, wait, wait." Alicia waved her hands, making the screen pixelate while it tried to buffer to keep up with her. Our internet connection wasn't great, but it would have to do. I needed my best friend desperately. "I'm so confused. Start back at the beginning."

I shook my head and grabbed the can of whipped cream off my desk. I tipped my head back and let it whoosh into my mouth. It was on the list of Mom's 'No-No' foods, but I'd convinced her to stop by the grocery store on the way home so I could pick up a couple cans. And, by a couple, I meant three. She felt too bad for me to say no. I did grab the organic kind, though, so that was slightly better.

It was totally necessary. No way was I getting through this story without whipped cream.

"Chandler picked me up for his family picnic." I swallowed and stared at the whipped cream can. I was, for sure, going to need more than one.

"Yep, got that part."

"We drove to the lake."

"I'm with you."

"I met his parents, then his little brother, then his twin."

"And his twin was Asher?"

"Yes." I threw back my head and whooshed until whipped cream spilled over the sides of my lips onto the carpet.

Sorry, Mom.

Alicia started laughing. "Holland, come on! This is weird, but it's not fatal. We can figure it out."

I wiped my face with the back of my hand, then licked the whipped cream off. "It's a disaster, Alicia. A certifiable, freakish disaster. I'll tell you one thing: I am never going back to school. I might never leave the house again, actually. So, it's a good thing that someone invented FaceTime, Zoom, Marco Polo, Grubhub, Instacart, and—"

"Okay, okay, okay. Slow down and back up. I need the whole story. What happened after you realized Asher was the twin?"

The memory flashed behind my eyes. I groaned, dropping my head to my hands. "I was holding Chandler's hand, Alicia."

"Okay?"

The look on Asher's face was going to haunt me until the day I died. Which, come to think of it, might be very, very soon. Really, a body can only take so many socially awkward situations before it keels over.

"Okay?" Alicia said again, louder this time.

I steeled myself. Okay. Okay.

Okay.

"Asher looked at me, totally and completely confused. Then he looked at Chandler. Then he looked at our hands..."

Oh, this was so bad. It was so, so bad!

"What did he do?"

"His face got all white, then kind of reddish, then white again. His mom was like, 'Aren't you going to say hi to Holly?' And he looked at me, really looked at me. Like, looked at me all the way to my hairy soul and said, 'I thought your name was Holland, like the country.'"

"Your soul is hairy?"

"Alicia!"

"Sorry, sorry, sorry. I just can't really picture that. What did you do next?"

It probably wasn't useful to launch into a detailed description of the intense way Embarrassment squeezed every single one of my vital organs, or the amount of heat that spread up the back of my neck to my cheeks. Alicia didn't need to know all that, especially because it was happening to me again right now as I remembered that moment.

What right did Asher have to look at me all accusingly when he was the one who never called or texted me and completely avoided me since Thursday? I hadn't done anything wrong, and I was the one squirming like I'd hidden Oreos under my bed.

"I dropped Chandler's hand, for one. My palms were so sweaty, and I didn't want to gross him out. And then I stammered a lot."

Like, a lot, a lot. It was way more difficult than it should have been to explain that my name is Holland but Chandler called me Holly. My eyes kept shooting between the two boys, not wanting to offend either one of them and failing brutally.

"Then, Asher glared at Chandler, and was like, 'Her name is Holland. You should call her Holland. Maybe she doesn't like to be called Holly.'"

"Which is true," Alicia nods.

Yeah, it was, but I didn't want Chandler to feel bad about it since it was just a misunderstanding.

"And Chandler laughed and said he was positive my name was Holly because Holland is the name of a country."

"What?"

I shook my head and went on. If I stopped now, I was never going to get through this. "And Asher said that Chandler is the name of a city, so that was a stupid point. Then Chandler said that Asher was a stupid point, and it just went down the steepest hill in the world from there."

"Okay." Alicia sucked in her cheeks and chewed the insides. This was how she processed all life events.

With a fish face.

It would be so nice if Alicia had something completely and profoundly awesome to say that would fix everything. I had no idea what that would look like, but I knew if anyone could do it, Alicia could.

"What do you mean exactly by 'downhill'?"

Oh yikes. Now scenes from the afternoon were flashing in front of my eyes in a profoundly unhelpful way.

Flash: Asher shoving Chandler and telling him to back off.

Flash: Chandler shoving him back.

Flash: A full-on WWF wrestling match without sparkly jumpsuits but including a chair across the back (Chandler picked up one of the camp chairs and laid Asher out with it) and a leaping pile drive (Asher jumped off the picnic bench onto Chandler). It only ended when Zack tried to join in the fun and they both turned on him. That's when their mom and dad, who were watching with their arms around each other and sentimental looks on their faces, told them to wash up for lunch.

"I can't even, Alicia. There are no words to describe the downhilliness of this day."

"Okay." Alicia propped her elbows up on her desk and pressed her fingers together in a very mastermindish pose. "You know how you and I used to fight over the same Barbie doll when we were in preschool?"

"Ball Gown Barbie."

"Right. Between the two of us, we had about a billion dolls, and we still always fought over who got to play with that one."

"Yeah..."

"And it wasn't even ours!" Alicia laughed. "It was my mom's. She hated it sitting around, not getting played with."

"Right..." As much as I really loved random trips down memory lane, I needed to go get another bottle of whipped cream out of the fridge.

"Do you remember what my mom did to get us to stop fighting?"

Alicia's mom was a life coach, so no doubt it was something to do with changing our brains or processing our emotions.

"She sat down with us and said that our fight over the Barbie was a branch. We were too good of friends and too good of people to fight like this over a doll that didn't really matter in the long run."

I had a vague memory of that. "What's the connection, Alicia? I'm barely following."

"Okay, so, we talked it all out until we figured out that the real reason, the trunk of why we were fighting was that I was angry at you for something. I think it was because you got that new dress for Easter, the pink one with the brown sash, and all I had was my sister's hand-me-downs. And you were angry at me for something."

"Yeah, I was mad because you had so many siblings to play with and I didn't have any at the time." I scratched my chin. "So, wait, are you saying that Asher and Chandler are fighting because they have problems with each other and it has nothing to do with me?"

"Well, yeah." Alicia shrugged her shoulders back and forth. "That works too. I was thinking more that the thing we fought over wasn't the reason we were fighting; there was a trunk or a root to that branch, right?"

"Sure. Yeah, okay."

"And I'm saying the reason *you're* so upset about this isn't because of what happened with these guys today; that's a branch. You're upset because of something deeper, and I think if we can figure out what that is, you'll feel better—at least good enough to face them both at school on Monday."

Wow.

"Are you sure you want to be a nurse, Alicia? You don't want to go to The Life Coach School? Cause you kind of have this brain stuff down."

She laughed and shook her head. "Focustrate, Hols. What do you think the real problem is here? You should close your eyes; it's easier to go deep if you're not looking at me looking at you."

I did what she suggested and leaned back in my chair. As I took each new, deep breath, the world around me faded. I couldn't hear the buzz of the computer anymore, or that weird old clock at Alicia's house. I was back at the lake, watching Asher and Chandler fight over the hand sanitizer and wet wipes as they tried to undo the mess they had made.

Asher keeps shooting me glances, sometimes confused, sometimes hopeful, sometimes frustrated. Chandler is busy boxing his brothers out and subsequently taking an extremely long time to wash up. Kathy hums as she sets out containers of lettuce and tomatoes, and Linus checks his phone.

That's right; he's a senator.

I remember that Asher told me that. He's probably crazy busy. Just one more reason why I feel increasingly uncomfortable at this picnic. They should be spending this time together as a family, since it's super limited, and not fighting or watching each other fight.

Kathy hands me a plate and tells me to go ahead; the boys know to wait while the ladies go first. I mechanically put together a hoagie without the bread—it looks store-bought and mass-produced—and add vegetables to my plate. Kathy is right behind me in line, chattering about random things

I don't exactly hear. I can feel Asher's eyes on me, and it's really starting to bug me.

Again, what right does he have to be so upset? I should be upset.

I am upset.

Oh!

I open my eyes. "I'm upset."

"About what?"

The words come on their own, like they've been waiting to burst forward for days. Which, come to think of it, maybe they were. "I'm upset at Asher. Like, really, really upset at him."

"Okay, why?"

This part is a little harder. It's more raw. "Because I really liked him."

"Liked?" Alicia tips her head to the side. "Or like?"

Now we've stepped in it. It was just going to get all hot and messy in here now.

"I don't know, Ali. I'm so confused right now. But, here's the thing: when I met him on Thursday, he was such a dork. His friends are dorks and they're all super weird, but I loved it. I totally loved it. It felt like being in Durango with you and everyone else."

"So, you think we're all dorks?"

"Well, yeah."

"That's fair," she shrugged. "So, you really like Asher?"

"No," I shook my head. "I mean, I don't know. I mean, I did like him, but then he didn't text me back and—"

"Do you think that might have been a fluke, like maybe he gave you his home phone number by accident or something?"

"No," I said. "I thought about that. If it was a land-line, it would have texted back immediately. It always says you messaged a landline and it didn't go through. Anyway, I saw him on his cellphone in Spanish. So, that means he got all my weird texts and just decided I was a nerd."

"Oh, Holland." Alicia's voice dripped with sympathy. "That's not what happened. You're amazing. I think you're mad at Asher because you liked him and he cut you off. Is that right?"

That was totally it. And then, on top of that, he got super mad about me showing up with his brother. He wrecked the picnic so *hoard*.

This whole thing really was Asher's stupid fault.

"So, now tell me how do you feel about Chandler."

How did I feel about Chandler?

I had no idea.

How *did* I feel about Chandler?

"Chandler is really hard not to like. He's super good-looking, Alicia. Like, *super* good-looking."

"But they're twins."

Oh yeah, I guess I didn't explain that part yet. "They're not identical."

If they were, I would have figured this whole thing out a lot sooner and spared myself a boatload of angst today.

"Asher has brown hair and blue eyes. He's tall and kind of adorable, but Chandler is like Chris Evans but with blond hair and super green eyes. He's really built, kind of too good to be real, actually. He's gorgeous, Ali."

Suddenly I remembered how Asher described his brother to me. Too perfect. Now that I've met him, I couldn't agree more.

"Is he nice though?" Alicia sounded wary, and I didn't blame her. The guys at our school in Durango who were super gorgeous were not very nice at all.

"That's the funny thing; he really is. He's super nice. He loves that I'm quirky, and I never feel like an idiot with him." I sighed and fiddled with the whipped cream can in my hands. "He's so beautiful, and he likes me. I'm just...whatever. I don't know. He makes me feel awesome...special... You know, like, seen."

"Super nice, super gorgeous? Sounds like a winner to me," Alicia laughed.

When she put it that way, yeah. I mean, duh. It's not every day I meet a guy that's the whole package who is also interested in me. I would be a fool to pass that up.

"Right?" I lifted one hand. "It's pretty simple, actually. Whatever I felt about Asher before, he's the one who chose to ignore me. I texted him a bunch of times, and he didn't respond to any of them. That was his choice, so that means he can choose to be mad about Chandler and me if he wants to. It really has nothing to do with me. As your mom likes to say, I can't make him feel anything. So, he'll have to work out his own stuff with his brother."

"And what about Chandler? Wasn't he kind of immature about this whole thing too? You said something earlier about a canoe race?"

Yeah, but as I thought about that more, it was really Asher who goaded him into it. Of course Chandler wasn't going to back down from that. He's a sports guy and super competitive. So that makes pretty much everything that happened today Asher's fault.

Again.

"I'm pretty sure Chandler was just humoring Asher and also trying to show off for me. Which is understandable, right? He brought a girl to the family picnic, who ends up knowing his brother, then his brother starts setting up competitions like he has something to prove."

"Did Asher win any of those competitions?"

"Not a single one. Not even the watermelon seed spitting contest."

I actually won that one. Having twelve-year-old brothers has its perks. I get tons of practice.

"Ouch." Alicia winced. "I kind of feel sorry for the guy."

I would have if he wasn't such a… a…something. Nothing he did made any sense. I was better off with Chandler. At least he was predictable.

Predictable enough that he was going to call me Holly forever. Now it wasn't just about hearing my name right or wrong; it was about saying it to spite Asher. That was Asher's fault too, actually. If he hadn't made such a big deal out of it, Chandler wouldn't keep doing it. So what if Chandler called me Holly? It's not like he did it to be mean. And it wasn't a bad name, it just wasn't mine. I could live with it. Maybe eventually I could talk him into calling me Hols like my mom and Alicia.

"You still there? Earth to Holland." Alicia waved her hand back and forth in front of the camera.

"I'm here. Thanks so much for hashing this out with me. I just needed to get it out of my head."

"Of course. I have a question though."

"Yeah?"

"How are you feeling about all of this? I mean, what are you making it mean?"

That was such a life-coach question. The correct answer was that I was an idiot for not putting two and two together. That lake disaster could have been avoided if I'd simply found out Asher's last name beforehand. Then I would have known they were brothers. It would have taken two seconds. Why didn't I ever ask Asher his last name? That was so stupid.

So, so stupid.

When I didn't say anything, Alicia let out a breath. "Yeah, that's what I thought. You're blaming yourself, aren't you?"

Blame pretty much had a permanent residence on the top of my head. He was heavy too; having him up there gave me a serious headache.

"Hols, this is not your fault. Both of those guys need just as much credit for how that played out as you do. Actually, scratch that. They are more at fault. They were complete neanderthals. Don't you dare take responsibility for how they acted."

"But I—"

"No," Alicia lifted one hand. "Not your fault. Keep saying that over and over until you believe it."

I wasn't sure that was ever going to happen, but I promised her I would try and then thanked her again for listening.

"That's what friends are for, chica. Anytime. Do you need help with anything else before I go tackle my Physics homework?"

I picked up the whipped cream bottle and turned it around in my hands. "Too bad you aren't here to help me dispose of all this whipped cream. I might have over bought. I was emotionally shopping."

"Completely understandable considering the circumstances."

"Yeah, but my poor mom. I thought she was going to barf when I brought all that chemically induced whipped cream out of the store. She grossed out worse than the time Dad won that cake at the elementary school cake walk. Remember that one?"

"Ugh, how could I forget? So much red food coloring. So much!"

"It really looked vile." I pushed my hair behind my ear so it could stop tickling my nose. "Mom wouldn't even let us try it. She threw it away and then made gluten free honey muffins instead." I sighed. "I wish I could throw this day away."

"Oh, Holland." Alicia pooched her bottom lip in solidarity sympathy. "I think you better hang on to that whipped cream. I have a feeling you're going to need it."

CHAPTER TEN

"Have a heart that never hardens, and a temper that never tires."
Hard Times

I had all of Sunday to consider my life choices and formulate a plan before I had to see Asher or Chandler again. Somewhere in the middle of Sunday School, while the teacher spoke about personal revelation, I had some of my own.

I wasn't going to worry about it anymore.

I'd been ignoring my phone since I left the lake. There were five messages from Chandler and even more missed calls. I was too scared to open them because I wanted to keep pretending none of this was real. Now I was going to face it. The twins had just as much responsibility for what happened at the lake as I did. It wasn't my job to figure it out. I was going to go to school and take it from there.

That's it.

It was going to be really uncomfortable to wait and see what happened, but it felt right. And I knew enough to know that when something feels right at church, you go with it.

For the rest of the day, I took a Sunday nap, played a ridiculous number of rounds of Uno with the twins, listened to Grandma tell me stories from when she was my age, and helped my parents make dinner. Really, they made dinner; I just made a salad, but it was an amazing salad, so there was that.

When I headed to school Monday morning after finishing my morning college class, I took Confidence with me. We're not always very good friends, me and him, but today was different. For once, we were on the same page.

I walked to my locker like I owned the world, and I even remembered the lift-up trick to get it open.

First try.

Thank you, Chandler.

Then things got a little dicey. I dawdled at my locker until the first bell rang. Confidence was wishy-washy that way. Because my locker wasn't anywhere near Spanish, I slid into my seat right as the second bell rang. Almost tardy. That wasn't the bravest decision of all time, but I think it was understandable. I wasn't sure what Asher was going to do when I saw him today. I mean, I wasn't sure what to expect from him anymore.

Asher glanced over his shoulder as I arranged my Spanish things all over my desk. I purposely ignored him. It wasn't hard once Señor Herrera announced a pop quiz.

Sacre bleu! I was in so much trouble.

Wait, that was French. Yeah, so not feeling good about this test.

But I could feel grateful for it.

With all the Spanish verbs from chapter one taking up my brain space, I didn't have any room left to pay attention to Asher. The bell rang before I was finished, so I stayed after class for a minute or two to scribble in the remaining answers.

I knew I'd have to face him sooner or later. I couldn't hide from him forever, not with him knowing my locker combination, my entire schedule and, oh yeah, I sat with his friends at lunch. But the longer I put it off, the better.

I'd be more prepared later. I was sure of it. Whenever that magical, all-encompassing *later* happened to be.

I stood up and almost bumped into a guy lounging on the desk in front of me. "Oh, sorry. I didn't see you there."

"No worries." He ran a hand through his hair, making his biceps pop. It was too contrived to be attractive. "You're Holly, right?"

"Sort of." I stopped moving and looked at him differently. Was he actually waiting there to talk to me?

"Cool. Hey, listen, you're the girl dating both Chandler and Asher, yeah?"

I opened my mouth to protest that statement fiercely. He didn't notice and just kept talking.

"I gotta tell you, Chandler's the guy you want. The dude is cool, you know? You should choose him. Or if you get bored, choose me. I'd show you a good time." He laughed. "Just kidding. For sure date Chandler."

I had no idea what to say. Bewilderment sat on my tongue.

"Anyway, catch you later. You know, if you want to hang out sometime if you don't choose Chandler, which you should." He pointed both arms at me as he exited the classroom.

What the what just happened?

I didn't even want to think about it.

I turned in my quiz and headed out the door to the gym. Asher was nowhere to be seen, thankfully. I half expected him to be waiting outside Spanish for a full confrontation. I let out a long breath and looked forward to a nice, quiet, drama-free walk to the girl's locker room.

"Holland! Hey, Holland!"

I turned around, completely caught off guard. It was a girl's voice, and not one I recognized. I didn't recognize the actual girl, either. She had long blonde hair curled into darling ringlets that my fingers itched to boing. I stuffed my hands in my pockets to get rid of the temptation.

"Hey! Sorry, are you Holland?" She fell into step beside me, sucking in air like she'd searched the whole school, nay, the whole world to find me.

"Yes." I chewed a corner of my lip. "Have we met?"

"No," she held out a hand, which I shook briefly. "I'm Michaela."

"Nice to meet you, Michaela."

"You too!" She stopped walking and grabbed hold of my elbow so I would join her. "Hey, I have to tell you, I know you're trying to decide between Chandler and Asher. You should totally date Asher. He's the nicest guy in the world. And you can totally trust him. When we were in kindergarten, he took the picture that the teacher colored to his desk to see it better and the student teacher thought it was his. She made this big deal about how amazing his coloring skills were, how he stayed in the lines. She gave him a sticker and everything. But then he stood up and told everyone it wasn't his picture. He couldn't take credit for something he didn't do. Isn't that so adorable?"

"I—"

"Chandler's nice too and all, but he isn't like Asher. You won't regret it if you choose him."

Was she getting *paid* to endorse Asher like this? What the heck?

She kept looking at me like I was supposed to say something now, but what in the world was I supposed to say to that campaign commercial?

"Um, thank you for sharing that with me."

Michaela blushed. "It's no problem. You're new here. I just thought it might help you make up your mind."

"Yeah, um, thanks. But how did you know about, um..."

"Oh," she waved her hand in the air. "Everyone knows."

Like, everyone, everyone? I looked around, expecting to see posters with Chandler or Asher's faces and slogans like *Vote Chandler as Junior Year Boyfriend. Chandler is the one for you.* Or maybe *Don't be Rash, uh, er, vote for Asher.* Or better yet, *Vote Asher the Hope Dasher.*

Not very flattering. But one hundred percent accurate.

"How does everyone know?"

Michaela shrugged. "It's not a huge town, you know. People talk. Anyway, I'll let you get to class. It was nice to meet you."

"You...too." I waved, but she had already disappeared into the crowd. I rounded the next corner towards the locker rooms and was almost to the door when I heard my name again.

"Holly?"

I turned around and saw another girl headed my way. Outwardly I smiled; inwardly I sighed. I had a feeling it was going to be a very long day.

·♥·♥·♥·♥·♥·

By the time I made it to lunch, four other people shared their opinions with me. Two more in favor of Chandler, two for Asher.

So, I guess that meant they were tied?

It wasn't until I got to the commons, in sight of Asher's friend group, that I realized sitting with his friends meant sitting with him. I mean, obviously I knew that already; it just didn't sink in until I was confronted with the reality.

Maybe I should just go eat in my truck.

Tenley looked over her shoulder at the very moment I was turning away and jumped to her feet. "Holland! Good! You're here!" She stomped over to me, grabbed my hand, and pulled me to the corner.

Everyone else sat in their usual spots except Asher. He was near the drinking fountain, kind of hiding to the side of it, staring at the floor.

"Sit." Tenley pointed to the floor across from Asher.

Since I was the only one standing now that she dropped to her bottom, I figured that command was for me.

"I'll stand, thanks." I didn't really love that she was talking to me like I was a dog or a toddler.

Tenley tipped her chin back and sighed so hard I felt the air tickle my chin. "Okay, seriously, you guys are ridiculous. And we don't have time for ridiculous. We only have a few short months to pull this fundraiser together." She waved a finger between Asher and me. "So, you're just going to have to get over yourselves."

Dara, her hair in cinnamon roll buns on either side of her head, lifted a hand to cover her mouth. I'm positive I heard a snicker, but when she lowered her hand again, her face was blank.

"Smooth," Ethan grinned.

"We don't have time for smooth." Tenley slapped the carpet with her palm. "Now sit your butt down right there, Holland, and help me think of an official club name. All I have is Save Runaway Careers From The Evil Money-Grubbing Corporations Club, and that is just not working for me for some reason."

"It is kinda in your face." Ryker took a huge bite of pizza.

Bryan nodded. "Not subtle."

"I never claimed to be subtle." Tenley grabbed my hand and gave a yank. "Why aren't you sitting?"

Why wasn't I sitting? Because Asher was right there, fuming into his Yoplait. His agitation was so palatable that it left a bitter taste in my mouth. I couldn't just sit there and eat like nothing was wrong.

"I'm going to go." I took a step back. "I'll call you later, Tenley. You can fill me in on what you guys talk about, and we can brainstorm whatever else you need help with, okay?"

I thought I got away with it for a second, then Tenley dove for my legs. My knees buckled and I had two choices: fall on my rear or sit on purpose. I chose the second option, but resented it the whole time I sank to the ground.

"Let's just say it, okay?" Tenley blew her hair out of her eyes. "Holland, Asher is ticked that you showed up at his family picnic with his brother because Chandler always poaches the girls Asher likes, okay?"

Asher's head jerked up. His eyes narrowed into angry slits that tried with all their might to zap Tenley into oblivion. "Seriously?"

"Asher," Tenley scooted to face him, "Holland is upset that you never called her or responded to her texts, and also ticked that you're ticked, okay?"

Not okay!

How in the world did she know that?

Tenley glanced at me, then rolled her eyes. "You asked about Asher answering texts at lunch, remember? Then you got really quiet and all sad. Anyone with half a brain could put those pieces together."

"I didn't put those pieces together," Ethan said.

"Like I said," Tenley lifted one hand. "Anyone with half a brain."

Ethan turned to Bryan. "Did she just insult me? I can't tell. Sometimes Tenley's compliments and insults sound exactly the same."

"It was an insult." Ryker lifted his chin. "Clearly an insult."

"Oh good," Ethan smirked. "I was worried. If it had been a compliment, the world would be about to end, and I have tickets to the Suns game this weekend."

Tenley glared at each one of them for so long that I started to inch backwards. If she was distracted enough, I might be able to sneak away and end the insanity.

Except I wasn't that lucky.

Her hand shot out and gripped my kneecap. "Now that we understand each other, can you guys act like adults instead of big, talking babies? Put your garbage behind you for the greater good because I really need everyone's help. This is important."

Asher shifted, drawing my eye to him. Now that I knew he and Chandler were brothers—no, twins—I could see the resemblance. They both had that slight dent in their chin like someone put their thumb there but didn't press very hard. And even though they had different colored hair, the hair itself was thick and cut in the same style. They sat the same way, kind of hunching their shoulders, and had the exact same mannerisms.

I wish I'd made that connection sooner. Maybe things could have turned out differently.

"Come on!" Tenley's patience was gone with the wind. "Suck it up you big babies. We have work to do."

I swung my eyes away from Asher and focused on Tenley instead. "What do you need me to do?"

But she kept looking at Asher. "Well?"

"Well what, Tenley?" His voice was hard and jagged. "What you just did doesn't resolve anything; it just makes everyone uncomfortable. Facing things head-on isn't always the way to fix them."

Tenley reeled back like she'd been slapped, and who could blame her? I certainly felt the sting. "I'm trying to save Runaway Careers. It should be important to you too, you know."

"What if it isn't?" He finally looked up, his eyes darting like he was searching for an exit. "What if I don't care? What if I'm sick of being a Whittaker? Would it really be the end of the world if we let that stupid tradition go?"

"Harsh," Dara breathed out.

"Look," Tenley lifted a hand, but Asher didn't wait to find out what she wanted him to see. He was on his feet the next instance, kneading his lunch bag between his hands.

"I'm out."

Before he could walk away, Tenley stood and faced him with her hands on her hips. "I'm trying to help—"

"Maybe your help isn't all that helpful. Did you ever think of that?"

Asher stepped around her and stalked across the commons.

Tenley blinked and let out a slow breath.

"Heavy," Dara said. "Ten, are you okay?"

She dropped back to the floor, her torso swaying slightly.

"You know he's not mad at you, right?" Ethan reached over and tapped Tenley's shoe. "It's just his thing with Chandler."

"He'll figure it out," Bryan added. "He has to have his Chandler moment and then everything will be fine again. Right back to normal."

Ryker crumbled up the trash left from the package of cookies he just inhaled and dropped it in the center of his tray. "Remember in third grade when Chandler took Asher's favorite cross trainers 'cause he lost his? Asher was a bear for almost two weeks."

Tenley nodded slowly, her eyes gradually coming back into focus. "Yeah, I know. That doesn't mean it's okay, though. He can have his Chandler moments, but I'm tired of him treating everyone like crap because he has some stupid inferiority complex about his brother. It's getting old."

"You're not wrong," Bryan agreed.

While they talked, I tried to become one with the wall. I knew deep in my soul this wasn't my fault, but it was getting harder and harder to believe that was true. If it weren't for me, there would be no problem between Chandler and Asher right now. Asher wouldn't have blown up at Tenley, and they wouldn't be sitting here trying to convince themselves and each other that Asher wasn't the biggest jerk in the whole entire world.

Maybe if I tried hard enough, I could apparate.

"Hey, are you Holland?" A girl with violently violet glasses slid across the floor beside me.

"Yes."

Too bad for me.

"I heard about you and the Whittaker twins. My name is Stephanie."

"Nice to meet you," I sighed.

She nodded, knowingly. "I know, right? So annoying."

I blinked. "What do you mean?"

"The whole thing with Chandler and Asher. It's so annoying."

I totally couldn't deny that, but I also wasn't sure what she was getting at.

"Every time they do this, I'm like, seriously?" She rolled her eyes.

"Every time?"

"Oh, yeah." Stephanie's glasses slipped down her nose when she nodded. "At least once a year they have some kind of battle royale over a girl or a car or their cell phone. I'm just sorry you're in the middle of it. The last girl they fought over had to switch schools because it got so crazy."

"The last girl…"

It was like a bucket of ice water splashed into my belly.

"Her name was Monica. We were really good friends." She looked over my shoulder, then sighed. "Anyway, I just wanted you to know that at least one person in this school isn't going to place a bet or try to convince you that one is better than the other. I think the whole thing is archaic." She squinted. "And also stupid. If you need someone to talk to, let me know, okay? I sit over there during lunch." She pointed to the wall next to the bookstore.

I nodded, not trusting myself to answer. My patience was hanging by a wisp of tinsel.

When I turned back to Asher's friends, they were just wrapping up their group therapy session. Tenley was all business again, her notebook spread out in front of her.

"I love Dara's suggestion. Let's call it the Extracurricular Club. Then we'll be set if there is anything else we need to save this year. What do you think, Holland?" She looked over her shoulder with a smile.

"I like it. Hey, can I ask a question?"

Tenley nodded but didn't look up from her notes.

"What happened with the other girl Asher and Chandler fought over? Monica?" It was so embarrassing to ask, but I had to know if I was just a new toy thing or if either one of them really liked *me*. Was I just the girl of the moment?

Ryker blinked. "I forgot about that."

"I didn't." Bryan turned a page of his book with a scowl. "She was my lab partner. When she transferred, I had to do the rest of the year by myself. You try pouring liquid slowly and adjusting the Bunsen burner at the same time and see how that goes for you."

Dara patted his shoe. "Might be time to let that one go, Nerf herder."

"We obviously all have issues from this," Tenley sighed. "Do you really want to know, Holland? I mean, really?"

I didn't have to think about it. "Yes."

She set her notebook aside. "Why?"

Since Tenley liked to have all the things out on the metaphorical table, I decided to say exactly what I was thinking. Danger signs blinked in the back of my brain and Uncertainty tried to give a speech, but I shut the door, then pushed a trunk in front of the door. A heavy one with lots of books. Then, just for good measure, I stuck a sumo wrestler on top of the trunk.

"Because I really thought Chandler liked me, and now I'm thinking he just likes competing with his brother. Is that it?"

Tenley tapped her pencil rapidly on the floor. "What about Asher?"

"Asher obviously isn't interested," I said. "He never called me back or anything, and that was before I even met Chandler. So it doesn't matter. I just need you to tell me if they do this all the time because I don't want to be that girl."

It was quiet for a minute. Everyone exchanged glances that I couldn't interpret. Finally, Dara spoke.

"They do like their competitions, it's true, and sometimes they do duke it out over girls. I don't know that they do it just to fight, though. Asher really liked Monica a lot, and she decided she liked Chandler better. That happened with Jetta too."

"And Kaylee," Ethan added.

Tenley put a hand on my arm. "It doesn't matter what happened in the past. Those were all unique and stupid circumstances, just like this one is. It's not like Asher or Chandler begins a new year with a goal to like the same girl as his brother and start a high school-wide war. You know?"

That made sense, sure, but it didn't make me feel better.

"Look, what matters is what you think and feel. You, Holland. If you like Chandler, date him and see what happens. If you like Asher, date him. This is about the three of you, not anyone else and definitely not the past." Tenley stared at me. I couldn't tell why exactly, but it seemed like she wanted to be sure I agreed before she went on.

I could sort this out with myself later. Right now, Tenley needed help with Runway Careers.

I nodded, then she clapped her hands. "Okay, we're good. Then back to business. We have a teacher sponsor already, Mrs. Marlow."

"She's so cool," Dara said.

"She really is," Tenley said. "And her husband is all muscle if we need someone to encourage people to participate in the club."

Ethan groaned. "Are we the mafia now?"

Tenley ignored him; she was really good at that. "So, we need to put together some fundraisers. The faculty gave us until Christmas break; I think I told you that already. If we don't have the money by then, they want us to drop it."

"Why? Runway Careers isn't usually until March." Ryker picked something out of his teeth and then sucked it off his finger.

"Ew," Dara said, wrinkling her nose.

"Yes, but we have to book things in advance. If we don't have the money by December, we won't have time to get the rest of the stuff in line."

Ethan nodded once. "Right, gotcha."

"So, give me some ideas, people. Fundraisers, go!"

People started throwing out ideas like candy at a parade.

"Wrapping paper sales."

"We could walk dogs!"

"Cakewalk."

"Bake sale."

"We could put on a play and charge admission!"

"Enchilada sale."

"Car wash."

"Carnival."

"Service auction."

"Cookie dough sale."

"We could make friendship bracelets!"

And then the parade stalled. Tenley stared at her notebook for a moment, where she'd written down all the suggestions. With a scrunched face, she crossed out some things and circled others until she was satisfied enough to sit up. She held the notebook in out at arm's length and twisted her torso slowly so all of us could see it.

Bake sale, cakewalk, car wash, and enchilada sale made the cut. Everything else was crossed out.

"What is a cakewalk, exactly?" Bryan squinted at the paper. "You don't actually walk on cake, do you?"

Tenley let out a huff of air. "Sometimes... Really, did you grow up under a rock?"

"Or in a dragon cave," Ethan elbowed him.

"Ha ha. Just tell me what it is."

Tenley glared at each of us in turn. "Do the rest of you know what a cakewalk is?"

I did, but I was kind of afraid to say anything. Tenley was the master of the hairy eyeball. After a moment of glaring, Tenley looked as if she were about to lose faith in all humanity. I raised my hand like a grade schooler and immediately felt ridiculous.

Oh well. The only thing to do now was talk. Everyone was looking at me. I might as well.

"If I remember right, a cakewalk is when people bring cakes—donated, I think—and put them on display with a number. Then those numbers go on the floor and people walk around, stepping on the numbers while music plays in the background. Whatever number you land on when the music ends, you buy that cake."

"So," Ethan's forehead wrinkled, "you have to buy the cake no matter what? What if it's lemon and you're allergic to lemons?"

"No one is actually allergic to lemons, Ethan. That's ridiculous." Ryker rolled his eyes.

"Peanuts, then."

Tenley raised her hands so everyone would stop talking and look at her or risk that hairy eyeball again. "The cakewalk I've been to was similar to that, but there was a winning number per round. When the music stopped, the person on that number got to go pick a cake to buy, whichever one they wanted. So, that cures the allergy problem."

That was a way better idea. This could actually be really fun.

"We could do it as part of a carnival," I suggested. "You know, people buy tickets to play the fishing game and the one where you pop balloons and…" I drew a blank.

Tenley was scribbling so fast she had to stop to shake her hand out three times. Words tripped over themselves as she muttered them. It was impossible to hear what she was saying, but I think it was good.

"Come on, Ten, we are on the edge of our seats here," Dara said in her best Princess Leia voice. "What are you writing?"

Tenley's sigh was full of contentment. Her shoulders relaxed away from her ears as she ran her hand along the notebook paper, gazing at it lovingly.

I'm not even exaggerating. She really was.

When she finally opened her mouth to speak, the words came out almost lazily. "We're going to do a carnival the first week in December. I'll email you your assignments. We don't have much time to pull it together, so check your email, people." She gave one last glare to put the fear of email slacking into each of us, and then smiled. "This is going to be epic."

Chapter Eleven

• ❤ • ❤ • ❤ • ❤ • ❤ •

Thank goodness I only had one more class before I could leave. I spent the whole time warding off notes urging me to date Chandler or Asher. I'd seriously had enough. If I had to sit through another class like that, I wouldn't be able to hold back Anger any longer.

And it wouldn't be pretty.

I lugged my stuff out of creative writing, mourning the fact that there had been very little creativity and next to zero writing the whole period. At least, not on my part. Everyone else in the class should have turned their notes in to the teacher instead of me. Some of those works of fiction were worthy of a Pulitzer.

When I turned the corner to the hall where my locker was waiting, my feet faltered. Why was Chandler standing near my locker? I didn't want to see him yet. I was still deciding whether I wanted to see him or his stupid brother ever again.

Yeah, I know I told Alicia I liked the fact that Chandler was interested in me, but after a full day of Whittaker campaigning, I was sort of done with both of them.

His face lit up when he saw me. "Holly!"

I dragged my feet the rest of the way to my locker. "Hi, Chandler." He stood in front of the lock so that I couldn't ignore him by spinning the combination. I just had to stand there awkwardly, staring at his shoes.

They were the same shoes he wore on Saturday. Obviously, he'd cleaned them up after Asher filled them with mayonnaise; there was no trace of it anywhere.

"Holly." His voice was louder than it should have been if the only person he was talking to was me. I was, like, inches away. But, then again, maybe he was trying to be heard over the crash of lockers and general noise of too many bodies crammed into one hallway. "We have to talk."

"Do we?"

He lifted my chin with his finger. Which might have been an adorable gesture if I actually wanted to look at him.

I didn't.

I kept getting images of him dangling a raw crawdad over Asher's mouth, daring him to eat it. 'Come on! Where's your man card?' When that didn't work, he ate it himself. It wasn't huge, but still. Something like that sticks with a person, kind of the way the grayish brown shell bits stuck in between Chandler's teeth when he smiled at me triumphantly.

"Yeah, we do," Chandler said firmly.

"About what?" I wasn't going to make this easy. It would be good for him to stand there awkwardly, feeling out of place and uncomfortable. Then maybe he would see how it felt to be me on Saturday.

Chandler ran a hand through his gorgeous blond highlights. "The lake. We need to talk about what happened. You should have told me you knew Asher."

I finally raised my eyes to his. "I didn't know he was your brother. You never mentioned him once until the drive to the lake, and then you never said his name." I was not taking the credit for this debacle. Chandler was equally at fault, just like Alicia said.

Chandler stared at me incredulously. "How could you not know we were brothers? Everyone knows! Come on, someone must have mentioned it."

I stood up straighter. "I come to school late and leave early. I don't see or talk to pretty much anyone who isn't in my classes."

"You can't tell me no one in your classes mentioned us."

I blinked. Did he think people sat around discussing the ins and outs of his relationship with Asher instead of listening to the math lesson or history lecture? Actually, that wasn't a totally off-base assumption, considering how many people felt the need to campaign for one twin or the other.

All day.

Okay, his question wasn't that conceited.

"Nope," I shook my head.

He still looked skeptical.

I sighed. "Can you scoot over? I need to get in my locker."

He stepped aside and watched me twirl the combination. When I opened it without a problem, he smiled. "Remember when I helped you with that?" His voice was full of nostalgia even though that was literally three days ago.

"Thank you for the trick. It's lots easier to open now."

Chandler puffed out his chest. "Yeah, no problem."

I exchanged my books, then closed my locker. "Okay, well, I guess I'll see you later." The hall was beginning to clear out, which meant the bell was probably about to ring.

"Wait, hold up. We still need to talk."

I was hoping he forgot about that. "Yeah, I guess."

"Look, Holly. Things really got out of hand at the lake. I get that, but you should have stuck around so we could sort it out. I didn't even know you left."

"Yeah," I said, surprising myself by speaking my thoughts out loud. "That might be because you pelted Asher with water balloons, then launched yourself out of your sinking canoe and tackled him into the water."

"It was shallow; he was fine."

"Was he? Even after he got that fish stuck in his swimsuit?"

Chandler cringed. "You saw that?"

Yeah, I saw that. I also saw the bucket of mud Chandler dumped over Asher's head and, shortly after that moment, when Asher pantsed Chandler. Luckily, they were both waist-deep in the water, so no one was scarred for life.

Namely me.

Okay, I was still pretty much scarred for life, but I was coherent enough to realize it could have been a whole lot worse.

"What about Asher, huh?" Chandler stretched his hands over his head so his shirt partly rolled up. A couple of passing girls stopped to watch. Too bad for them, he dropped his arms before his abs came into view. "Maybe you noticed when he mocked everything I said, then threw that jar of pickles in my face?"

I was sitting next to Chandler when that happened, so, yes, I did notice. It's just that all the stuff that happened while we ate lunch was overshadowed by the shenanigans in the water. For a second there, I really thought they were going to drown each other on purpose.

"Look, Holly, I didn't come over here to pick a fight. The opposite, actually. I wanted to say I'm sorry for everything that happened."

I wish it was that simple. I wish he could say he was sorry and everything would be normal again. No matter how many words came out of Chandler's mouth, we were still in the middle of a disaster.

"I don't know how to navigate this, Chandler. I think it's probably better if none of us ever see each other again."

That was the only solution I could see where no one got hurt.

"No." Chandler took my hand and held it in the space between us. "Come on, we can figure this out. I really like you, Holly. Will you give me a chance to prove it?"

There probably aren't very many girls who could resist the earnest look on Chandler's perfectly chiseled face while he was holding their hand tightly in his. Add to that the totally irresistible scent of his cologne, and it was only natural that every single one of my defenses started to crumble.

"Give me a chance," he smiled. "Please?"

Before I could answer, the sound of stomping feet drew my attention away from Chandler. Asher was marching up behind us in his best impression of a rampaging bull elephant. "What's going on here? The bell is about to ring. You're going to be tardy again."

He was talking to Chandler, glaring at him like he wanted to singe his eyebrows with one good stare. Asher ignored me so thoroughly that he accidentally bumped my shoulder, breaking the contact I had with Chandler's hand.

"You know if you're late to class one more time, you'll get suspended from the football team." Asher crossed his arms. "And you know how much this school *needs* you."

Chandler gave Asher a withering look. "That is my business, bruh. I already have two parents, so you can keep your fat nose out of my stuff."

Asher snorted. "That would be great. I'd love that. Unfortunately, everyone in the world thinks I need to be my brother's keeper." He crossed his arms over his chest. "And, by the way, *bruh*, we have the exact same nose."

That caught my attention. I studied their noses and came to the conclusion that Asher was right; they did have the exact same nose.

I wish noticed that sooner.

"Look, you guys..."

Asher looked at me for the first time, his eyes smoldering, but not in a good way. It was like he wanted to transport me to the fiery center of the earth with those eyes. Far, far away where he never had to look at me again.

At least, that's what I got out of it.

I gulped, "I really think—"

Chandler talked right over me like I wasn't even there. "That's not the point, Asher, and you know it. You always do this, bruh. You gotta get over me. Seriously, get your own life."

"That's what I'm trying to do. That's what I've been trying to do since, like, birth. Too bad every time I turn around, you're there, stealing my soap, eating my cereal, butting your big butt in the way of every girl—"

"By the way," Chandler said in a mocking voice, "we have the same butt. If mine is big, yours is too."

Wow.

That was...Wow.

Where was that warning bell when a girl needed it? There had to be something wrong at the office. It usually rang by now, didn't it? Maybe I should go check. Yes, I should definitely leave and let these two discuss their butts in private.

I took a slow step backwards.

Chandler's hand reached out and grabbed mine, holding it tightly so I couldn't move any further. "You're making this so much worse. Here I am, trying to smooth things over, and you're just screwing it all up again. Like usual. Why don't you go so I can talk to Holly."

"Her name is Holland, you freak! Why is it so hard to get through your stupid, thick skull?"

"Come on, HOLLY." Chandler glared at Asher. "Let's finish this talk somewhere else."

I didn't want to go anywhere unless it was home, and I really didn't want to finish this talk. I pulled on my hand, trying to get it out of Chandler's grip. Asher noticed and smacked his brother on the shoulder.

"Let her go. She's trying to get away."

"Don't touch me, you crashy punk." Chandler let go of my hand to punch Asher in the shoulder. "Get over it. She's not going out with you."

"Guys," I tried again.

I don't know why I bothered. Neither one of them seemed to notice I was there anymore.

"Get your hands off me!" Asher grabbed Chandler's wrist and twisted his arm. "Holland's not going out with you either. You think you're the greatest thing that ever walked. You're not, you're just..." He grunted as Chandler swung around and caught him in a headlock.

"Gimme a break," Chandler said through gritted teeth. "I'll bet you anything Holly likes me better than you. That's what's really bothering you, isn't it?"

They wrestled each other to the ground, legs and arms flinging all over the place. I stepped away, trying to stay out of the way. They yelled things back and forth that were impossible to interpret. Only my name was discernible here and there. Well, my name and Holly's.

"Hey, you guys, I'm going to go now. I can tell you're busy, so I won't disturb you. You just keep doing what you're doing. No worries. I can find my own way to my car." I kept talking as I backed away slowly. When neither one of them responded, I figured I was safe to turn around and walk away. I increased my speed as I got farther down the hall to put as much distance as possible between myself and the twin tornado of terror.

The bell finally rang as I pushed the doors open to go outside.

Well, it was about time.

Chapter Twelve

"No one is useless in this world who lightens the burdens of another."
Doctor Marigold

When I got home that afternoon, the first thing I did was check my email. Tenley said she was going to email carnival assignments, and I desperately needed a way to take my mind off the stupid Whittaker twins.

Behold, the longest email in the history of emails.

Complete with diagrams and a detailed portion for each carnival game, along with the name of the person in charge of making it happen.

I was in charge of the cakewalk.

Which made sense, since I was the only person who knew what that was, but it still made Anxiety crash through the windows and start a ruckus.

How was I supposed to find people to donate cakes? I knew, like, three people in this whole town.

Before I could really work myself up, I heard Grandma's bell ringing downstairs. Dad was locked in a project and Mom was at the gym, so I took this timely opportunity to step away from the screen and breathe. Breathe in down the stairs, breathe out down the hall, breathe in into Grandma's bedroom.

Breathe out.

"Hey! What do you need?" I walked over to the side of the bed and took a seat.

Grandma laughed with a slightly mocking note. "I didn't want to bother you; I know you're busy. I tried to get up myself, but I knocked over my cane and..." That laugh again.

"Hey, no problem! I needed a break. Where are you trying to go?"

"The restroom." She rolled her eyes.

"Hey," I grinned, "when nature calls, it's no joke."

I helped her stand, then grabbed her cane and handed it to her. "I'll walk with you, okay?"

"You really don't need to do that."

"I want to." I looped her free hand through my elbow and clasped her hand there with mine. "You're doing me a favor, really."

We took a few, shuffling steps and then stopped to rest. Grandma's smile was forced. I couldn't tell if she was in pain or just really, really embarrassed. What could I do to distract her?

"I just got an email from Tenley, one of my new friends," I said in a cheery voice. "She's putting together a carnival in December to raise money, and I'm helping her. You should see the pages and pages of notes, Grandma! She's even more meticulous than Gramps was!"

"Oh, my! What are you raising money for?"

Oh good, it was working. Grandma looked interested instead of frustrated.

"Um, Runway Careers."

"Runway Careers!" Grandma looked up, her face brightening. "I just love that Runway Careers! I decided to be a seamstress after I attended during my last year in high school."

"Really?"

"Why do you look surprised?" Grandma's eyes twinkled. "Did you think I am too old? They didn't have Runway Careers back with the dinosaurs and such?"

"No!" I nudged her gently. "I just didn't realize. You've never talked about it before."

"Well, you've never asked," Grandma shrugged. "Why do you need to raise money? Doesn't the school put it together? They did when I went there."

"Yeah, I guess they are out of money. They had cuts or something, and Runway Careers isn't completely necessary, so it had to go."

"Oh, no. Runway Careers is definitely necessary. I couldn't even begin to tell you how many people have found their chosen career because of that event. Your father did, your grandpa, me, most of my friends. Oh, it's such a good experience. Everyone should have the opportunity." Grandma paused. "Although, I suppose you already have your career decided, yes?"

I nodded. "I'm going to be a nurse." And Alicia was going to be a doctor, and we were going to work together at a hospital in a big city until some rich bachelors swept us off our feet. Not twins though.

I'd just about had it with twins.

Grandma pursed her lips. We were just steps from the bathroom door when she said, "I want to help. What can I do?" A flash of uncertainty went across her face as if she was asking the question to herself instead of me and didn't like the answer.

But I had my own little flash, and mine was brilliant. This was the perfect thing to get Grandma's mind off her ankle. She'd lived in Prescott forever; she knew everyone. She'd have no trouble figuring out who could do what. It was perfect!

We stopped walking, and Grandma inched her way along the wall into the bathroom. I waited in the hall until she came out.

"Grandma, I think you are the solution to all of my problems!"

Okay, I was exaggerating; she wasn't the solution to *all* of my problems. There was probably very little she could do to fix the mess with Asher and Chandler, for example, but she was definitely the solution to my carnival problems.

"Are you up for going to the kitchen? I need a snack, and I want to pick your brain."

Grandma nodded. "Whatever is left of my brain is yours to pick."

She didn't lean quite as heavily on me as we walked to the kitchen. That was a good sign. I helped her into a chair and went to the fridge. Hummus and vegetables sounded awesome.

"What are you fixing?" Grandma asked, twisting in the chair to look at me.

"Hummus."

Grandma made a face.

"I can get you something else, though. What sounds good?" I set the hummus and a bag of cut carrots on the table.

Grandma leaned forward. "Promise not to tell?"

I zipped my lips.

"There's a secret cupboard behind the buffet where I hide all the treats your mother doesn't like. You'll have to scoot the buffet over a bit and you'll see what I mean."

I walked to the buffet, not knowing what cupboard she meant until I got there. Just the edge of a door peeked out.

"Before your family moved in, I stashed all my good stuff in that cupboard and moved the buffet to hide the door. I knew your mother would throw it all out."

I pinched my lips together to keep from laughing out loud. There was no doubt my mom would do exactly that. She had immediately attacked the fridge when we got here. Two bottles of Sweet Baby Ray's BBQ sauce and a bottle of ketchup were in the trash two seconds later. Victims of their ingredient lists.

High fructose corn syrup. *Shudder.*

I used my shoulder to move the buffet enough to open the cupboard. Inside were stacks of Oreo packages, bags of chips, and boxes of Lorna Doone cookies. That was just the beginning. There was a year supply of junk food in there. "What do you want?"

"A Lorna Doone sounds lovely, with a glass of milk."

I pulled out a box, moved the buffet back in place, and headed to where Grandma waited patiently. "How in the world did you move that thing? It weighs a ton!" I kept picturing her sitting on the floor with her back to the buffet, pushing with her shoulders.

I really hope that wasn't what she did.

"Oh," she took the glass I handed her and set it on the table, "I had Asher Whittaker come do it for me. Don't worry."

Good thing I hadn't picked up the milk jug yet. Hearing Asher's name sent a tremor through my limbs. After it ran its course, I grabbed the milk and poured some into Grandma's glass, then sat across from her.

"Do you want some?" She took a cookie from the package and held it out to me.

I shook my head.

"No? Well, let me know if you change your mind. I can't think of anything more lovely than a milk-soaked Lorna Doone. I'm glad your mother consented to let me keep my evil cow's milk full of hormones and antibiotics in the same fridge as her organic rice milk."

My mom and grandma had irreconcilable food preferences and teased each other constantly, but they really, really loved each other. Why couldn't Asher and Chandler do that? Love each other for their differences instead of going to war?

I picked up a carrot and swirled it through the hummus, then just stared at it.

"Anything wrong?" Grandma reached for a napkin in the center of the table and wiped her milky fingers.

I shook my head, then shrugged.

"Come on, out with it, love." She eyeballed me. "Don't be coy; you're the one who coaxed me out of my cave. You're going to have to deal with the consequences by telling me what's bothering you."

"Who says anything's bothering me?"

Grandma lowered her eyebrows.

"Okay, something is bothering me." I took a deep breath. I didn't want to ask the question, but I had to. "How well do you know Asher and Chandler Whittaker?"

Grandma's hand hovered above her milk. "What an interesting question. How well do *you* know those boys?"

Interesting question, indeed. Apparently, I didn't know them at all. Neither one of them was showing up as the boy I thought he was when I first met him.

Grandma sat back and folded her arms. "I think I need some more information before I say another word."

That was all the encouragement I needed to effectively spill my guts. I told Grandma everything, every interaction I'd had with those guys from day one to that afternoon.

When I finished, I felt drained.

"Oh my," Grandma whistled through her teeth. "That is a story and a half."

"Yeah." I finally took a bite of the carrot so I could chew instead of think. My brain needed a break.

"Let me ask you something, Holland." Grandma leaned forward and rested her elbows on the table. "How do you feel about those boys?"

"That's the thing, Grandma. I don't know." I blew out a gust of air. "I mean, I really liked Asher when I first met him, but he's not the same guy now. Plus, it is really hard to overlook the whole ignoring my texts thing."

"Yes, that is out of character." Grandma's eyes narrowed. "I'm sure there's more to that story than we know."

I shrugged. It didn't matter anymore. "And, honestly," I blushed as the words came out, "I thought Chandler was really hot, and it was super flattering that he was interested in me. But then he got so competitive that it was like I wasn't even there anymore. But, then again, he was the one who found me and apologized first. Asher acts like the whole thing is my fault. I really don't know."

"Sticky." Grandma pursed her lips. "This is very, very sticky."

"Yeah," I sighed. "Honestly, I don't want to talk about it anymore. I shouldn't have brought it up. I was just so confused and you mentioned Asher, and then I wondered what you thought of them." I tapped the table lightly. "What do you think about them?"

Grandma reached across the table and covered my hand with hers. "Honey, it doesn't matter what I think."

"Of course it does!" My eyes flew to her face.

"You know what I mean. I could love 'em both or hate 'em both, and it makes no difference whatsoever. You need to decide what *you* think about them. That's what matters."

I took a deep breath and let it out with gusto. "I know."

Grandma patted my hand before pulling away. "You'll figure it out. You're the best kind of girl to handle this."

"Am I?"

"Of course, because you care about people. You'll do what's best for you, and you'll do what's best for them. That's the Holland I know."

But what if that Holland had no idea what was best for everyone?

"Now, about your carnival? What do you need help with?"

It took my brain a few minutes to transition. I shook myself. "I'll be right back." I jetted to my room to get my phone. It would be easier to show Grandma the email from Tenley than to try and explain it.

I plopped back into my chair across from Grandma and opened my phone, then slid it over to her. She read while I caught my breath.

"My goodness, you weren't kidding!" Grandma looked up a few minutes later. "This young lady puts your Gramps to shame, and he was quite the organizer. What is your responsibility here?"

I leaned over so I could see the screen and scrolled until it got to the cakewalk. Grandma peered over her glasses.

"Cakewalk! I haven't been to a cakewalk in years! They used to do them at church all the time when I was a girl. Well, that's a fun responsibility right there. You couldn't ask for a better one."

"What were they like when you went, Grandma?"

"I seem to recall the cakes were numbered, and when the music stopped, they drew a number from the hat. If you were on that number drawn, that's the cake you got. But I have to say that I would have liked to pick my cake. Especially since I was buying it. It's nice to have some say in flavors and how much you pay."

I totally agreed. "So, we have the cakes with prices arranged on a table. Then a circle of numbers, yes?"

Grams nodded.

"Then we have music and a caller who draws a number out of a hat. I really like that. If your number is called, you go to the table and purchase the cake of your choice."

But was that going to hurt a donator's feelings if every cake was except theirs? I pictured a lumpy, lopsided cake with sliding green frosting all alone on the table. That would be the cake I made. I'm not much of a baker.

"That sounds perfect." Grandma clapped her hands. "Now, about those cakes. What are your thoughts on how to get them?"

"I don't have one," I sighed. "We don't have any kind of budget to buy them. It's probably too much to ask a store or bakery to donate, like, twenty cakes to the carnival, isn't it?"

"Perhaps."

"And I don't know twenty people in this state, much less this city. Not well enough to call them and ask them to make a cake to donate, anyway. And I can't offer to pay for ingredients or anything."

"You shouldn't have to do that."

"No?" I tipped my head to the side. "Do you think people would be willing to make a cake for free?"

"Absolutely," Grandma grinned. "I've been in this town a long time, Hols, and I've seen amazing things. Forest fires, tragic accidents, blizzards—the people here take care of each other. Let me make some phone calls—prime the engine, so to speak—and then I'll give you a list of people you can petition. What do you say to that?"

Hallelujah came to mind.

"Is that too much for you to do right now? I mean, it's kind of my responsibility. I don't want you to have to do it for me. Especially when you're trying to get better."

"There is nothing better than service to lift the soul. Now, it might not fix my ankle, but I feel better right now than I have in weeks."

"It's the cookies," I gestured across the table.

Grandma laughed. "No doubt they did some good in their own way. I am happy to help you, Holland. I think I might need it as much as you do."

I scooted out of my seat and around the table to throw my arms around my grandma. "You are a lifesaver, you know that?"

"Oh, now, enough of that nonsense." She squeezed my arm with her hand, then swatted me. "How about you put these cookies back into hiding before your mother comes home and sees them. We don't need that kind of trouble."

I did, and just in time. Mom breezed into the kitchen as I shoved the buffet into place. Grandma picked up her crumb-coated milk glass and held it in her lap until I got over to her and took it covertly. While Mom put groceries away and asked about our days, I rinsed the glass free of all evidence and set it next to the sink.

"Dinner at six, okay? We're having stir fry. Oh, good, Mom, you got a snack." Mom looked at the hummus and veggies. "I'm surprised. I didn't think you liked hummus." She smiled, "Or vegetables."

"I don't." Grandma rested her hands on the table like she didn't have a care in the world. "I was keeping Holland company while she ate."

"Well, that's nice. I'm glad to see you up and smiling."

"I'm glad to be up and smiling."

Their banter could go on for hours; they both enjoyed it so much. I had to break in or be stuck there forever, watching the verbal tennis match.

"Want me to help you back to your cave, Grandma? I need to finish up some assignments." And also process what Grandma said to me about Asher and Chandler. I think she had a valid point. Until I figured out what I wanted, I was just going to get tossed between the two of them like a favorite chew toy.

"Yes, ma'am." Grandma held out her arm. I took it, then led it to my shoulder. She put some pressure on as she stood, then leaned more into the cane than she did into me.

"If you finish early, Hols, come help with dinner," Mom said. "I'd love to hear about your day. I feel like I haven't had a chance to talk to you in ages."

"Absolutely."

Grandma and I made our way through the house to her bedroom. At the door, she let go of me and carefully covered the rest of the distance to her bed. Once she was safely seated, she leaned her cane on the nightstand and rested her eyes on me.

"I think you know, deep down, which one of those boys you like better."

That was not what I was expecting her to say, not even close. "Really?"

Grandma nodded. "I think the reason this feels so difficult and frustrating is because you like him so much and he's behaving so badly."

Give the woman a crown. My grandma was the queen of the generalized statement.

"Which *he* would that be, Grandma?" I smiled slowly.

She wagged a finger at me. "You know exactly who I mean. Now, I'm not telling you what you know, Holland. I'm telling you what I think will give you a chance to open your mind to all the possibilities. Your brain is stuck on the now, but people aren't made up of one moment, my girl. They are a beautiful disaster of millions of moments. Think about everything, not just one thing, and I think you'll know exactly what to do."

I narrowed my eyes. "That sounds suspiciously like life coaching. Didn't you say it's a bunch of hoo-hoo?"

"I did." Grandma flicked a hand across her cheek. "But just because it's hoo-hoo doesn't mean it isn't true."

"That might be a profound statement." I smiled. "Want me to get your cross-stitching supplies?"

Grandma waved a hand at me. "You go get your stuff done; I'm going to read."

"Good idea. See you at dinner." I turned towards the stairs but stopped when Grandma called my name.

"Yeah?" I peeked my head back in.

"I love you, Holland." She settled back on her pillows, easing her leg onto the bed. "And I like that twin better, too."

I told her I loved her back and then shook my head all the way back to my own room.

Why did I always complain about adults always telling me what to do as a kid, and now that I'm almost an adult, I'd give anything for them to boss me around? It was weird. Like, how awesome would that be if Grandma said, 'I definitely know from years of life on this earth that you should for sure hang out with ________. You'd have the best chance of happiness and mutual love with him'.

That twin.

Him.

He.

I let out a sigh and plopped into the chair at my desk. Yeah, not confusing at all.

Clear as mud.

Chapter Thirteen

"Trifles make the sum of life."
David Copperfield

Life has a way of helping you out when you're in the middle of a weird crisis involving twin brothers that you didn't know were twins before you sort of started liking both of them.

Yeah, strangely specific. I know.

The following weeks were so bonkers that I didn't have a single spare minute to figure out what to do about Asher and Chandler. I barely even saw either one of them.

Once Grandma gave me her master list of awesome bakers who were willing to put together a beautiful cake for free, I divided my time between calling all of them and helping Tenley build carnival games from tutorials on YouTube. Her parents were saints. By the last week in November, every spare space in their living room and garage was filled with carnival games and supplies.

Somehow I made it through all of the building Saturdays without seeing Asher more than once. Tenley anticipated chaos and separated us. She put him in the garage and me in the living room. I caught a glimpse of him when he came inside for a drink of water, and that was it. The rest of the work days, I hung out with Dara, dressed as whatever character she was at the moment, and the rest of the guys. That was nice. I got to be someone other than the girl the Whittaker twins were fighting over.

The week before the carnival, I spent every spare moment calling the people who were making cakes to make sure they were still good to go and then giving them details. I'd said it so many times that I could do it in my sleep. "Please drop off at the south door of the school gym on Friday, December seventh before five o'clock."

And, amazingly, every single one of them did just that. On Friday at four forty-five, I stood in the gym next to a beautiful table housing not twenty but fifty gorgeous cakes. No sliding green frosting or lumpy bumps to be seen.

I really owed Grandma for this one. She had seriously saved the day. It would have been fabulous if she felt up to coming, but they'd put the screws in her ankle just a couple days ago, and she was in a lot of pain. I would have to take a billion pictures for her. Everything looked amazing.

The fishing station was in the corner opposite me, with Ethan untangling the fishing lines. We'd already done that three times, and they still found a way to tangle. I swear, someone could not have purposely tangled the lines as badly as they somehow tangled themselves. It was kind of amazing and completely obnoxious at the same time.

Ryker was in charge of the beanbag toss next to the fishing booth. It was irresistible, apparently. Everyone who walked by joined Ryker in practicing their beanbag skills. It was a good thing we didn't have a school toss team because most of those bean bags ended up in Dara's duck pond. The only person who could make it in a hole of the sturdy cardboard box we'd rigged for the beanbag toss was Ryker, and he stood, like, ten feet away.

Must be hard to be that fantastic.

Dara had to fish sopping bean bags out of the inflatable pool that was originally intended for bobbing for apples until Tenley stopped to think how disgusting that was. Now it was full of bobbing rubber duckies, all shapes and sizes because they came from various homes. It was almost alarming how many people had rubber duckies lying around and were willing to donate them. There was a whole garbage sack full of more in the cafeteria in case anything happened to the ones in the pool. A small net with a long handle leaned against the table, ready to go when we were.

A loud fffftttttttthhhhhttt sound came from Bryan's station where he was blowing up a billion balloons. Luckily someone let us borrow an electric blower-upper, or he would have passed out a long time ago. His game was probably going to be the best one, though. People would enter the plastic pool at his station, which was filled with balloons. Then they had to try to pop them by sitting on them. Whoever popped the most in one minute won a piece of candy.

Actually, that was the prize for everything: cheap, bulk candy so that all the money could go to Runway Careers. It sounded lame when I put it like that, but everybody loved candy. It would be totally fine.

My station was all set with the cakes—priced according to how fancy they were—numbers on the floor, and a hat full of matching numbers. My phone was ready to play a shuffle of nursery rhyme songs that wouldn't morally offend anyone.

It was time to check on everyone else. I started with Bryan because I had a feeling he was going to need help blowing up those bazillion balloons.

For sure I was *not* going to check on Asher, whose ring toss was right next to my cake walk. I could feel his eyes on the back of my head whenever I wasn't facing him, and I was so not going there right now. Tonight was about raising money for Runway Careers. We'd put so much work into this, and it was time to focus. The hope was that this event would be so successful, we wouldn't need to do any other fundraisers.

Tenley walked over to Bryan's station the same time I did. Her hair flew around her in crazy whisps, and her hands white-knuckled a clipboard.

"Do you guys think we have enough stuff?"

I picked up a balloon and put it in place, then pushed the spout to get the air moving inside. It was too loud to reply for a few seconds.

"What do you mean by 'stuff'?" Bryan asked. "Like, prizes?"

"No, booths." Tenley waved her hands wildly. "Are there enough activities to keep people occupied for three hours?"

"There's seven booths with your dunk tank," I said.

"Sick," Bryan twirled the balloon around his fingers to tie it. He was becoming a master at that. It took me way longer to tie my balloon. "That dunk tank, seriously, how did you do that?"

"I can't take credit." Tenley blew some hair out of her eyes. "I didn't make it or anything; I just borrowed it from another school."

"That's awesome. The mayor is going in there," Bryan said. "How'd you rig that?"

"He called me and volunteered. He wanted to help. I guess he decided to go into politics after Runway Careers his junior year."

So many people had decided their futures from this one event. I was so excited to see it in action.

"Sick," Bryan said again.

"Anyway," I went on, "seven booths and the pony rides outside."

"Also, sick."

"Yes, thank your brother for me, Bryan." Tenley's smile started to curl up, but she got distracted and it dropped.

"Will do. He's happy to do it. He bought his farm right after high school because—"

That's right, because he went to Runway Careers.

Mind boggling, really, how the school board could decide this event didn't matter when it so very much did. To a lot of different people, apparently.

"It's going to be fine." I put a hand on Tenley's arm so she'd look at me. She tried, she really did, but her eyes kept darting all over the place. "If everything runs out or people get bored and we need something to do, we have that DJ who said he'd turn it into a hoedown, remember? Great back up plan, by the way."

"Yes," Tenley nodded. It gained momentum as she kept at it. "You're right. Back-up plan, options... It's fine."

"Look at it this way." Bryan pulled a full balloon off the spout. "In the grand scheme of things, none of this matters."

Tenley stared at him.

I rolled my eyes. "Great perspective, Bryan, but maybe not super helpful at the moment."

He shrugged and wrapped the balloon end around his fingers. "I'm just saying."

"Okay, well, I'm going to go check on Asher's ring toss." Tenley gave a little wave and hurried over to Asher. He stooped over the two-liter soda bottles filled with sand so the rings didn't knock them over. This was probably the third time he'd rearranged them.

Not that I noticed. I wasn't glancing over at him every couple minutes. It was an assumption.

Really.

"It's just a carnival." Bryan reached for another balloon. "Tenley needs to relax. It's not like the fate of the known universe hangs in the balance."

That was true, but the fate of Runway Careers might.

Just then, Dara joined us dressed as Captain Marvel. With the three of us filling balloons, we were done in no time. Done, meaning we stuffed as many as we could into four big garbage bags. There were more balloons to blow up if we needed them, but it looked like there were plenty to me.

At six o'clock everything was ready and everyone was in place. Our teacher sponsor sat behind a table at the entrance so that no one could enter the carnival without passing her. Her being there might not have made a difference because she was so nice and kind of tiny, but she brought her husband, who was a huge dude with biceps the size of basketballs. He leaned against the wall like he was auditioning for the Secret Service. Sunglasses and everything. The only things missing were the ear piece and whatever heat those guys were usually packing.

A line was already forming in front of the ticket desk. I must have been more uptight about it than I thought because a steady stream of breath eked out like I had a slow leak. I didn't realize I'd been holding that.

The first people into the gym were a cute family with five kids bouncing from excitement. Excitement was super good. They went straight for Dara's duck pond. Dara had Hawaiian music playing in the background; it looked super fun.

The gym filled steadily. I lost track of how many people were at which booth as more people crowded around mine. There were many who had never heard of a cake walk and needed me to explain how it worked. I almost considered writing the information on my forehead with a Sharpie marker. The good news was, once a few people tried it out and walked off with their showstopping cakes, word got around and the need for explaining waned.

"Congratulations!" I clapped for the newest winner, a cute little girl with round, fuchsia glasses and freckles. "Find your parents and pick your cake, then take it to the front to pay, okay?"

She was too busy hopping up and down to answer, so she just nodded.

Tenley hovered around the cake table to make sure no one stuck their fingers in the icing and that the people who chose a cake actually made it to Mrs. Marlow to pay. Her dunk tank was only happening every hour, so she had the free time to help me out. We probably should have realized that it would be impossible for one person to run the cake walk and monitor the cakes at the same time, but it worked out. And now we knew for next time.

Everything went smoothly for about an hour.

Just one hour.

I was between cake walks and straightening the numbers taped to the floor when I heard someone shout, "Hey!"

Chandler and some guys I didn't recognize were at Asher's booth. Chandler had a handful of rings but wasn't throwing any of them. He stood at defense as Asher got in his face.

"You can't do that; it's not how you play the game. In fact, it's cheating. You're disqualified." Asher made a grab for the rings, but Chandler moved them out of reach at the last minute.

"Give me the rings, Chandler. You can't do that."

"I wasn't cheating."

"See that line right there? That's where you stand. Then you throw the ring onto the bottle."

"Bruh, that's what I did."

"No, you stood here, and then you dropped the ring over the top of the bottle."

"For reals? Chill out. It's just a game."

"Yeah, a game you cheated at. Give me the stupid rings."

"Try and get them."

By this time, they were attracting more attention than just mine. Several people had stopped what they were doing to watch. I put my hands on my hips, wondering if I should step in or something. I hesitated because I didn't have a great track record with stepping between those two.

Chandler waved the rings in the air, taunting and mocking with each swish. Asher glared at him instead of jumping for the rings like Chandler clearly expected him to do.

"Come on, baby butter. Try and get them. What's wrong? You think you can't?"

Asher scoffed. "I'm just waiting for you to grow up and give them to me."

"I think you're scared. Come on, you want a bigger man card. Jump for them."

"I am not going to jump for them."

Chandler waved the rings close to Asher's nose. Unable to resist, Asher made a grab and missed. Chandler thought that was incredibly funny.

Asher did not.

"Wow, Chandler, you're so cool. It's so super cool to cheat to win. Is it really that hard to throw a ring on the top of a bottle from two feet away? Let's talk about that man card, yeah?"

A few girls giggled.

Chandler froze.

His eyes darted around the room like he was suddenly aware of how many people were watching his interaction with his brother.

"I can do it from your stupid line."

"Yeah? Prove it."

More eye darting. "I don't need to prove what I already know. It's fact."

"Actually, facts get proven all the time, Chandler. Come on, are you scared?" He hooked his thumbs into his armpits and waved them up and down like chicken wings. "Bock, bock, bock."

Chandler threw the rings at Asher, hard enough to make his head jerk backwards. For sure hard enough to stop all the clucking. Rings scattered across the floor with a series of thumps.

I glanced around the room, catching Tenley's eye. Obviously, I couldn't see what my expression was like, but it must have been something awful because Tenley started towards Asher's booth. At the rate she was going, it would take forever. There were just too many people in her way.

I, on the other hand, had a clear path to where they stood, facing off and glaring. It would be really easy for me to intervene. I couldn't just stand there and let things escalate.

Could I?

Before I talked myself out of it, I ran around the cake table. Chandler was closest, with his back to me, so I stopped there and grabbed his elbow.

"Hey." I had to pause to breathe; my heart was in my throat, and also I needed to think of what to say because my brain was apparently impersonating Cheese Whiz.

Chandler looked down at my hand on his arm. A slow smile spread across his face. He slid his arm across my shoulders and pulled me into his side. "Hi, Holly. There you are."

Asher's nostrils flared. "Super mature, Chandler. Why don't you pick up those rings and hand them to me?"

"I would," Chandler twirled my hair around his fingers, "but I'm kind of busy right now."

Asher made a sound similar to a super ticked-off bull. I'd only seen one once when some guys in Durango decided to test the theory that bulls got crazy when they see red.

It did not end well.

I tried to pull away from Chandler, both because he was making me uncomfortable and because I was not neutralizing the situation in this position, but his other arm came around me and pulled me close to his chest. My arms were pinned to my sides. Before I quite knew what was happening, Chandler leaned forward to kiss me.

I'm sure he would have succeeded if Asher hadn't blown his top and leaped at his brother. Chandler let go of me in the impact, landing hard on his back. I staggered to get my balance, then watched in complete and total horror as Asher and Chandler started a ginormous wrestle fight on the gym floor. For lack of a better description, they looked like a couple of dogs scrambling all over each other. Complete with biting and growling.

I guess they were playing street rules.

As the boys rolled around, the crowd moved back, creating this wobbly circle around them. Tenley reached my side about the same time Chandler ripped the shoulder of Asher's t-shirt.

"What do we do?" I gasped.

"Mrs. Marlow's husband is trying to get through. I guess we let him handle it?"

We scooted back as the boys rolled towards us. Tenley cupped her hands over her mouth to shout her opinion at them, but the chanting and yelling from the crowd drowned out whatever she was trying to say. It was for the best; I doubt she wanted those words recorded for future posterity.

"Where is he? Where is he?" I stood on my tiptoes, trying to find the super buff husband. He was gargantuan; it shouldn't have been hard.

The crowd shifted again to make room for Asher and Chandler. It happened before I could register how close we were standing to the cake table. They slammed into one of the legs, making it buckle. With super human skills, I vaulted over the boys and grabbed the table end as it sloped toward the ground.

A cake wobbled and fell to the floor at my feet. That was okay. I had the table. Losing one cake wasn't the end of the world. I held the table level for just one tiny moment before my feet slipped out from under me and I fell on my rear. Two more cakes zoomed by, making a terrible splat on the ground. As I scrambled to get my feet under me again, another cake slid right into my face.

Butter cream in my hair, crumbs in my eyes, fondant up my nose.

It caught me so off guard that I let go of the table entirely and tried to wipe the guck out of my eyes. Now I had a front row seat to the rest of the cakes piling into my face and lap.

Tenley made it over to me in time to catch the last one, a two-tiered white cake with sugar glass bubbles, donated from the wedding cake bakery. She held it aloft and looked down at me. "I would help you up, but I don't know where to put this."

Between the mess that was the Whittaker twins, the crowd of people moving around, and the table turned playground slide, there weren't many options.

"It's alright," I told her, then slowly rose to my feet. My eyes were stuck on each demolished cake. Understanding tried to convince me it was an accident; both Asher and Chandler had been provoked. It wasn't a big deal. But Understanding is pretty soft spoken and isn't easy to hear when Anger steps in.

I stared at Asher and Chandler rolling around like animals, not even aware they wrecked my booth, popped Dara's kiddy pool, and essentially ruined our entire fundraiser. Anger began clouding the corners of my vision.

"STOP!" I screeched. The people standing around me jumped, but the twins kept right on wrecking everything. I stooped down and picked up a platter that held the remains of a gorgeous cake covered in fondant polka dots. It was mostly intact, except for a chunk pulled out of the side like someone attacked it with a spoon. Too ruined to salvage, but still in tact enough to throw.

That's right. I was going to throw a cake. It just seemed like the right thing to do.

I stomped over to Asher and Chandler. "STOP IT!" I lobed the cake at their stupid heads. "STOP IT RIGHT NOW!"

My voice didn't really carry above the noise in the gym, so I had to rely on the cake to deliver my message.

It did a great job.

Both of them stopped trying to strangle each other and peered at me with wide eyes, as if they'd just woken up and had no idea what was going on.

Mr. Marlow finally made it through the crowd and grabbed each boy by his collar. I'd never actually seen anyone do that before; it was strangely satisfying. I stood where they could see me and jabbed a finger into the space between them.

"What in the world is wrong with you guys? Do you even care that you just single-handedly wrecking-balled the whole carnival? Do you care about anything other than your own stupid selves?"

Chandler glared at Asher. "It was his fault. You saw. He totally attacked me."

My gaze shifted to Asher, who examined his shoes. "Holland, I'm so sorry."

"Do you think *sorry* is going to fix this? It's not. I get that you guys have your weird man card competition, but what I don't get is how you could let that destroy the hard work of so many people." Tears ran down the sides of my cheeks. Not because of sadness, but because of anger.

I was just so mad.

"Holland," Asher looked at me, his eyes red-rimmed.

"Don't talk. Don't either of you say a word to me right now, maybe never again. You started this stupid competition, but I'm going to end it. You are both repulsive. I don't want to date you, I don't want to talk to you, I don't want to *see* either one of you ever again."

And with those parting words, Mr. Marlow jerked Asher and Chandler to their feet and plunged forward, disappearing into the crowd.

Chapter Fourteen

"A word in earnest is as good as a speech."
Bleak House

Cleaning up was the worst. I could barely see through the tears to pick up anything. Tenley had to leave every now and then to sob in the bathroom. She'd come back with shining cheeks and bright eyes.

Not in a good way.

Some of the people who were there during the spectacle stayed to help clean up. It was really a matter of determining what was salvageable and what was trash. Unfortunately, most everything was the latter.

I was supremely grateful Tenley saved that last cake because when we were done mopping the gym floor, we all sat around it and devoured it. There weren't any utensils to be had, so we grabbed handfuls and effectively stuffed our faces. It felt amazing in the moment, but I was so sick I could barely sleep that night.

The next morning, I woke up with a migraine. I've never had alcohol, but I imagine that's what a hangover felt like. My brain was raw, everything hurt, and I wanted to sleep until the end of forever.

My family tiptoed around me all morning. By the time they got to the carnival the night before, it was all over. We were picking up the pieces of Tenley's shattered dreams. No one made me talk it out yet, for that I was grateful. I guess when a girl comes home from an event completely covered in cake and frosting, it was safe to assume it didn't go well.

Some time that afternoon, there was a knock at the door.

"I'm not home," I croaked and slammed my bedroom door. I was especially not home if either Asher or Chandler happened to be at the door.

I was serious when I said I never wanted to see them again. Anger might have worn off, but that had not.

There was a light tap on my bedroom door.

Seriously?

What part of 'not home' did my family not understand?

"Holland?" It was Tenley's voice. "I made them let me in. Can we talk?"

I checked the mirror on my closet before I opened the door.

Yeah, I looked like death.

"Hey, Tenley."

She tried to smile, but since she also looked like death, it did not come off very well. I gestured to my desk chair and then flopped on my bed. Tenley ignored the chair and flung herself onto the bed next to me with a groan. She brought her arm up and covered her eyes.

"Tell me it was all a bad dream."

"I wish I could."

Tenley turned on her side and propped her head up with one of my pillows. "What happened? It was going so well!"

I shrugged, but I also knew Tenley wasn't buying it. "It was my fault. I was trying to get them to stop fighting, and I made it so much worse. I should have stayed out of it. I thought I could help."

"That was not your fault!" Tenley narrowed her eyes. "It's the stupid Whittaker War. They've been doing this garbage since preschool. It's just never gotten this far out of hand before."

"I'm still sorry."

"Yeah," Tenley nodded. "I'm sorry too. But it's not my fault or your fault."

I picked at the yarn ties on my quilt. "How much money did we make before, you know, Armageddon?"

Tenley let out a breath and fell back into her devastation pose. "Two thousand dollars."

That was not enough.

The school board wanted at least five to reinstate Runway Careers. We'd hoped to bring in ten.

"And I'm waiting to hear back from the school custodian about the damages to the gym."

Just…fabulous.

"So, what's next?" I asked slowly. "Are we giving up?"

"No!" Tenley sat up, her eyes fluttering. "No, we are not! That's partly why I'm here—well, mostly to lament with someone who understands, but also to get your opinion. Let's plan another fundraiser. A car wash would be easiest. Do you think we could pull it together by next weekend?"

She looked so hopeful that I hated to shake my head. "It's December, Tenley. It's supposed to snow tomorrow. I don't think a car wash would work."

"Bake sale, then?"

The thought of more cake made my stomach churn. "No."

"No?" Her face dropped, and she sighed. "I know. You're right. It's not going to work. So, I guess that's it?"

"I guess," I said in a small voice. "I'm so sorry."

"Me too, and so are Asher and Chandler."

I blinked. "Have you talked to them?"

"No," Tenley laughed lightly, "I haven't. I should have clarified that. I meant they *will* be sorry. I'm not going to ever let this go. When one of them gets married, I'm going to stand up and tell this story all over again. I'm going to tell this story at their funerals. I'm going to haunt their children's children's children. They are going to be so very sorry they did this."

I walked Tenley to the front door. When I closed it behind her, I leaned my back on the door and thumped my head against it as I looked at the ceiling. Images of the day before flew across my mind like they needed to be seen.

Asher and Chandler rolling around like neanderthals.

The cake table sliding downward.

Throwing the ruined cake at them.

That one made me smile. The rest were just the worst. I took a deep breath and headed back to my bedroom. There was something I needed to do right away before I changed my mind. I pulled out a pair of clean jeans, slipped on a striped sweater, and twirled my hair into a messy bun.

That was good enough.

Mom and Dad were nowhere to be seen, and I didn't want to search or wait around for them because the longer I hesitated, the more likely I was to lose my nerve. The twins were eating cereal and reading *Calvin and Hobbes* at the kitchen table, so I'm not sure how well they were listening when I explained to them where I was going and asked them to let the parents know I wouldn't be long.

I'd never been to the Whittaker's house, so I texted Dara for their address. She was less likely to question me than Tenley and was usually was better about responding right away. This time was no exception. I cut their address out of her reply text and pasted it into Google Maps, then off I went. It was early on a Saturday morning, and the city was still waking up. I wound my way through downtown with hardly any traffic, which was good because it allowed me to focus my mental energy on what I wanted to say.

I turned off Gurley Street near Bosa Donuts and checked my phone to make sure I was going the right way. Up a hill and down a hill, around a wide corner, and I found myself in an older neighborhood with large homes built into the slope. I leaned forward to check addresses on mail boxes and slowed way down. The numbers were starting to match up. I recognized Chandler's car before I saw the house number.

This was it. I pulled against the curb and stopped my truck. A couple deep breathes, a whispered pep talk, and I was ready.

I walked up the steep driveway and a number of stairs to reach the front porch. My fist stalled for just a moment before it knocked three times.

I held my breath and waited.

Kathy answered the door almost right away, like she was waiting right next to it, expecting me.

"Holland! Come on in, dear. How are you?" She wrapped her arm around me and pulled me into the house. With her arm still firmly in place, she led me into the large kitchen where she set me on a bar stool. The whole walk over was filled with commentary. "I can't tell you how happy I am to see you. I wanted to talk to you. My boys, they, well, you saw. And it's so unfortunate. I hope you know it's not you. They do this. Their dad and I had a long talk last night. I should let them tell you. They're going to work to pay back what they destroyed. They're both so sorry. They'll tell you. Can I get you some orange juice?"

I nodded mechanically because she seemed to expect me to. My brain was stuck, processing what she said. I didn't catch up to the orange juice thing until she'd already poured a glass and set it in front of me.

"How about a muffin?"

"No, thank you." I doubt I could eat it right now. It was hard enough to choke down the orange juice.

"I'm so happy you came by. The boys were going to come to your house today to apologize. I'll let them tell you." She held up a finger, then left the kitchen. I was alone with my thoughts and the loud tick of the owl-shaped clock on the wall.

I sipped more orange juice, attempting to gather my words so they would be ready when Asher and Chandler appeared. Kathy hadn't said specifically that she was going to get them, but I assumed that was what she meant.

Footsteps sounded behind me. I turned slowly, letting the momentum of the twirly bar stool do most of the work. Asher and Chandler stood on either side of their mom. Asher was dressed in jeans and a t-shirt, his hair slicked like it was still wet, and tennis shoes on his feet. On the other side, Chandler was wearing plaid flannel pajama pants and a tight white shirt. His hair stuck up all over the place, and his feet were bare. Asher looked down; Chandler looked up.

"Hey, Holly," he yawned and gave me a little wave.

Asher didn't say anything.

I rose to my feet, careful not to knock over my juice. Kathy squeezed the boy's shoulders. "I'll be in the living room if you need me."

I waited for her to leave, even though she was probably going into the living room to eavesdrop. That's what my mom would have done. It felt better without the extra pair of eyes staring at me, even if there was another pair of ears listening to my words.

I clasped my hands in front of me and looked at Asher, then Chandler. "I came by this morning to talk. Can we sit somewhere?" Standing there was super awkward, like I was the judge and jury, and they were on trial.

"Let's sit at the table in the dining room." Chandler waved a hand toward a room on the other side of the kitchen and then skirted the bar counter on his way to the fridge. "I'm gonna eat while we talk; let me grab some cereal."

Asher and I started for the dining room at the same time, bumping shoulders.

"Sorry," he muttered. "You go ahead."

I did, without looking at him or saying anything. The only sound was the clanging in the kitchen. Chandler joined us a few minutes later with a ginormous bowl of cereal that sloshed onto the table when he set it down. Chandler ignored the mess and shoveled a large spoonful into his mouth.

"Are you going to clean that up?" Asher asked, his voice tense.

Chandler shrugged; his mouth was too full to answer.

Asher scraped his chair away from the table and stomped to the kitchen. He ripped a paper towel from a roll like it mortally offended him and then stomped back.

Chandler swallowed hard. "Bruh, I was going to clean that up."

Asher snorted.

"I was, dude!"

"Give me a break, Chandler. You never clean up your messes."

Chandler's eyes flicked over to me. "I'm not the only one making messes around here, you know."

Asher stopped wiping to glare at his brother.

I'd seen that look before.

"Okay, seriously, both of you be quiet." I held out my arms. "If either one of you says one more word, I'm leaving."

Chandler gave a snarky smile and pretended to zip his lips. Asher did some glaring, saying more that way than he could have done in words, but at least they weren't yelling at each other. It wasn't perfect, but I would take it.

"This," now my hand waved between the three of us, "has gotten out of hand. Not only did we wreck the carnival that Tenley and everyone spent so much time planning..." I paused here to breathe in and out. Anger was building again, and I knew from experience that nothing good came when Anger was driving the bus. "...and wasted time, resources, and money. But the worst part is, there's not enough money for Runway Careers. You guys might not care about that, but it's a big deal to a lot of people. We let them down. Us. We did."

Asher raised his hand.

"You can talk if you promise you won't say anything mean to or about Chandler."

Asher scowled, but after a deep breath, he looked at me. "You didn't do anything, Holland. It was me and him." He jerked a thumb across the table at Chandler, who had just lifted his bowl to drink the milk left at the bottom.

"Thanks for saying that, but it was my fault too." I took a deep breath. "I haven't done anything to discourage you guys, and it's gotten out of hand. We should have had this conversation a week ago and saved everyone a lot of trouble."

"That wasn't your responsibility either. We could have sorted things out just as easily as you could."

Why was he so determined that it wasn't my fault? It was. I knew it was. I'd spent a lot of time thinking about this and I made myself face a hard truth. I liked the attention. I didn't discourage them because I liked how it felt to have them both fighting over me. I'd never had two guys like me at the same time, ever. I was flattered. I was stupid. They were both gorgeous and Pride loved it. This was as much my fault as it was theirs.

Obviously, I didn't tell any of this to them. It was between me and me.

"Don't let me off the hook, Asher. This is on all three of us. So, we're going to sit here until we find a happy place, something we can all live with that will bring balance to whatever is going on here. Okay?"

Asher nodded.

"Chandler?" I asked.

He blinked and glanced over his shoulder. "Sure, yeah, let's do this. I'm meeting everyone at ten. We're going to the mall for laser tag. You should come with, Holly."

Asher let out a heavy sigh.

"Thanks, but let's just do this one thing first and then we can talk about that, okay?"

Chandler saluted.

"Okay." I wasn't sure how to start. I felt like what we needed more than anything was to understand where everyone was coming from. Then we could ditch Mystery and Assumption and just deal with what we knew. That felt right. "I'll tell my side of the story first. Maybe if we all share our sides, we can figure this out. Sound good?"

Chandler stretched his hands behind his head as he nodded. Asher leaned forward, his eyes intent on me.

"Okay, I met Asher on a Thursday, my first day of school. He helped me find my locker and classes, then invited me to eat lunch with his friends." I peeked sideways at Asher. "It was incredibly nice. I had a really good time. That was exactly what I needed on my first day; I was seriously freaked out to start school in a new place. So, thank you for that."

Asher nodded, his eyes never wavering.

"Then, Asher gave me his phone number." This part was harder. The sting hadn't really gone out of the experience yet, even though it was months ago. "And I texted him a couple times that night, and in the morning. He never said anything about the texts, and he avoided me after that."

Asher sat up straight. "Wait. Sorry, can I talk?"

Shame did a little number on the back of my neck. I'd been so bossy. Yikes. I didn't mean to be; I just hated it when they sniped at each other, and I was afraid if either one of them started talking again it would turn into another brawl, leaving broken dreams and broken furniture in its wake.

"Yes, you can talk."

"I know it's not my turn, but I'm kinda confused, Holland. I didn't see any texts from you. I didn't get them, anyway. The next time I heard anything from you was when you showed up at the lake with Chandler." His eyes were so intensely focused on my face that it was like he was trying to see into my soul. That or he was trying painfully hard to ignore Chandler.

"You're jumping ahead," Chandler smirked.

That was true. Now the story was all out of order. "Let me finish, okay. We'll come back to that."

Asher nodded but didn't lean into the chair again. His back was straight and his face tight.

"I met Chandler on Friday afternoon when my locker was stuck and I..." I blushed, "was yelling at it. He helped me open it, then invited me to hang out with him and his friends after football practice." I skimmed over that memory quickly, not wanting to say something hurtful about his friends but not wanting to lie either. It was best to say nothing at all. "After that, he invited me to the lake. You both know what happened at the lake and from then on."

"Cool." Chandler tapped his fingers on the table. "I'll go next. Holly was screaming at her locker. I thought it was funny, so I invited her to John's house to watch a movie. We held hands."

Asher sucked in a breath.

"Then I invited her to the lake. I didn't know you knew her, man. It wasn't like the other times. She's hot and real and really fun to be around, so I wanted to hang out with her more. That's it." Chandler shrugged.

Asher's face was beginning to blotch with red patches.

"Asher, it's your turn. Are you ready to talk? Like, calmly?" I seriously doubted it; he certainly did not look like he was ready. He was all tensed up like he wanted to throw hands.

My question seemed to be what he needed to get a hold of himself. Maybe it was saying the word *calmly*, or maybe it was those extra seconds that gave his brain a chance to connect with his frustration. Either way, it worked. He took a deep breath and unclenched his fists.

"I met Holland," he stressed my name and looked at Chandler, who was obliviously tracing patterns on the tabletop, "on Thursday, like she said. And I already told you guys I never heard anything again until the lake. That's it. That's all."

"I texted you, Asher." I pulled my phone out of my pocket and unlocked it. I clicked on his name and slid the phone over to him. "See, a couple times." Heat crept up my neck. "Okay, more than a couple times."

It wasn't until Asher had a secure hold on my phone that I started to remember what those texts said. I'd lost sleep agonizing over them, and now I'd given him the very means to refresh his memory of how weird I am.

That was brilliant.

I couldn't afford to let Insecurity in right now. I had to keep Confidence and Determination by my side, or I was never going to get through this. And we had to get through it. If we didn't come to a reasonable truce between the three of us, then the school, and possibly the town, would be reduced to a smoldering crater by the end of the year.

So, yeah, I was just going to let Asher think whatever he wanted to think about those texts I sent. They didn't mean anything about me. They were just words.

"Didn't you already read them?" I asked, holding out my hand for the phone.

Asher didn't give it back. He looked up, that adorable grin in place. "No, I didn't already read them. I told you, really, I never got these texts."

"But I texted the number you gave me." I scooted the few chairs over so I could see the screen over his arm. I clicked on his name, and the number came up for him.

"No," Asher groaned. "No, this is my home number. The landline."

"That can't be right." My forehead crunched into a billion wrinkles. "When you text a landline, it always shoots back a message that the text didn't go through, specifically because it's a landline. Watch." I entered in my home number and sent a text.

Hey, you

Not even two seconds later, a response came.

Error msg: The number you entered is a landline. Text cannot be sent. Contact your service provider to set up text to landline option.

I showed the screen to Asher. "Try the number again," he said.

I entered the number by hand with Asher's help, sent a hello text, and waited.

Nothing happened.

Chandler yawned with a loud exhale that ruffled the placemat in front of him.

"It's got to be bugged or something," Asher said. "That's really weird."

I looked at him, my face just inches from his. With a start, I scooted back to my original chair. "So, I was texting your landline? You didn't see my messages?" That was a relief in a roundabout way, but also extremely confusing. "But, why didn't you tell me it was a landline? Or give me your cell phone number?" He had one; I'd seen him with it.

"I gave you the landline because," Asher glanced at Chandler, who had his cheek mushed into his fist and was staring into the distance, "um, because Chandler never uses it and I didn't want him to answer your call. And I didn't give you my cell number because I didn't want Chandler to see it."

No, that still didn't make sense. "How would Chandler see a text on your phone?"

Asher's eyes widened. "Chandler and I share a phone."

"And the car," Chandler piped in.

"We swap," Asher said. "When I have the phone, Chandler has the car and vice versa. I gave you the landline so you wouldn't text on Chandler's day. I never explained?"

I shook my head.

"Right," Asher flopped against the back of his chair. "I didn't explain on purpose because I didn't want something like *this* to happen again." His hand swung into the air, between Chandler and I, then dropped to the table top. "Great job, Asher. That turned out great. Just...great."

This was a lot. My brain sort of reeled. He never got my texts. He wasn't ignoring me like I thought.

"But, you avoided me," I said in a small voice.

"When?"

It felt stupid to bring it up; it was such a long time ago. "Right after I sent the texts. I thought you got them and didn't respond because you thought I was a dork. Then you didn't show up at lunch, and I thought you were making up excuses because you were sorry you gave me your number in the first place, like you regretted..."

Asher leaned forward, his face earnest. "I don't remember the specifics, Holland. I don't know why I wasn't at lunch or whatever else I did that looked like I was avoiding you." He took a long breath. "I never thought you were weird. I never avoided you on purpose. I thought you were amazing. The perfect girl, actually." He stopped talking as if he just realized people could hear him.

I blinked and sat back, my emotions twirling all together like a tornado. Relief, confusion, regret, hope...and a whole bunch of others. "Asher—"

Chandler slapped the table with his hand so loudly that I jumped. "Hey, it's getting close to ten. Let's get out of here. Have you been to the mall yet, Holly?"

My brain was having the hardest time switching its focus to Chandler. I knew I should because it was polite to look at the person asking you questions, but I wasn't done puzzling out Asher. And I really didn't want to hang out with Mylee and the rest of Chandler's friends.

That broke the spell. Now my mind could go back to work on our current dilemma. Whatever happened in the past had happened, for whatever reason. I couldn't change it.

The fact that Asher thought I was perfect—whatever that meant—didn't take away the fact that he acted like a caveman at the carnival. I needed to know something, and I needed Courage to help me ask the question. I carefully brought it to the front of my mind, then looked from Asher to Chandler with searching eyes. Eyes ready to see every twitch of the lip and flick of the eye. I was ready to attach meaning to all of it.

"Do you guys like me?"

That came out so juvenile. I regrouped and tried again.

"What I mean is, do you both want to date me?"

"Yes," Asher said.

Chandler let out a breath, his eyes swiveling to Asher, and said, "Yes."

Asher reached forward, but not close enough to touch me. "The real question, Holland, is if you want to date either of us after everything and...everything. Especially after yesterday."

That was a very good question. I'd come to their house ready to talk it out or tell them off, but somehow the anger was all gone. It was like I'd sprung a slow leak at some point and lost it all.

What did I want?

Now that I knew Asher didn't blow me off on purpose, I was curious if we could become something. I liked how quirky he was, and his smile was fantastic. I didn't like his temper or this weird competition with his brother, though.

Oh yeah, his brother.

I'd held Chandler's hand. I'd encouraged his attention. I liked him...didn't I? Chandler was so dang attractive and fun to hang out with, but he was also kind of self-centered, which I really didn't love. I'd seen it especially today, though I think it was there all along.

I did want to date them.

But I was really attached to Wary.

"I don't know. I mean, yesterday was awful."

"It was," Asher nodded. "I can't tell you how sorry I am about that."

"I can," Chandler said. "Really sorry. That was uncool. I'm really, really sorry."

Asher turned his head purposely so he couldn't see Chandler. "I've been thinking. If you'll give us another chance, I'd like to try and make it up to you."

"Yeah, me too." Chandler added.

Asher paused for a second, then went on. "Here's what I think. How about we go on three dates each, and at the end of those dates, we have another round table discussion like this one, and you can tell us your decision. What do you think about that?"

"Another discussion?" Chandler groaned as he stood up. "Great. That works. I'll go first, Holly. How about we catch dinner tonight?"

"Come on, Chandler. Give her a second."

"What?" Chandler stretched his arms above his head.

"Thanks for the offer, Chandler," I shook my head, "but I want some time to process all this before we start the dates." Confidence was really shining; I hope it decided to stick around. "Actually, I think I'd like to take a break from all of this until after Christmas, and then we can start the dates next year and see what happens?"

Asher nodded. "I think that's a great idea."

"Cool," Chandler said.

I stood up. "But I just have to say this last thing. The dates need to be normal, okay? Nothing huge, no one-upping. Just normal dates you'd take any girl on. The simpler the better. Does that make sense?"

The last thing I wanted was air balloon rides, ski trips to the Alps, and bragging rights.

"Correct answer." Asher's grin did something weird to my stomach. "That sounds great. I'm in."

"Yeah, me too," Chandler said.

"Okay, I'll think about it over the break. And if you guys decide you're not interested, that's okay too. Okay?"

Sheesh, how many times can a person say *okay* in one sentence?

"Sounds cool. I gotta run, but that's all good." Chandler's voice raised as he headed down the hall. "See you at school on Monday, Holly."

"Bye," I called.

"Here." Asher stepped aside. "I'll walk you to the door."

We took a few steps in silence, but it wasn't settled; I could tell there was something major on Asher's mind. He reached for the door handle, then froze. His free hand raked through his hair, making it almost as messy as Chandler's bedhead. "You really didn't know Chandler was my twin?"

"I really didn't. You guys aren't identical, you don't act anything alike, and your friends are totally different. How would I make that connection?"

"No one told you?"

I thought about that. "No. I mean, you talked about your brother, but you never said his name or that you were twins. Maybe Tenley mentioned your brother... I don't know. I don't think so. So, no I had no idea. I really didn't come to the lake as his date to punish you for ignoring my texts."

Asher ducked his head. "How did you know that's what I thought?"

"I figured." It didn't take a genius to come to that conclusion.

"I thought you met him, liked him better, and then never called me. That's why I got so ticked." He laughed. "What's the opposite of serendipity? Not a happy accident, a trainwreck?"

"Karma?"

No, that didn't sound right.

"Fluke?"

Asher laughed some more. "Tragedy?"

I pulled out my phone and googled *the opposite of serendipity* because now I was curious if that was a thing. "Zemblanity!" I turned the phone so he could see the screen. "Unhappy, unlucky, unexpected discoveries."

"That's it!" Asher raised both fists in the air. "We are total victims of zemblanity."

"I actually kind of love that word."

"Me too."

I looked up at Asher's face and felt something warm slide down my throat into my belly. "I'm going to avoid you at lunchtime this week, just so you know. I'll tell Tenley so she doesn't ask a billion questions and bug you about it. I think that will be more fair. Don't you?"

He nodded. "Except that I don't really care about fairness right now." His hand slid down the length of my arm until his fingers locked into mine. "Did you really hold Chandler's hand?"

Well, technically, he held mine. Since I couldn't seem to get air to move at the moment, I just nodded.

"Did you kiss him?" His eyes flicked to my lips and his head slowly moved closer.

My breath caught.

Asher froze. "Never mind. I'm sorry. I shouldn't have asked that. It's none of my business." He let out a deep sigh that tickled my lips. "I'll call you after Christmas, okay?"

My head wobbled like a doll with bad seams. Asher let go of my hand and stepped away. It was easier to think and breathe, but I eyed the distance between us with distaste.

"Bye, Holland."

Somehow I said good-bye and made my way down the stairs without falling on my face. My knees felt like jelly, and my legs felt like I'd run ten miles uphill. The whole drive home I thought about that moment when it sort of looked like Asher was going to kiss me. It would probably haunt me until the end of time.

Because...why didn't he?

Chapter Fifteen

• ♥ • ♥ • ♥ • ♥ • ♥ •

"This is a world for action; not for moping and droning in."
David Copperfield

Tenley called me before I made it to my front door.

"Hey, what's up?"

"You sound happy." Tenley's voice was just as bright as mine. I wondered if that meant she almost got kissed too.

"So do you."

"Well," Tenley paused, "that's because I am. I just got off the phone with Mrs. Whittaker."

"Yeah?"

"Yeah, she's so upset about what the twins did. She called the school board and convinced whoever is in charge to give us extra time. We have until the end of January to raise the money!"

"Tenley! That's awesome!"

"It is!" She let herself indulge in a laugh for two seconds, then her voice snapped to all business. "So, here's what I'm thinking. Let's do a raffle. There's no set up or anything. We can get businesses to donate things like coupons and gift cards, then have everyone sell a billion tickets. Then just you and I will do a live stream for the winners. See? Nothing to get wrecked. Then we can hand out the prizes. Easy peasy."

That did sound easy peasy. "I think that's a great idea, Ten!"

"Yeah? You're in?"

"Totally!"

"Great! Dara's here now; we'll come get you and start petitioning businesses."

I stared at my front door. I was so close to home and yet so far away. There was no way I could tell Tenley I was unavailable in favor of a bowl of popcorn and a Dickens novel.

As lovely as that sounded.

"I'll check in with my parents and call you if that's a problem. Otherwise, see you soon."

I opened the front door and went straight to the kitchen. The twins were gone, but Mom stood at the sink, washing dishes. Her ear buds were in, so I placed a hand on her arm to get her attention.

She jumped at least a foot into the air. "Holland, you're home!"

"For about three seconds." I quickly filled her in on the time at the Whittakers and my plans with Dara and Tenley. I talked fast, but it still took a long time.

"So, you're okay?"

"I'm okay," I nodded. "I think we have a good plan."

"I do too. I'm impressed, honey. That took courage."

"Yeah," I sighed. "It was really hard, Mom."

"Well, you can certainly do hard things."

I laughed. "Thanks for that. So, I'll be gone for a couple hours, then let's watch a movie tonight. Maybe pop some popcorn?"

"Yes!" Mom clapped her hands, spraying bubbles in all directions. "I'll tell the guys not to plan anything. What do you want to watch?"

"Surprise me." I grabbed an apple and one of mom's homemade granola bars from the fridge to hold me over. I still hadn't eaten breakfast.

"Here, take this too." She handed me a baggie of vegetables and cheese cubes. "I don't want you to get stuck eating fake food while you're out and about."

I smiled and thanked her, imagining the look on Tenley's face while she sipped her milkshake and I crunched a carrot stick. She was getting used to it; the comments came much less frequently.

I guess that's what it means to make friends: you learn to love each other even when you're both super weird.

The doorbell rang just as I slipped my purse over my shoulder. I swung the door open to reveal Tenley and Dara on my front porch.

"What do you think?" Dara spun around, and her long black and purple cape swung a wide circle. That was eye catching, but not nearly as much as the headset of black, twisty horns she wore.

"Maleficent?"

"Bingo!" Dara stopped twirling and fingered the tips of her horns. "I made it last night out of Styrofoam, stuffing, and pipe cleaners. My mom helped me."

Her mom must be a wizard. The horns looked real. Even when I leaned in for a closer look, I couldn't see any trace of the materials they used.

"You look just like her." Even her make-up was flawless.

Dara smiled. "Thanks! My mom used to work for a theater. She was in charge of props and costumes. If you think this is cool, you should see what the woman can do with a glue gun and old newspaper."

Just then, Tenley cleared her throat; I was just surprised she put up with our chitchat for as long as she did. "Let's get moving. We're burning daylight." She swung her arm wide and marched us down the driveway to her car. It took a second to get Dara's horns through the car door, then we were off.

"Where to first?" I sat in the backseat, in the middle so I could make faces at Tenley in the rearview mirror whenever she happened to glance back. That wasn't the real reason I sat where I did—I wanted to be able to see both girls in the front seat at once—but it was certainly an added perk.

"The mall," Tenley said. "I know someone who works at JCPenney. They said they might be able to do something for us."

"Plus the Christmas decorations will be up. So fun!"

Tenley rolled her eyes, but I was with Dara. Strolling through the mall all festive with Christmas decorations sounded amazing to me. I'd been to Prescott Gateway Mall once before, sort of. The mall was like an outdoor-indoor thing, and I just skirted the edge when I went with my mom to Michael's. Tenley parked us near the entrance of the indoor portion and started gathering her things.

"Are you sure you want to start there?" Dara lifted a hand in the air. I hadn't noticed that her fingernails were now three inches long and deep purple. It was wicked cool. "There aren't very many stores open inside the mall anymore. I think we'd have better luck if we started outside."

"You're not wrong." Tenley pushed her car door open. "But JCPenney is inside, and it's flipping cold out here. So, inside we go."

We hurried inside the building and stopped just inside the door. Tenley wasn't wrong either. I hadn't noticed the cold as much earlier, but now that the wind had picked up, it had a bite.

"This way." Tenley took the lead at a ridiculous pace, weaving around people on her way to JCPenney. I tried not to smash into anyone while looking around at the same time. There were a lot of stores I recognized: Claire's, Journeys, Hot Topic, to name a few. There were also a lot of stores I didn't recognize. Not to mention a bungee jump thing. I wanted to slow down and take it all in, but Tenley was on a mission. She didn't look to the right or the left.

Once inside JCPenney, my head stopped spinning. This was a familiar place with not so much to process. My eyes could stop darting all over the place, and my head could stop asking, "What's that? What's that? What's that?"

Tenley led us to the back of the store, near the bathrooms. A tall guy with a goatee bent over the drinking fountain. He looked up as we got closer.

"Tenley!" He wiped his mouth with the back of his hand. "Right on time."

"Duh, what'd you expect?" She extended a hand. "You know Dara. This is Holland."

"Holland." He said my name like he was savoring the flavor. His eyebrows rose significantly.

"Stop it, Benjamin. You promised you wouldn't hit on my friends anymore." Tenley looked at Dara and me. "It's so awkward when he does this."

Dara nodded knowingly, but I was completely lost.

"This is my brother Benny," Tenley explained. She probably noticed the confused look on my face. "He's an idiot."

Even after knowing they were siblings, I couldn't see it. Benny was tall and wafer thin with hair cut so close to the scalp he looked almost bald. Tenley was tall too, but not so thin that she looked like she was going to blow away with the next big gust of wind. Their eyes were different colors, and Tenley's nose was closer to a pug while Benny's was long and thin.

"Great start." Benny rolled his eyes and I suddenly saw the resemblance between the two of them. "You go ahead and ask me for a favor now, little sister."

Tenley huffed. "I'm already doing the dishes for you for a month, so don't act all victimized. What did you find out?"

Benny crossed his arms and leaned one shoulder against the wall. "The salon will give you a coupon, same with the jewelry counter. The store itself will donate five one-hundred dollar gift cards."

I hadn't had time to determine what I was expecting, so I was blown away with the generosity. "Wow, that's awesome!"

Benny winked at me, and I was sorry I'd said anything. I'm sure he was a nice guy and all; I just wasn't the kind of girl who could juggle three guys at once. My hands were totally full with Asher and Chandler.

"It's okay," Tenley scowled. "I was hoping for more."

"As usual." Benny shook his head. "How about you tell your favorite brother how awesome he is for getting you five gift cards and two coupons for your little raffle. Thank you, Benny. You're the best."

"Thank you, Benny," Tenley mimicked in a mocking voice. "You're the bestestest."

"I'll take it." Benny glanced at Dara. "Love the costume, by the way. Not as hot as Wonder Woman, but way more impressive."

Dara gave a low bow.

"When do you think you'll wear the Wonder Woman costume again?" Benny scratched behind his ear.

"Summer," Dara laughed. "Have you been outside? I'm not wearing that thing in this weather."

"Too bad."

Tenley punched him in the shoulder.

Benny yipped and clutched his arm. "What?"

"You know what you did. Cut it out."

"What?" he said again, but this time it was obvious it was contrived. He did know what he did. That much was obvious.

Tenley punched him again, this time in the other arm. "We're leaving. See you at home. Don't forget to bring the coupons and stuff with you. I need them tonight."

I chanced a look back at Benny as we walked away. He watched Dara mostly as he massaged both shoulders.

I skipped to catch up to Dara. "What do you think about Benny?"

"Does anyone think about Benny?" she giggled.

Tenley laughed along with her.

So, yeah, I was not going to pursue that subject. I was all set to drop it when Dara peeked at me over the side of her headdress. "Why did you ask?"

I shrugged. "No reason."

We passed a mom with a baby in one arm and a toddler skipping along beside her. When the toddler saw Dara coming, she screamed and ran behind her mom.

Dara and her costumes had become so normal to me that I sometimes forgot most people were not used to seeing another person walk around dressed like a movie or comic character. I gave the little girl a smile as we went by. She was too busy hiding between her mom's knees with her eyes squeezed shut to notice the gesture.

"No, really. Why did you ask?" Dara stopped walking.

Tenley and I stopped too, then moved to the side so we weren't blocking the walkway.

"I just..." I twirled a piece of hair that had come loose from my messy bun.

"We both know what you're going to say. Just spit it out." Tenley tapped her foot.

Wait, they did? I got stuck for a moment, trying to figure out how they knew. Tenley cleared her throat loudly to get me back on track.

"I think Benny likes you," I blurted out as smooth as broccoli.

Dara blinked.

"Okay," Tenley said. "That is not what I thought you were going to say."

"What did you think I was going to say?" I was curious.

Apparently Dara was curious too, but about something totally different. "Why do you think Benny likes me?"

Tenley answered. "I thought you were going to say Benny was a creeper."

Then I answered Dara. "He looks at you differently. He was kind of a creeper to me, but it was different with you."

"No," Dara shook her head. "He said he wanted to see my Wonder Woman costume—which, by the way, is just a skimpy swimsuit. That's creepery."

True.

"I still think he really likes you. What he said wasn't the best, but the way he said it was different. Maybe something about his eyes? Have you known him for a long time?"

"Since she moved here," Tenley said.

Dara chewed her lower lip. "I was nine."

"Yeah, so, that makes sense. If he's known you since you were a little girl, he probably doesn't know how to tell you he's interested. Right?"

Tenley shrugged.

Dara didn't say anything for a long time, then she shook herself. "No, it's too weird. Where are we going next?"

"Dillard's." Tenley looked relieved. "This way. Let's go." She took off at a walk that was way closer to a jog. I didn't even try to keep up with her. Instead, I stayed with Dara to keep her from tripping over her cloak at these high speeds.

Tenley paused at the entrance and waited for us to catch up. "So, here's the plan: we split up. One of us goes to customer service to ask what they can do for us, another goes to the makeup thing, and the other talks to clerks. There are a billion of them in this store, so I'll do that. What—"

A loud laugh broke off Tenley's instructions.

A girl laugh.

Followed by whispering.

And then a bunch of guys laughing.

Dara groaned, and my stomach dropped into my toes. Those voices, they were familiar. Not in a good way. I suddenly remembered that Chandler invited me to the mall with him and his friends.

When I finally summoned Courage to back me up and took a look around Tenley, there they were. Mylee, Janis, John, Chandler, Dillan, and a couple other guys I didn't know. They were all staring at Dara's outfit and laughing uproariously. Well, most of them were. As soon as my face peeked out from behind Tenley, Chandler choked on his laugh.

"Holly?" His face was a mixture of confusion and disbelief. I could almost hear his thoughts.

What is she doing here with *them*?

A little someone I like to call my pal rose up inside me. Indignation doesn't show up often; I'm a pretty easy-going girl. In the past, it usually appeared in the face of grave injustice. I wonder if that makes me a superhero?

Whatever, I for sure wasn't going to let Chandler's friends get away with mocking Dara. Not one of them was better than anyone else. I don't care how big their houses were or how many designers they wore.

"Hi, Chandler!" I gave him an easy smile. "How's it going?"

He stepped away from his heckling friends. "I thought you couldn't come to the mall. You said you were busy."

"I am busy." I lifted my chin and linked my arm through Dara's elbow. I hadn't lied to him; I also hadn't known we were coming to the mall. "Dara, Tenley, and I are gathering donations for a raffle. It's the fundraiser we're doing next for Runway Careers."

"Runway Careers," one of Chandler's friends mocked.

"Lame!" another supplied.

Chandler didn't acknowledge his friends. His eyes kept skipping from Tenley, who scowled with all her might, to Dara, who tried to turn the lot of them into snakes with her mind powers. I didn't know that for sure; I just assumed that what she was doing based on the look on her face.

When he looked back at me, I kept my gaze steady with Defensiveness's help. Chandler could think whatever he wanted about my friends, just like I got to think whatever I wanted about his friends.

He reached out a hand. "Come on. They can finish up without you. I want to show you the laser tag. It's fire."

Dara started to pull away, but I tightened my grip on her elbow.

One of the guys I didn't know made a toddler noise that sounded like a bodily function. "Why are you wasting your time, Chandler? Leave the nerds alone. Let's go."

I tipped my head to the side, keeping my eyes on Chandler's face. Nerds, huh?

Chandler's expression creased into frustration. He took a couple long steps to reach my side and kept going. That is, after he grabbed my arm and yanked me away from Dara. When we were out of eaves-dropping distance, he leaned in close.

"What are you doing here with them?" His breath was minty when it puffed into my face, but his words smelled sour.

Yeah, I totally called it. I knew that's what he was thinking.

"I told you. I'm helping them gather donations for the raffle."

"Those are Asher's friends."

"And?"

"And I don't think it's cool that you're hanging out with them right after you said we're not starting this competition until the new year."

I had no idea what he was saying. "Okay?"

Chandler's words came out in a rush. "It's like sports psychology, you know? Be the ball? If you're around people who think Asher is better, you'll start thinking Asher is better, and that gives him a head start."

Seriously?

"Tenley and Dara are my friends, Chandler. We've been hanging out together without Asher since my first day of school. They never say anything about Asher."

"Maybe not out loud." He tapped the side of his head. "It's psycho-logical."

"No," I shook my head. This was completely ridiculous. "It's really not."

"I'm just saying, if you're going to hang out with Asher's friends, you'll have to hang out with my friends to even it out."

That was not happening.

"Tenley and Dara are *my* friends, Chandler."

He glanced over at them, standing there waiting for me while his lovely friends mocked them with whispers and stares.

I'd had enough.

"I'll see you in January." I pulled away from him and started back towards my friends. Chandler's sigh was so heavy it ruffled my hair in the back. He grabbed my hand and pulled me back.

His hands trailed up my arms until they met behind my back. He played with the ends of my hair and sighed again. "Look, I don't want you to leave mad. I really like you, Holly."

His words were pretty and his hands were distracting, but Defensiveness was still my constant companion.

"Are you saying that because you want to win?" I asked.

His head jerked back like I slapped him. "What's that supposed to mean?"

"That means that I think you like this competition with your brother more than you like me. I don't think you're interested in me at all. Did you know my name isn't actually Holly? It's Holl-LAND. Like the country."

"Why didn't you just say something?"

"I did, Chandler, like, three times. That's my point. If you really liked me, if you were really interested in me, if you were really falling for me, you would remember my name. And you wouldn't care who my friends were," I added, trying to pull out of his grip so I could get back to them. Chandler was literally throwing them to the wolves right now.

His grip tightened.

I could feel his heartbeat against my collar bone and just like that, Defensiveness fled. It was powerless in the face of so much Chandler. His woodsy cologne, the stubble on his chin that rubbed my temple, his arms so tight around me his biceps popped.

I was either bewitched or completely shallow.

For almost a whole minute, I forgot all about Dara and Tenley, Asher, and Chandler's terrible taste in friends.

When that minute was over, I yanked myself backwards, catching Chandler off guard. His grip broke, and I stumbled for a moment before I found my balance. It was much easier to think with distance between us. I stared at him, trying to catch my breath and my sanity.

His lips curled into a smirk. "Holly, come on."

"Holland."

The smirk grew. "Holland, whatever. Come on, you clearly want this."

I did.

I mean, did I? I honestly didn't know what I wanted. This was exactly why I said I would start dating those bozos in *January*. I needed space to clear my head.

Chandler took a step forward, but I held out both hands. "Stay right where you are. I'm going to finish helping Tenley and Dara, you're going to go do whatever you do with your friends, and we will talk next year."

Before Chandler could answer or move closer or confuse me more, I bolted to Tenley, grabbed her hand and Dara's arm, and dragged them both the rest of the way into Dillard's. I didn't stop until I reached the women's underwear section. It was the only place I could think of that Chandler wouldn't follow.

Well, maybe he wouldn't.

I hoped he wouldn't, anyway.

"What was that all about?" Dara asked breathlessly. "What is going on with you and Chandler?"

"I don't know." I hid my face in my hands. "I don't know."

"Cause that back there, that was something."

I groaned and sank to the floor, right next to a rack of blue and yellow flowered bras.

A sales clerk appeared out of nowhere. "Can I help you?"

I peeked through my fingers to see her eying me uncertainly.

"Oh no, we're fine," Tenley said. "My friend just loves these bras so much, she's overcome."

Dara snorted.

Nice one, Tenley.

The salesclerk nodded like that made a lick of sense, and told us to let her know if we needed help, then she got out of there as fast as her stilettos would let her.

Wise woman.

Dara and Tenley plopped onto the ground next to me. Dara still covered her mouth so I couldn't see how funny she thought this whole thing was.

Well, I was glad someone was amused.

"This is simple," Tenley said, pulling a pack of gum out of her purse. She offered me a piece, but I shook my head. Dara took one, probably because chewing could cover up her Cheshire Cat smile.

"Is it?" I kneaded my fingers together. "Is it simple?"

"Yep," she nodded. "You're making a big deal out of nothing. The only thing going on here is hormones."

I groaned again and flopped onto my back.

Hormones.

Fabulous.

Chapter Sixteen

"Happy, happy Christmas, that can win us back to the delusions of our childhood days."
A Christmas Carol

After I recovered, we gathered gift cards and coupons from Dillard's and twelve other stores in the mall. Some stores, like JCPenney, gave more than one thing for us to raffle, so Tenley was thrilled and Dara was optimistic.

I was a zombie.

When Tenley dropped me off at my house, I only had enough energy to drag myself through the front door and up the stairs to my bedroom. I collapsed face down on my bed.

"Holland is home!" Rhett bellowed.

Brett added, "And she's dead."

He wasn't wrong. There were too many feelings to sort through, too many things to figure out. I rolled onto my side, grabbed my fluffiest pillow, and held it close to my belly, then let myself drift to sleep.

At least in my dreams I was safe from the Whittaker twins.

Mostly.

The last week of school before Christmas break went by in a blur. It was then that I discovered the greatest advantage to having a modified schedule: I got there too late to see anyone before school, and I left early. Lunch would have been a hiccup except for the fact that I found a table in the back of the library with a lovely view of the classic fiction section. I shared my meal with Señor Ebenezer Scrooge.

Tenley and Dara knew I was hiding from Asher and Chandler, so they left me to it until Friday. They found my table just as I finished up my second read through of *A Christmas Carol* and had to wait until I got to the last line.

"God bless us, everyone."

"Amen," Dara said with gusto. Today she was dressed as a Christmas elf with jingle bells on her pointed shoes. She was adorable, actually. I wish I had a matching outfit.

Tenley dropped a huge roll of raffle tickets onto the table. "Help me with these. We're making groups of one hundred. That's how many raffle tickets we each need to sell over Christmas break."

"We're only selling three hundred tickets?" Dara took some scissors. "How much are they?"

"A dollar a piece, and no, that's not all we're selling. I meant one hundred per person in our Extracurriculars Club. That's the three of us, plus Bryan, Ryker, Ethan, and Asher. Also, Mrs. Whittaker told us to send extra home with Asher, as part of the twins' penance, so I thought I'd give them three hundred, one hundred and fifty for each of those cretins."

"That's a none hundred total." I pursed my lips. "If we sell them all, that's only a nine hundred dollars. Is that enough?"

"No." Tenley shoved the papers closer to me. "But that's all the raffle tickets the school has left over from the booster club fundraiser."

"Um," I hated to ask, but I had to know, "how much money did we make from the carnival before it went south?"

Dara gave me a sympathetic smile.

"Two thousand dollars," Tenley sighed. "The Whittaker's paid for damages, thankfully, so we didn't have to use any of our money for that."

Tenley looked exhausted. I knew better than to ask if Runway Careers was worth all this stress, so instead I used my brain juice to focus on how I could help her. We needed three thousand dollars more to reach the goal of five thousand by the end of January.

Three thousand, three thousand. Come on, brain. How do we come up with three thousand dollars?

"What if we charged more than a dollar per ticket?" I blurted.

Tenley blew some hair out of her eyes but didn't say anything.

"I mean, if we charged five dollars, that would be more than enough money to hit our goal." Also, there wouldn't be so much stress on selling *all* the tickets. It would be nice to have some wiggle room.

Not bad, brain. Not bad at all.

Tenley's eyes filled up with tears. Yeah, she was stressed. "Holland, that is so obvious it's ridiculous. I think that will work!"

I appreciated her enthusiasm, but now I was having a party with Second-guessing. "Do you think people would pay that much for a raffle ticket?"

"Yes," Tenley nodded firmly. Dara echoed the word, giving it more power. "It's for a good cause. Plus, the prizes are really, really good. Oh my gosh, I'm so relieved! I think we can do this!"

We counted and ripped in relative silence. Satisfied silence. Cozy silence.

And then...

"So..." Dara's voice was hesitant, "how's it going avoiding the boys, Holland? Is it working?"

"Surprisingly, yes," I said. And it was true. I couldn't believe it, but I hadn't seen either one of them all week. Well, except for the back of Asher's head in Spanish.

Apparently, I spoke too soon.

"Asher Whittaker."

His voice flew through the library like it had a jetpack.

My head snapped up. "Where is he?" I couldn't see him, but I could hear him.

Dara set her stuff down and tiptoed to the edge of the classic fiction bookcase. "He's by the checkout desk. He's talking to the librarian. Maybe he lost his card or something? No, he had a hold. Oh crap, he saw me." She stood up straight and waved like everything was normal. "Hide," she hissed out of the corner of her mouth. "He's coming over here."

That was great advice, but there was nowhere to hide.

I looked around frantically until Tenley put her hand on top of my head and pushed me under the table. I pulled my backpack into my chest and huddled into a tiny ball. I must become one with the floor.

I had such a good Whittaker-free streak going. I was almost myself again. The last thing I needed was a confusing encounter that jumbled everything up.

"Hey, Asher." Tenley's voice was too loud. She didn't sound natural.

"Hey, what are you guys working on?"

"Oh, nothing," Tenley said at the same time Dara answered, "Raffle tickets."

The chair across from me scraped back from the table. "Do you need some help?"

"No!" both Dara and Tenley said.

There was a pause, in which I tried to pull myself into a smaller ball. Or disappear completely, whatever worked. I wasn't picky.

"Why are you acting weird?"

"I'm always weird," Dara said immediately.

"Not like this."

"What do you mean?" Tenley's laugh was horribly chintzy. If we all survived this moment unscathed, I was going to make her take acting lessons from Dara.

"Like, you want to get rid of me? Why do you keep looking over my shoulder?" Asher's chair moved as he twisted around.

Tenley's foot started to twitch. "I'm not."

"No, really. What's going on?"

"We're almost done, so you don't need to help. It's good, we're good, it's good. You can go now."

Okay, forget what I said about acting lessons from Dara. The way she was babbling was even more suspicious than Tenley being weird. Maybe she needed a script to stay in character.

I measured the distance between each person's chair, wondering if it would be possible to sneak out from under the table and run like heck without Asher seeing me.

"There's an extra chair," Asher said.

"I like to have two, in case one offends me," Tenley said.

Asher tapped the table with his fingers. From where I sat, it sounded like rain on the rooftop. "Or, someone else was here too. Someone who doesn't want to see me. Someone who didn't have time to escape before I sat down." Asher's face appeared under the table. "Hi, Holland."

I dropped my head to my knees. "You can't see me."

He laughed, a delicious sound that warmed me to my toes. "What are we? Two?"

"Maybe," I muttered and made no move to get up. If I sat there long enough, he might forget about me and go away.

"Holland?"

I peeked out of my arms.

Asher's eyes were clear blue, like looking at a summer sky. "I'm leaving, okay? You don't have to hide under the table anymore. Have a merry Christmas."

"You too," I croaked.

He was gone by the time I climbed back into my chair.

Christmas vacation dawned clear and cold with two beautiful weeks of Christmasy freedom. I used the time leading up to Christmas Eve wisely by getting ahead on some college assignments, shopping for gifts, and rereading my favorite Christmas books: *The Mansion* by Henry Van Dyke, *The Best Christmas Pageant Ever* by Barbara Robinson, and *Mr. Dickens and His Carol* by Samantha Silva. And after I read that one, I had to read *A Christmas Carol* all over again.

On Christmas Eve, I helped the boys make gingerbread men for Santa Claus. It took a while because they had to look like each member of our family. I wasn't much help with baking or decorating, but I was a whiz at cutting out dough. The twins did the mixing, I did the cutting and arranging on cookie sheets, then they baked and decorated.

I also supervised.

So, of course, everything turned out perfectly.

We arranged cookies on a platter with a glass of milk and put some organic carrots on the table with the feathery green stems still intact. Mom always insisted that reindeer flew better when they ate clean. Once that was done, we changed into matching pajamas and gathered around Grandma so she could read *The Night Before Christmas*. Dad usually did that part of the tradition, but since we were with Grandma this year and the tradition started with her parents, it seemed like the right thing to do.

I curled up on the floor at the feet of her rocking chair, next to the Christmas tree. A candle flickered from the arm of Grandma's chair. It cast cozy shadows on the wall, like the ghosts of all Christmases past were listening too. I settled in and let her words wash over me.

The children were nestled all snug in their beds...

The moon on the breast of the new fallen snow...

As dry leaves before the wild hurricane fly...

Clement Clarke Moore certainly had a way with imagery. I loved how the pictures danced in my head like sugar plums.

Christmas was so magical.

I pulled my fluffy blanket tighter across my shoulders and stared at my family while Grandma read. The twins lay on their stomachs with identical legs waving in the air while they sucked peppermint candy canes. Their freckles stood out in the dim light, and their tousled hair made them look about half their age. Mom and Dad snuggled on the couch next to Grandma's chair. Dad held a mug of hot cocoa with one hand, and his other was draped across Mom's shoulder. She propped her legs on his with her head resting on his shoulder.

Then Grandma, with her silvery voice and animated face, sat in the plump rocking chair holding the book so we could all see the pictures. There was nowhere in the world I would rather be.

"Happy Christmas to all, and to all a good night." Grandma closed the book with a sigh and rested it on her knees. Her hands swept across the cover. "You know, this was your great grandfather's book. An artist friend he knew in Germany painted it by hand. It's the only copy like it in the world. It was one of the few things my grandparents brought with them when they immigrated."

"That reminds me." Dad untangled himself from Mom's octopus limbs and stood up. "Who's ready to light the tree?"

The twins cheered as they scrambled to their feet. I took Dad's seat next to Mom and watched as they counted down, then lit the tree for the first time that season. As always, it took my breath away. It didn't matter how many times in my life I'd seen a Christmas tree lit; that first time in our house on Christmas Eve was something special.

Grandma's eyes glistened. "I love this tradition. Thank you for continuing it with your own family."

Dad perched on the edge of her recliner and bent close to squeeze her shoulder. "Of course, Mom."

Brett toyed with one of the ornaments, a red one with a white hand print that he made when he was in preschool. "Why do we wait until Christmas Eve to light the Christmas tree? All my friends have their tree lit up for the entire month of December."

"We're special," Dad said.

"Yes, that." Grandma smiled at him. "But also because, when my father, your great grandfather, was a little boy in Germany, they didn't have strings of lights for the tree. They decorated it with candles."

"Real candles?" Rhett's eyes widened. "Holy fire hazard, Batman."

We all laughed. Grandma waited for the sound to fade before she went on. "Yes. That is why they only lit the tree on Christmas Eve. Just for that one night. My father loved it so much that when I was a little girl, we would put the electric lights on the tree, but we wouldn't plug them in until Christmas Eve."

"Coooooooool," the twins breathed.

Mom filled up everyone's homemade cocoa and we sipped while we stared at the lit tree. My eyelids grew heavy. I set my mug to the side and rested my head on the back of the couch. This is what I needed to get my head on straight. A beautiful, peaceful moment without any reminder of World War Whittaker. Christmas sparkled in the air like snowflakes. There was peace on earth and goodwill to all teenage boys. I was positive it would all work out. I didn't need to worry about it anymore.

With my family surrounding me and the magic of Christmas hugging me tight, I drifted off to sleep.

Alicia video-called me at ten the next morning.

"Happy Christmas, Harry!" She spread her arms out wide as soon as my video finished buffering.

I giggled. "Happy Christmas, Ron!"

Alicia's face got serious. "I've been thinking."

"Yeah?"

"Really, you should be Ron and I should be Harry, you know, since your hair is red and mine is dark brown. I don't know why we haven't thought of this before. It's a gross oversight."

I shook my head with a smile. "What did you get for Christmas, you weirdo?"

"Well..." She gave the word a billion extra syllables. "Someone awesome sent me scrubs with cactus on them. Cactuses? Cacti."

"Aw, you're lucky to have someone so awesome as a friend."

"I know, right?"

"Well, someone awesome sent *me* compression leggings that are dusty rose colored and fabulous."

"Lucky ducky!"

"I know, right?" I mimicked her voice perfectly. "Thank you, by the way. I love them!"

"And I love the scrubs. I'll wear them when I start my internship this summer."

My hands dropped to the table, making the laptop wobble. "Shut the front door. You got it?"

"Yes!" Alicia let out a shriek that she'd probably been holding in for days. "I just saw the acceptance letter in my email yesterday."

"That is amazing! I am so excited for you!"

Alicia nodded, quickly at first, then it gradually slowed down. "I wish you were here interning with me. It seems weird that we're not doing this together."

"I know." Something squeezed my middle for a moment and wouldn't let go. "I wish I was there with you too."

We stared at each other with sad faces for a couple of minutes before Alicia waved her hands around. "Okay, that's enough wallowing; it is what it is. You'll be here next year, and we'll live out all our interning together dreams then. Right now, I want to hear this carnival story. Your texts didn't give me enough information."

I groaned. "You really don't want to hear it, trust me."

"Oh yes, I do! The more you think I don't, the more I really do." Alicia lived her life hand in hand with obstinance. "Plus, if you tell me now that you've had some space and are in a fabulous mood, it will start to feel different, you know?"

I did know, and she was right. As I plunged into the debacle that was the carnival fundraiser, I found myself giggling instead of cringing, laughing instead of crying, and spinning it with shades of irony instead of tragedy.

"And then, I got so mad that I picked up a ruined cake and threw it at them to get them to stop rolling around like a twin dust devil."

"You did not! What happened to Holland the Meek? The girl who was too nervous to ask the teacher for a bathroom pass and made her best friend do it? The girl who stuttered whenever she bought her ticket at the movie theater? What has Arizona done to you?" Alicia stared at me through the screen.

"Funny things happen when Anger steps in, you know?" I shook my head. "I probably wasn't showing up as my best self at that moment, but it felt so amazing to catapult that cake at their heads. SO amazing!"

Alicia pulled her sleeve down to wipe her eyes. "I wish I could have seen it."

"Actually, I bet someone filmed it. I'll ask around."

"Please do. I really want to share that moment with you. I feel so sad that I missed out on this pivotal experience in your life!" She placed a hand over her heart.

"You're silly."

"And you're awesome! What happened after you tossed the cake at them?"

"They stopped fighting. Then, um, I yelled at them a lot and Mrs. Marlow's super buff husband dragged them both away."

"You yelled at them?"

"Yeah." I swiped my finger across my laptop keyboard to get rid of all the dust. "I basically told them I didn't like either one of them at the moment and they were the worst."

"Holland!" Alicia applauded. "Way to speak your truth, my friend."

I let out a laugh and ducked my head. "Yeah, my filter broke."

"Sometimes it needs to. So, what now? What's the status?"

"Of my filter?"

"No, you stinker. With the guys. Asher and... What's the other one's name?"

"Chandler."

"Yeah, him. What did you decide to do? Same plan? They're both on life support? Any thoughts of pulling the plug?"

I laughed all the way from my belly. "Same plan, yeah. We'll see how those first dates go before we pull any plugs."

"Wow, so you're really going to do it?" Alicia held up one hand. "You're going on a date with each of them—"

"Three dates."

"Three dates with each of them, and then you're going to choose one? Like on *The Bachelorette*?"

"No." I wrinkled my nose. The one and only thing Alicia and I never could see eye-to-eye on was *The Bachelorette*. She was borderline obsessed, and I thought the whole thing was borderline Looney Tunes. "We're going to sit down like civilized human beings and decide what to do next."

"How very diplomatic."

"Right?" I narrowed my eyes. I didn't like her tone. "What?"

"What?"

"What are you thinking that you're not saying?"

Alicia's eyes shifted away from the screen. "I should really clean my closet."

"Alicia!"

"Okay, fine. It's just not very romantic, you know?"

"What isn't romantic?" I was trying to piece together what she was saying and could only think that her closet wasn't romantic. That couldn't be right. I don't think I'd ever met a closet that was.

"The plan," Alicia said. "It sounds so clinical."

"I thought we liked being clinical," I teased.

"I love it, I totally do, but I would think *you'd* want something more Mr. Darcy-ish. Are you really okay with this date checklist and discussion?

I mean, was it your idea? It sounds like something a guy would come up with."

A guy did come up with it, but I agreed to it, so there was that.

"Holland?"

"I'm thinking."

I hadn't stopped long enough to consider whether I liked the idea or not. I was just so glad they agreed to a solution so easily. Now that Alicia brought it up, I let the idea mull around my brain. Sure, it would have been nice if the dates came about in a more natural, normal way. But this wasn't really a normal situation. Even if I wanted to fall in love with one of them like Marianne fell in love with Colonel Brandon, it wasn't realistic.

I let out a sigh.

"What?"

"Oh, it's nothing. It's fine."

"Don't give me that garbage, Hols. I know you better than that."

"It doesn't matter. I might wish it was different, but it's not. What does your mom always say? When you argue with what's real, you lose every time?"

"Yes, except that you also can talk to people and change the circumstances and make boundaries. You know? You don't have to just deal with it."

I tapped the table with the pad of my fingers so it didn't make any noise. "What would you do, Ali?"

She sucked in her cheeks in an impressive fish face. "Tough call. First, I would need to figure out how I feel about the guys, I guess."

It's not like I expected her to have the answers to everything, but I guess maybe I did somewhere deep inside because her answer was a tremendous letdown. "I don't know how I feel about the guys; that's why we're doing the dates."

"So you can choose one?"

I shook my head. This all had made perfect sense when I was sitting in the Whittaker's dining room, but now it made absolutely no sense. "I'm not choosing one or the other. I guess I'm hoping the dates will make it obvious which of them I should date."

"Holland!" Alicia gave me a teacher look, the kind I used to get when I gave the wrong answer and the teacher thought I should have known the right one. "You know it doesn't work like that, right? You can just make a decision and then choose to be happy with your choice."

That took us right back to the place where I was the person choosing one of them and rejecting the other. That wasn't a comfortable place. "I like them both, Ali. And I don't want to hurt either of them."

"So, you want the dates to make it so these guys know if they want to be with you or not? Are you hoping one will bow out, is that it?"

"Yes." That was exactly what I wanted. Ideally, either Asher or Chandler will just decide he doesn't like me anymore and I will end up with the twin that does like me. It could be either one. I really did like them both.

"What if that doesn't happen, Hols?"

"Then, I guess it gets messy." I really didn't want messy though.

"Holland?" Alicia's voice lowered, dripping with sympathy. "I know you hate this."

"I do," I sighed.

"I need to say something, okay? Because you're my best friend and I love you."

Foreboding settled on my shoulder.

"You are such a nice person who hates conflict, so I think you're prepping yourself to settle for whatever the Whittaker twins decide. You're probably telling yourself you'd be happy with either one of them, maybe even going so far as to tell yourself you'd be fine if they both decide they don't like you."

Okay, everything she said was true. It was creepy how she knew things about me that I hadn't been able to put into words.

"It's like the nursing thing."

"Wait," I blinked. "What nursing thing?"

"Holland." Compassion surrounded my name when Alicia said it.

"You don't really want to be a nurse." She gave me a small smile. "You hate to see people suffer. You hate it when others are in pain. It would tear you up if someone died that you were helping."

"I..." The word trailed off when no others gathered to back it up.

"You love the thought of the two of us rooming together and having a life plan because it's safe." She sighed. "Do you remember that sleepover when we talked about all this?"

My mind went blank, like my laptop when there were too many tabs open and it just shut down.

"I told you about that experience when I went to the hospital to visit my Grandpa, and I was intrigued by all the nurses, remember? They were so kind and helped him so much that I decided that's what I wanted to do with my life. And then you said—"

"Me too," I whispered.

"Yes," Alicia nodded. "But, is that what you really want? Really?"

Tears welled up in my eyes, making it very difficult to see. "I don't know."

"See, that's it!" Alicia pointed at the screen. "That's the key. You don't know because you don't stop to decide what you want, Holland. What do you want?"

I sniffed. "You mean, with the twins or with a career?"

"Let's start with a career. That might be easier to wrap your head around."

"I don't know, Ali. I've planned on being a nurse with you for so long that I can't even think what other careers there are." I wiped my eyes with the back of my hand. This was hard to face, but I felt lighter somehow, more free.

That's how I knew I was on the right track.

"Teacher, firefighter, office assistant, engineer, actor, accountant, baker—no, not that one, yikes." Alicia's words dissolved into giggles.

"Not nice," I giggled with her.

It felt so good.

"The sky is literally the limit, Hols. You can do whatever you want! What do you love? What are you passionate about? What do *you* want to do?"

I didn't have an answer to those questions, but I was going to give it some thought. I told Alicia I'd talk to her later and lay on my back, looking at the ceiling. There was something thrilling about the thought of doing what I wanted to do just because *I* wanted to do it.

A shiver of possibility went through me, leaving goosebumps on my arms.

Chapter Seventeen

"An idea, like a ghost, must be spoken to a little before it will explain itself."
The Lamplighter

If Tenley was surprised that I shanghaied her at lunch on the first day back to school in the new year, she was really good at hiding it. She just watched as I laid out notebook pages and explained all the ideas I'd had about Runway Careers. There were many; I'd thought about pretty much nothing else since my talk with Alicia.

"Wow." Tenley pointed to the drawing I'd made of possible seating arrangements and decorations around the runway. "That looks amazing. I love the centerpieces."

They were just simple glass jars with pinecones and greenery in the center. Beautiful, but simple. We could round up most of those things with zero cost.

"What's the catch?" Tenley set down the paper with three different menu ideas and eyeballed me. Her hairy, scary eyeball. "Why did you spend so much time on this when you're supposed to be taking a break?" she went on.

"No catch," I said as I shook my head. "Really. I just want this to happen, and I'm willing to do whatever has to be done to make it happen. With or without the funding."

Tenley's eyeball didn't move.

"Okay. I recently decided that I don't want to be a nurse, so I need another career option. I'm hoping I'll figure it out at Runway Careers. Is that bad?"

"Nope." Tenley looked down at my papers. Suspicion had obviously left the building. "That's perfect motivation." She sifted through a few more papers, then pulled out her phone. "I'm going to take pictures in case something happens to these. Once everyone gets here, we're going to talk."

I nodded and concentrated on finishing my lunch while she did that so I could give full attention to our talk when the time came. Dara was already there with us, but it took a solid fifteen minutes for Bryan, Ryker, Ethan, and Asher to meander their way to our corner. With only ten minutes left in the lunch period, I had to sit on my hands to keep from jumping out of my skin.

Tenley called us to order by crumpling up her lunch bag and throwing it at Ethan's head.

"Bruh!"

"Now that you're all paying attention, let's talk about raffle tickets. I'll start. I have fifty billion relatives who are way too rich and complete suckers. I sold all of my tickets." She made a big production of patting herself on the back. "Asher, you're next."

Asher's eyes flicked to me for just a moment. I hadn't spoken to him or Chandler since before Christmas break. I knew we needed to have a date conversation, but my mind was too focused on Runway Careers to even think about it.

"I sold all the tickets Dara gave me. The money is in my locker."

"Awesome!" Tenley punched the air. "How many did Chandler sell?"

"Um..." He looked at the ceiling. "Like, none."

"What?"

"Yeah, I just did it. No big deal."

Tenley scrunched her face. With surprising self-restraint, she turned to Dara. "How about you, Belle?"

Dara fluffed the ends of her gargantuan yellow dress. My brain pulled a squirrel moment and got distracted wondering how she fit at her desk or in her car while wearing that thing.

"Um, yeah. I only sold twenty five."

"Okay," Tenley nodded with great precision. "Is there a reason?"

Dara sighed. "I'm the worst?"

"No, you're not!" I held out a hand. "We still have a couple of weeks until the deadline, right? We can sell them. We'll help you."

"Yeah," Dara finally looked up. "Except…"

"What?" And there was Foreboding, plopping down on my lap.

"I talked to a lot of people. Um, people who gave money or resources to the carnival. They were upset. They didn't want to spend any more money on something that might…um…" She glanced at Asher. "Sorry."

"No." He shook his head. "I'm sorry."

Tenley sighed deeply. "How did the rest of you do?"

Ethan sold twenty five with the same reason as Dara. Ryker forgot until this morning and still had all of his. Bryan sold half, I sold all of mine, but that was only because my mom took them to the gym.

"We're short," Tenley said while I was still working out the numbers in my head.

"No we're not." Bryan held out his phone with the calculator app in view. "That's exactly three thousand dollars."

Tenley shook her head. "I don't want to meet the goal. I want to exceed it. The administration isn't going to take us seriously if we do the bare minimum." She stood up and grabbed her backpack without warning. "I'm going to take a walk; I'll see you guys later."

"I'll come with you." Ethan scrambled to his feet.

The rest of us gave each other discouraged stares as they walked away.

"We'll figure it out," I said, trying to coax my old pal Optimism out of the shadows. It might have worked if Despair hadn't been hanging onto my back like a monkey.

Dara nodded, gathered her things and left, her dress swishing gorgeously across the commons. One by one, Ryker and Bryan made their excuses and left until it was just Asher and me in the lunch corner.

"You know," Asher said as he ran his hand through his hair, "it might not be the worst thing if this tradition died."

My head jerked up, my expression probably reflecting how horrified I was to hear him say that.

"I'm just saying, it's been around forever. It's not even necessary anymore with the Internet, and it's causing so much drama. It might be time to let it go."

I shook my head, too furious to trust any words to come out.

"I know you think I'm a jerk for saying things like this, but Runway Careers has gotten way out of hand. My grandpa started it and even he hates it. Originally, he did it to help people figure out what they wanted to do before they went to college. He had no idea it would turn into such a huge, elaborate thing. Last time I talked to him, he told me he wishes they'd stop doing it too." He glanced at me and went on. "You weren't here last year, obviously, but it was crazy. They hired professional models to wear career costumes and had an MC. There were sparklers at the end of the runway. The food was catered, and some of it was super weird. It cost everyone months of headache, tons of money, and for what? There was a huge uproar because one of the models came wearing a skimpy nurse outfit, and someone threw up after eating too much coconut shrimp. That's not what my grandpa started."

Somewhere in the middle of his speech, Fury curled into a calm, fluffy kitten. Asher was right. I wasn't there before. I had no idea what Runway Careers was supposed to be like. As I pictured what he described with sparklers and loud music, something inside me died a little. That's not what I wanted Runway Careers to be either.

"What would Runway Careers be like if you planned it?" I asked, wrapping my hands around my legs so I could rest my chin on my knees. "If it could be whatever you want."

Asher looked at a point somewhere over my shoulder. "I'd make it plain and simple. Students would announce their parents or whoever came with them, and those people would just wear what they normally wear to work. There would be cookies or something easy at the end, and a meet and greet so students can ask the people questions about their careers. No fuss, no strobe lights, no jazzy music."

A new vision of Runway Careers was forming in my mind.

"If it could be like you just described, would you want to do it this year?"

"Yeah, I guess," Asher shrugged. "But no one would like it. They're all used to having a huge production."

"Asher, is your Grandpa still alive?"

"Yeah. Remember? He lives right by your grandma."

I forgot that. "Like, across the street, or..."

Asher smiled. "How about I take you over there? For one of our dates? We could have dinner too, so it's more date-y."

"Did you just say 'date-y'?" I tried to hide a smile and failed dismally.

"Yes." He narrowed his eyes. "Judgy much?"

"I'm not judgy. I've just never heard-y someone add an 'ee' to the end of a random word like date."

Asher shook his head with a laugh. "Anyway, what do you think? Would that be a fun date?"

We probably needed to talk about the dates in general before I thought anything about that one specifically. "What did you and Chandler decide? How do you guys want to do this?"

"We thought, if it works for you, that we could start this week. We'll each take you on a date for the next three weeks, and then we'll all talk it out, like you said."

That is what I said, before Alicia recommended I figure out what I want. I still hadn't done that. I was too caught up in all my thoughts about making Runway Careers awesome. Oh well. I had three weeks to figure out what I wanted. That was plenty of time.

"Correct answer, that sounds great. Are you free tonight?" I asked. I wanted to talk to his grandpa as soon as possible.

"Hey," Asher said, rolling his eyes, "I'm supposed to ask you."

The bell rang then, and I stood up automatically. Asher did too, but he grabbed my backpack so I couldn't leave yet.

He held it out to me, his blue eyes bright. "Holland, I would love to take you out to dinner tonight. Are you available?"

"Yes," I nodded. "But—"

"AND," he raised his voice to drown out mine. "I'd love it if you'd accompany me to my grandparents' house for a visit afterwards."

"When you say 'accompany', I think of a piano."

Asher squinted. "You're supposed to think of the Regency Era and be super impressed."

"Oh," I grinned. "I'll do that next time."

Asher let go of my backpack. "I'll pick you up at five. I have the car today."

"Where are we going to eat?"

"Surprise." He held out a hand. "But don't worry, it will be healthy. Tell your mom that so she likes me better."

I laughed. "That's savage, sucking up to the parents. You're playing dirty."

"No," Asher's face got serious. "I'm playing to win."

Asher arrived five minutes before five-o-clock. I was pacing in front of the door, wondering if I'd dressed appropriately. It was hard to look cute and date-y when whatever I put on was covered in a puffy down jacket. Plus, my hair was already flying out of the side French braid I'd attempted. I watched five YouTube videos trying to figure it out and then gave up and called for my mom to rescue me.

She came into the living room to answer the door but stopped when she saw me pacing. "Are you going to get that?"

I shook out my hands. "Eventually."

"You're nervous," she said with a smile.

I nodded.

"It's okay to be nervous. You can still go and have a great time. Just take the emotion with you."

Right now, Nervous was glued to my chest, so it was hard to breathe. It also, somehow, curdled my belly, making me think that I might throw up the apples and peanut butter I'd eaten about an hour ago. I didn't want to take Nervous anywhere except back up to my room and under my covers.

The doorbell rang again.

Mom moved the curtain and stood back so she could peek through without being seen. "He's waiting. Holland. He looks adorable, and SO nervous." She let the curtain drop, a sassy smile in place.

I see what she did there.

By letting my nerves keep me frozen on this side of the door, I was fueling Asher's nerves on the other side. I took a deep breath and squared my shoulders. Okay, Nervous. Let's do this. My hand shook as I reached for the door, but I got a grip just fine and pulled it toward me without a hitch.

Asher's finger was poised over the doorbell for a third ring. His hand dropped when he saw me.

"Holland. Hi."

"Hey, Asher." I glanced at my mom, who made shooing motions with her hands. "I'm ready."

Wow, that wasn't lame at all.

"Me too," Asher grimaced. "I guess, let's go?"

I nodded and shut the door behind me without looking at my mom. I didn't want to see the expression on her face confirming what nerd bombers we were. It's not like we never talked. We'd had conversations that went okay. Why was this so stinking awkward?

Asher went around to the driver's side of the car, then smacked his hand on the hood and hurried to my side. "Let me get that for you." He opened the door, almost taking the end off my nose. If I hadn't dodged out of the way at the last minute, it would have been bad.

"Sorry, sorry." Asher waited for me to get all the way in and then shut the door softly. I could see him muttering to himself through the windshield as he walked around the front of the car. When he opened his door and slid in, he said "sorry" three more times.

"It's okay," I said.

"Yeah, cause nothing says awesome date like an ER visit with a broken nose." He stuck the key in the ignition and turned harder than was necessary.

I put my hand on his arm so he would look at me. "Can we just pretend we're not on a date? I am so tense. I don't know why, but this feels like so much pressure."

Asher let out a long breath that hissed at the end. "Yes, please. I mean, sure, if that's what you want. I totally get it that you're intimidated by my man card, so I'll go along with whatever you want. You know, for you." He puffed out his chest and made the dorkiest face in the world.

I laughed all the way from my toes, letting some of my nerves fade away. "That's what I'm talking about."

Asher pulled into the street, his shoulders resting like they'd dropped a thousand pounds. "You can mess with the radio if you want."

I did, turning it until I came to a country music station, just to see what he would say. It wasn't recent country either; it was old-school, nasal, steel guitar country. Straight up Grandpa Morriss style.

Asher didn't even flinch.

After observing him for a couple more minutes, I swung the dial to a station that was playing classic rock.

Still no reaction.

Very interesting. I added this information to my mental Asher notes. I let the Beatles song finish, 'cause I liked it, then turned the dial until a new Taylor Swift song filled the car.

"Mercy!" Asher bumped the steering wheel with his palm a couple of times. "I call mercy. You can go back to the twangy country, you can bring on the Aerosmith, but if you make me listen to Taylor Swift, the chances are very great that I will perish."

"Perish?" I used the word to hold back my giggles. "Who says *perish* anymore?"

"Correct answer." He pointed at himself. "This guy."

I flipped the dial back to classic rock and settled in my seat. "Okay, so no Taylor Swift. What *is* on your playlist?"

"I could tell you, but that's too easy. Wouldn't it be so much more fun to find out for yourself?" He glanced at me. "Press the USB button to reveal my playlist. Dun, dun, dun."

Once the button was deployed, I listened carefully. I didn't know if it was possible to learn everything you wanted to know about a person by discovering what kind of music they listened to, but I couldn't deny that Curiosity was tapping on my shoulder.

"Coldplay," I nodded. "This is a great song."

"Yeah, and it just keeps getting better. I have great taste in music. Me and awesome songs are like this." He held up his hand to show me his first two fingers twisted together like a couple of wonky branches.

"What about movies?" I asked. "What do you like to watch?"

It was funny that I'd known Asher for months but didn't really know him. I don't think we'd had a chance to sit down and really talk since that first day I met him, when he walked me to the library.

And people can change so much in a couple of months.

"Correct answer: comedy." He grinned. "What about you?"

"You don't want to know."

"I asked."

"True. However, you really don't want to know."

"Why not?"

Well, that was easy. Maybe because every other guy I'd shared my favorite movies with turned green or fell asleep.

"Come on," he wheedled as he turned the steering wheel to make a sharp turn. "It can't be that bad."

"Okay," I breathed. "Correct answer: BBC movies like Charles Dickens' *David Copperfield* and—"

"Jane Austen," he nodded. "I remember you told me you love the books; it makes sense you love the movies too. What's your favorite classic?" he asked.

"I love *A Tale of Two Cities*. It's so horrible."

Asher's lips twitched. "It's horrible...and you love it?"

"That sounds weird, but I can't explain what I mean. It would ruin the whole movie. Have you seen it?"

"I don't think so. I haven't read the book either. What's it about?"

"Two cities," I said in a sassy tone.

Asher shook his head and just laughed.

I folded my hands in my lap. "I'm not going to tell you anything about it because it will for real spoil it. There's nothing like the first time you read the book and realize what's going on." I sighed. "I'm actually a little jealous you get to have that experience for the first time. I'd love to feel that way again."

Asher pulled the car into a parking lot and stretched his neck to look for an available space to park. It was jammed with cars. "How about you watch it with me?"

"Really?"

He eased into a tight spot and turned off the car. His body twisted to face me. "Yeah, that can be our date next week."

"You really want to spend almost three hours watching a movie where they talk funny and wear breeches?"

"Yes," he shrugged. "If you love it that much, I have to see it."

Heat flooded my cheeks. The way he looked at me was so…

Something.

"But let's not get ahead of ourselves. First date first. Are you ready?"

I looked around. "Yes. Where are we? I thought we were going to your grandparents' house?"

"Not this date, next date. They had something going on today." He pushed open his door, then jogged around to open mine. "Welcome to the country club. My dad's a member; he's obsessed with golf." Asher made a face. "The good news is, they let me rent out one of the picnic areas, and they have those outdoor space heaters, so we don't freeze our…"

"Yes?"

He shrugged and opened the back door to grab a mini cooler. "You know."

"No, I don't know. I have no idea what you were going to say. What would we freeze off?"

"But that's not all," he said, ignoring my sassafras as he nudged the door shut and casually reached for my hand. "I also made you food. All by myself."

"Really?" It was hard to think about anything else when Asher's fingers were entwined with mine. I had to do some serious tugging to get my mind to focus on what he was saying.

"Really, really." He pulled me to a stop while we waited for a car to back out. "It's going to be great." We walked into the front doors where a lady at the round desk greeted Asher by name. He paused to ask her about her kids, then turned down the hall and led me out a side door.

I caught my breath.

The grass might have been slightly brown, but the spread of the lawn against a backdrop of red rocks with the sun shining at an angle was absolutely gorgeous.

"Right?" Asher tugged me around the building where someone had set up a picnic blanket between two space heaters. I was glad to see those. With the wind picking up the way it was and the sun on its way down, it promised to get super cold outside.

Asher let go of my hand so we could settle next to each other on the blanket. He opened the cooler to pull out a thermos and two bowls. Then he froze.

"What's wrong?"

Asher sat back on his heels. "I forgot to bring spoons."

I leaned over the cooler to look inside. The only thing left was a container filled with something I couldn't identify through the frosted plastic. Definitely no spoons.

"I could go see if I can borrow some." Asher craned his neck behind him, but there was no one around.

"It's fine." I took the thermos and twisted the lid. "We can pour your soup into the bowls and sip it. Like that part on *Beauty and the Beast* when they eat their porridge."

Asher smiled. "Which one am I?"

"Duh." I shook my head and handed him the thermos. The lid was on way too tight. "Beauty."

He fluttered his eyelashes in the most obnoxious way possible. "Why thank you." When he handed the thermos back to me, his fingers brushed against my wrist. Fireworks went off in my stomach.

Simmer down, I told them. You were just holding his hand two seconds ago. What is the big deal? I set the bowls on the blanket between us and was about to pour when Asher cleared his throat.

"Hey, Holland?"

I looked up. "Yeah?"

"I don't know how to ask this..." His eyes darted around my face, never settling.

My fingertips started to tingle as I wondered what he was going to say. It had to be monumental if he couldn't even look at my face for one second. I held my breath as he opened his mouth.

"Is your butt wet?"

Chapter Eighteen

"Any man may be in good spirits and good temper when he's well dressed."
Charles Dickens

Chandler called me the next day to ask me out for Friday night. The only thing he would tell me was to dress formally.

I wasn't sure what that meant, so I called Tenley.

"Mr. Whittaker has all kinds of connections. Chandler's probably taking you somewhere fancy. Just wear a dress."

Which was great advice, except for the fact that every dress I owned now looked lame and hobo-ish. Which was why Tenley and I were at the mall three hours before my date, trying to find something that didn't make me feel frumpy or huge and didn't cost more than my truck.

Yeah, good luck.

"What about this?" Tenley held up a smashing dress with spaghetti straps and white embroidery along the skirt.

"It's cute, just not very warm." I'd have to put so many layers on to keep from freezing, I'd look like a snowman.

"That's fair." Tenley put it back on the clearance rack with a grim look. "I will find something or perish. I have never spent full price on anything in my life, and I'm not about to start. Or let you do it either. There's got to be something here that will work."

I admired her determination but sincerely doubted it. Not only were the dresses on her rack totally skimpy, but they were also mostly bright summery colors. I was normally a big fan of those, except that *fancy* was usually a black, gray, and navy kind of thing, wasn't it? I didn't remember

197

ever seeing a movie where the main character went out to a fancy thing wearing a bright orange tank dress with yellow flowers on it.

Tenley squeaked a number of hangers as she shoved them aside. "So, you never told me. How did it go with Asher the other day?

We'd been so busy with planning for Runway Careers that we hadn't had time to talk about much else. I chose to believe that was why Asher hadn't really said anything to me since he dropped me off Monday night.

"It was really fun."

Tenley stopped moving and gave me her hairy eyeball. "Was it?"

"Yes." I didn't mean to sound so defensive; it just sort of happened.

"Hm." Tenley focused on a dark blue dress with only one shoulder strap and a skirt short enough to qualify as a shirt.

I shook my head. My dad would freak out if he saw me in that.

"That's interesting."

"What's interesting?" I pulled out a modest purple dress with a long chiffon skirt. It was gorgeous, but prom dress fancy. I wish Chandler had given me more information. What did *formal* mean to him? Cause I had friends in Durango that thought formal meant wearing a button-down shirt instead of a tee.

"Well, I was just thinking about how Asher stares at you when you're not looking, like you're the Red Ryder BB gun on the other side of the store window."

"What? He does not!"

"Yes he does, and I was thinking about how you never really said anything about your date, and he never really said anything about your date, and that leads me to the conclusion that the two of you are either getting married secretly this weekend—"

"Right after my date with Chandler. How did you ever figure it out?"

Tenley ignored me. "OR your date was terrible, and you're both embarrassed."

I looked away. "It wasn't...terrible."

"I knew it!" Tenley skipped over to me and grabbed my arms so I couldn't keep messing with dresses. "What happened? Tell me everything."

"Fine." I pulled my wrists out of her grip. "But only if you stop looking through the skanky clothes and really help me find a dress."

"Deal!" She reached for a black frilly thing and waved it in front of my face. "Come on, don't keep me in suspense!"

I pushed the dress away, guiding Tenley's hands back to the metal bar where the dress belonged. "Okay, so, he took me to the country club for a picnic on the grass."

"Classic."

"Yeah?" I paused. What exactly did that mean?

"Of course he's going to try and impress you without going over the top. A picnic is casual, but the country club is unique. Good move."

"Yeah, so, he even made this beef and barley soup from scratch and a fruit salad, so the food was super healthy and homemade."

"Awww."

I nodded. "But I guess there was a problem with some pipes freezing or something and while we were getting ready to eat, the grass filled up with water."

"What?"

"Asher noticed it first. Then, when I stood up, my jeans were soaked and soggy."

Tenley groaned.

"We gathered the picnic stuff and went inside—or, we tried to, but the side door was locked, so we had to walk all the way around. By the time we got to the front entrance, my pants were stiff because they were frozen. They wouldn't let us in the front door because we were all muddy from sitting on the wet grass. Asher explained what happened, but the lady really didn't believe him. I think she thought we were trying to crash the country club or something."

"Didn't she recognize him?" Tenley peeked out of her hands. "The Whittakers go there a lot, Like, a lot, a lot."

I shook my head. "When we first went in, they did. But this time there was a new person at the front desk and she totally didn't believe our story. Asher finally told her we didn't want to come in anymore; he just wanted someone to go check on the sprinklers because they needed to be fixed. She agreed, probably to get rid of us, and we walked across the parking lot to Asher's car."

Tenley made a face. "What happened? I can tell it was bad; just say it."

"So, um, apparently Asher parked in a no parking zone, and they towed his car. It was gone. And, um, also, Chandler had the cell phone."

"What about your cell phone?"

"Funny you should ask. I knew I had it with me when we were at the picnic place because I took a picture of the view, but it wasn't in my purse anymore, so we walked all the way back to the front doors and tried again to beg the lady to let us in so we could go look for it."

"You are kidding me?"

"Nope." I tried not to smile. It really wasn't funny at the time. "No matter what we said, she was positive we were trying to do something nefarious. She threatened to call security and Asher said, 'Please do'."

"He did not!"

"He totally did. When security got there, they recognized Asher. The lady felt awful, I could tell. But instead of apologizing, she pretended we didn't exist."

"What next? I don't even want to know. Tell me."

I pulled out a gray dress with a pretty flared skirt and lace overlay. "Security escorted us to the picnic area. My phone was on the sidewalk by the heater. They asked us a billion questions about the flooded grass, then we asked them a billion questions about what happens when a car is towed. One of the security guys, George, was about to get off shift and offered to drop us off at the tow yard on his way home."

"Is that weird?"

"It might have been, except that he was probably as old as my grandma and super nice. He drove us to the tow yard, and the gate was closed. We missed it by half an hour."

"Oh my gosh. Are you making this up?"

"No!" I laughed. "I swear it is all true. I would tell you to check with Asher, but I really think he's trying to block the memory. Anyway, Asher smacked the fence with his palm and hit a piece of wire that was sticking up—"

"Ugh!" Tenley shivered. "Ugh, that gives me the creeps. Did he get cut?"

"He did," I nodded, remembering. "It was nasty, but luckily I had a first aid kit in my purse. So, that was fine. Then George drove us to Asher's house. Asher explained to his parents, then borrowed their car, and we drove to a lake—Watson. I think—to salvage the rest of the date."

"Good luck with that."

"Yeah. That's when we realized we'd left the picnic stuff in George's car."

Tenley banged her head against the rack in front of her.

Poor Asher. More than once that night, I wished I was a Fairy Godmother that could wave a magic wand and make everything work. He looked so miserable.

"It was okay, really. I had a couple packets of pistachios in my purse, for blood sugar emergencies, and there was a case of bottled water in the back of the car. We didn't starve."

"Seriously?" Tenley shook her head slowly. "What did you do?"

I smiled at the memory. It sounded bad, I know it did, but it wasn't. Not really. We cracked pistachio shells and leaned back in the heated seats and talked for a couple hours.

Really, it was one of the best dates I'd ever been on.

Tenley would think I was nuts if I told her that, so I shrugged. "We talked and stuff. It was fine. What do you think about this one?" I swung a red cap sleeve dress with a gorgeous circle skirt. I held it up to my chest to make sure it went at least to my knees.

It did.

But Tenley shook her head. "You should never wear red. Seriously. It just makes you look red all over."

I looked at the dress with sad eyes. "It's so pretty."

"Is there another color?"

I shifted through the dresses near it until I found one in navy blue. It wasn't as pretty as the red, but it was probably better for this fancy, formal date. Less eye-catching.

"Yes." Tenley took it from me and held it out. "Try it on. Also, how come you don't have a purple heart for surviving that date?"

"It was fine," I said again.

She handed me the dress and followed me to the changing rooms. "It was not fine; it was a train wreck. I don't think he could have planned it to go that bad."

I disappeared into a stall so I wouldn't have to answer.

"Did you get to talk to his grandpa like you wanted to?" Tenley asked.

"I didn't this time. Next time."

"Perfect! Hey, if that dress works, I have some red heels from prom last year. They could be your *wow* statement." Tenley's older sister was a fashion design major and lived at home. That was the other reason I begged Tenley to come with me. She might hate shopping, but she was really good at it.

I shimmied into the dress and zipped it up the back as far as I could reach. "That would be great, thank you!"

"No problem." Tenley turned around as the stall door creaked open. "Wow, Holland. That's the one. You look amazing!"

"Yeah?" I stepped over to the trifold mirror and twirled to check the back.

"Hold on." Tenley got the zipper the rest of the way for me. "There, perfect. Really."

I let my gaze fade and pictured this dress with red heels and my hair pulled part way back with wavy curls floating down my back.

Sold!

"Yep. This is the one." I skipped back to the dressing stall.

"How's the price?"

"Fair."

"Yeah, that means expensive," Tenley grumbled.

It was expensive, but it made my waist look tiny and my eyes pop. So I think that made it worth it. Plus, I could wear it to other stuff. It was casual enough for church and fancy enough for a homecoming or winter formal.

This dress was an investment.

I changed quickly and came back out with the dress hanging over my arm. There was no need to put it back on the hanger.

"I've been thinking," Tenley said as she fell into step beside me.

"Yeah?"

"How many dates do you have left? This one with Chandler, then one more with each?"

"Two more with each. Two more weeks after this."

She nodded thoughtfully. "How about you don't worry about Run-way Careers until this dating stuff is over? Me and the others can handle it until you pick a twin."

Pick a twin. It made me so uncomfortable whenever someone put it that way. I wasn't picking a twin any more than a twin was picking me.

"Are you sure? I want to help."

"I know you do." Tenley stepped around a toddler pushing a doll in a stroller. "That's so cute! But really, Holland, I think you have enough to worry about right now. Especially if you have any more dates like the one on Monday. Just focus on this and then you can focus on that, okay?"

"Okay," I agreed reluctantly. There was wisdom in what she said; I could feel it. "That's probably a good idea."

"It is, and you know what else is a good idea? Calling me as soon as you get home from each date. I want to hear every detail while it's fresh. This is good stuff."

Chandler knocked on the door of my house promptly at five-thirty. I took an extra second to fluff my hair before I opened the door.

He whistled.

And I rolled my eyes.

"No, really. You look hot." His eyes roamed downward and lingered on Tenley's heels. They were at least three inches high and a block heel instead of a thin stiletto. This increased my chances of surviving the night without breaking anything.

"Thanks." I pulled on my coat and tried not to listen as Self-Conscious whispered unhelpful things into my ear. Instead I looked out at the front yard as I closed the door behind me. "Hey, you got the car back!"

Chandler smirked as we walked down the front walk. "Yeah, Dad went and picked it up Tuesday morning when they opened but we had to catch a ride to school in Mom's grocery getter. That was cool." Then he muttered something that I didn't quite hear, but I thought I caught the word *Asher* as I slid into the passenger seat. Which meant I really didn't want to know what he said, so it was good Chandler shut the door on his words before any of them had a chance to come together and make sense.

When he got in and started the car, he turned to me. "I heard your date was trash."

My belly squirmed. We hadn't really set boundaries for these dates, but I sort of thought we wouldn't talk about them with the other twin. Of course they were going to be curious how each date went. That was understandable. If I were on the other side, I'd totally want to know.

Uncertainty sat in my lap like a fluffy cat. It felt wrong to talk about Asher when I was with Chandler.

Unfair.

Bad form.

"Um, what did he tell you?"

Chandler snorted and started the car. "Are you kidding me? Nothing. We don't talk. I pieced it together from what I overheard and what Dad said. Sounds like old Asher really knocked it out of the park there. So cool."

I felt the need to defend Asher begin to crawl up my throat. I hated that whenever I was with one of the twins, I had to defend him from the other.

Actually, what I hated was that I was the reason they bad-mouthed each other.

At least, I was the current reason.

What a mess.

Maybe this whole thing was a big fat mistake.

Uncertainty started purring.

Before I could figure out what to do, Chandler turned the radio on and then pulled into the street. "You don't mind if we put the game on, right?" He fiddled with the knob until a sportscaster voice filled the space. Chandler draped one arm over the back of my seat and drove in silence, except for the occasional hiss or cheer.

I didn't figure out where we were going until we pulled up to the country club.

"What..."

Chandler got out and tossed the keys to a valet, then opened my door and held out his arm like we were two hundred years in the past. I slipped my hand through his elbow and couldn't help but sigh when he swung us around. We strolled up the carpet to the front door. Our image reflected in the glass, making me catch my breath. We looked so fabulous together.

His tight pants and slicked hair, my amazing dress and calf-enhancing heels. I felt like a movie star as we walked through the door.

The receptionist scrambled to her feet and practically bowed when she welcomed us. She gushed and fluttered as she led us down a long hall to a dimly lit restaurant. There were fireplaces on every wall and another, large and ornate, in the center of the restaurant.

The receptionist left us in the capable hands of the host—her words not mine—and we followed his tuxedoed self to a corner table with the name *Whittaker* attached to a vase of roses.

"Wow," I breathed as I slipped out of my coat. The host whisked it away and left Chandler to pull out my chair.

I've never actually had a guy pull out my chair before. Sitting should have been intuitive; I've sat enough times without thinking about it. But this was different. I felt super stupid as I squatted, waited for him to push it in part way, then sat all the way in my seat. It was unclear if that was the way it was supposed to work; I was still pretty far from the table.

It was fine. If I scooted to the front of the chair, I could still reach everything comfortably.

So that's what I did.

I took the white linen napkin and draped it across my lap the way Emma did in the BBC film. When I looked up, Chandler was already examining the menu.

"Do you like steak?" he asked from behind the menu.

We didn't eat a lot of meat at my house. I don't think I'd ever had a steak before. Before I had a chance to answer, Chandler set the menu aside.

"You'll love it. It's amazing here."

A waitress sashayed to our table then. She clearly didn't get the memo that we were in high school because she offered us the wine list. Chandler pretended to look it over, then shook his head and asked for water with lime. At least, I hope he pretended. I was so busy trying to figure out what to do with the multitude of forks in front of me that I missed a couple things.

Like Chandler ordering for me.

The waitress never looked at me once. She smiled and cooed and bent waaaaaaay over when she filled Chandler's glass. It's not like we couldn't already see what was going on. Her shirt was crazy low cut.

Chandler handled it well. When she took her shake and bake away from our table, he smiled at me like nothing weird had happened. I took a sip of water and tried not to make a face. I wasn't a huge fan of lime. As discreetly as possible, I moved it aside.

"So." Chandler leaned forward. "You didn't say, was your date as bad as it sounded?"

My smile wavered just a little. "Um, it was okay. Sometimes stuff happens."

"Yeah," Chandler laughed. "That's really nice of you to say and everything, but the truth is, Asher is the biggest spaz in the world."

"I—"

Chandler went on like I hadn't said anything. "He tries hard, sure, but he's such a mess. This is what a country club date is supposed to look like." He spread his hands over the table like he was responsible for making it so awesome.

I nodded, pressing my lips together. Right when I needed a way to change the subject, I was at a complete loss.

Chandler pulled out his phone and swiped with his thumb. After a moment, he said, "Sweet!"

"What's up?" I asked and then wished I hadn't. If it was something to do with Asher, I might actually scream.

And that would be really awkward in a public place such as this.

"We won. John owes me fifty bucks."

"Who won?"

He turned his phone so I could see a scoreboard, but that didn't clear it up for me. "They've got the best quarterback in two years. Undefeated, baby."

Okay, I could work with that. "So, is that your favorite team?"

"For football, yeah." He took a sip of water and tucked his phone away. "Oh, hey, look. The guy is setting up."

I followed the direction of his arm and saw that the thing I thought was a fireplace in the center of the room was actually an organ. From this angle, it was so much more obvious. A man in a tuxedo with a red rose in the lapel shuffled sheet music.

"Check this out." Chandler leaned forward and grabbed my hand.

The organist flung out the tails of his coat and sat. After a dramatic pause, his white gloved hands flew across the keys.

My heart sped up as the music swelled. "What?"

Chandler nodded knowingly. "I requested it for you, Holly—I mean, Holland. Sorry. I remembered you said you like this song."

Tears pricked the corners of my eyes as the music from *The Phantom of the Opera* swept over me. It wasn't the beginning organ-pounding tune that is so well-known, but rather the sweet love song between Christine and Raoul. "All I Ask of You". It was my favorite song from any musical I'd ever seen. I couldn't believe that Chandler remembered that. I didn't think he was actually listening.

I squeezed his hand. "You are seriously so sweet."

He laughed, then scooted his chair closer to mine. "You sound surprised."

I barely noticed him lift my hair and run his hand along the back of my neck. I was so caught up in the music, mouthing along with the chorus. If I hadn't opened my eyes right then, I would have missed the part where Chandler leaned forward, his lips inches from mine.

"Oh!" I pushed him away and, in the process, fell off my precarious perch on the chair. I fell to the floor—modestly, somehow—and brought our pristine tablecloth with me. Chandler caught the glasses and silverware so only the table cloth slithered to the ground and covered my shame with its satin sheen.

That was a relief.

It was just too bad I had to come back out.

I pulled the tablecloth off my face and propped my palm on the seat of my chair. It took a couple false starts to get my heels under me before I could stand. I smoothed my hair and tried not to look at anyone. A couple of waiters and our waitress were already milling around, setting our table to rights.

When they left, my song was over and reality crashed in like a tidal wave. Speaking of spazzes...

I was such a mess.

"Sorry, Chandler. You caught me off guard."

He shrugged. "It's fine; they fixed it."

I didn't mean the table. "I, uh, wasn't expecting you to kiss me."

"No?" His eyebrows lifted in surprise. "Really?"

"We're in a restaurant. People are eating." It was a lame reason, but it also made sense. I know I don't really want to see people making out while I'm trying to eat dinner.

"Yeah," Chandler leaned one arm over the back of his chair so that it dangled at a weird angle. "I guess I didn't think about that. I was just feeling it, you know?"

No.

Maybe that was the real problem. I wasn't feeling it. I didn't have a clue he was about to kiss me. What did that say about me? Shouldn't I be acutely aware when a super hot guy was about to kiss me? Shame perched on my shoulder way too close to my ear, almost blocking out what Chandler said next.

"No worries. Maybe later."

Maybe later?

Our waitress came then, balancing plates like a boss. I would have spent a little more time with Overthinking, picking apart Chandler's flippant response, but I got distracted by the steak.

After the waitress glided away, I leaned forward so I could whisper. "Chandler, is the steak supposed to be sitting in liquid?"

He was already cutting into his like it was fine. Maybe it was fine. The problem was, I didn't know. "Yeah, it's rare."

"Rare?" I had a vague memory of a movie or something where they ordered a medium rare steak, but I had no idea what that meant. "As in valuable?"

"No." He stuck a large piece in his mouth and chewed. "As in mooing. It gets tough if you cook it more. You need all the blood there to keep it tender."

Blood?

Tender?

Mooing?

My stomach flipped over itself. Now all I could see was the field of cute baby cows at the Cutlip's ranch in Durango.

Mooing.

There was no way I could eat this. And there was no way I could eat anything else on the plate if that liquid really was blood because it was touching everything.

I suddenly understood why people become vegetarians.

Chapter Nineteen

·❤·❤·❤·❤·❤·

"There is nothing so strong or safe in an emergency of life as the simple truth."
Charles Dickens

Well, one good thing came from my date with Chandler: I decided I was *not* going to kiss either one of the twins until we figured out what we're doing.

I made the decision because when Chandler walked me to the front door, I could smell steak on his breath, and it gave me the gags. Since hurling and kissing do not mix, I went inside as fast as I could.

But as I obsessively thought about it all night, I realized that not kissing either one of them until these scheduled dates were over was a very good idea. We would all be able to make a better decision if we weren't jumbled up from getting physical and stuff.

So, it was official. No kissing.

The next week went by in a blur. I couldn't figure out if it was because I was dreading my date with Asher or looking forward to it. Even without the physical stuff to muddy the waters, I was a completely confused mess. When I saw Asher, my stomach jumped, and I was positive he was the one. It was weird, but that awful date made me like him more. It was endearing that he was such a mess. I felt like he gave me permission to be a mess too sometimes, and that was just really comfortable.

But then I would see Chandler, and my stomach would jump, and I was positive he was the one. He was so good-looking; every girl in the vicinity gave me evil glares when they saw us together in the hall. In my entire life, I couldn't remember a time when anyone envied me about anything. I was just way too average. Chandler made me feel extraordinary, and he was

211

so thoughtful. I still couldn't believe he remembered my favorite musical song. He was so charming. And funny. Every time he stopped at my locker, he had a new story to tell.

Yeah, the farther we went down the road of figuring this out, the more confused I got.

Confusion was now my middle name.

Asher texted me Thursday night to make sure we were good for our date Friday afternoon. It was a teacher prep day or something, so there was no school. I replied yes, and he said he'd pick me up at eleven. I almost asked what we were doing, but then I remembered his grandpa and *A Tale of Two Cities*.

I was ready to go at ten-thirty, wearing jeans and a sweater with my hair in loose curls to look a little less every-day. I took that extra half hour to text Tenley for advice on how to talk to Asher's grandpa. It took the entire thirty minutes to organize my thoughts.

When the doorbell rang a couple of minutes after eleven, I tucked my phone in my back pocket and opened the door.

"Holland, hey." Asher leaned in for a hug that would have been fine if Rhett hadn't walked by at that moment.

"Ewww, get a room."

My cheeks went insta-red. "This is a room, you pumpkin."

Brett jogged in then, his hands full of bags of cut vegetables. He stopped short when he saw Asher. "Who are you?"

"Holland's boyfriend." Rhett laughed like a hyena and shoved a handful of popcorn in his mouth. Most of it didn't make it, and the floor was now littered in kernels that looked like apricot blossoms.

"Clean up your mess, you heathen, before Mom gets home." I swung my purse on my shoulder and tried, with my eyes, to tell Asher to run for his life.

I'd be right behind him.

"Are these your brothers?" Asher asked, obviously not getting my hint. I'd have to be less subtle next time and just bolt for the car. "I haven't met them yet."

"Lucky," I said, but the word got lost or was ignored as the boys gathered in the center of the front room.

Asher lifted his fist toward Rhett. "I'm Asher. Who're you?"

Even if Rhett wanted to pretend he was too cool for school, he wouldn't have been able to pull it off. Asher had uncovered his Achilles Heel: Rhett loved fist bumps. He fist-bumped everything.

With great enthusiasm, Rhett bumped his knuckles to Asher's fist. More popcorn flew out of the bag and onto the floor.

I rubbed my temples.

"I'm Rhett, Holland's favorite brother," he smirked.

"Right." Brett rolled his eyes. "Favorite brother. That's probably because you hide her makeup and impersonate her on social media. She just looooooooves you."

"Wait, what?" I stepped forward. I didn't totally catch that part about social media.

My brothers answered, "It's nothing," in unison and went back to their conversation with Asher. I guess I should be happy they acknowledged me at all. They were already in the thick of reenacting the plot of their favorite Marvel movie. I knew from experience that it could go on forever.

"Hey, guys? We have to go. Asher's grandpa is expecting us." That wasn't technically a lie. It was an assumption. They were totally not the same thing.

The twins groaned. "Can you come back? I want to see your lightsaber. Will you bring it next time?" Rhett begged.

Asher had a lightsaber?

"Sure."

"Coooooooooooooooool!" Brett started up the stairs. "You should bring your brother too. I didn't know twins didn't have the same face. That's weird, bruh."

Asher deflated a little bit. "Yeah, I'm sure you'll get to meet him sometime."

When Asher turned to me, his face looked so puppy-dog sad that I reached for his hand. "I think you have a fan club."

"For now," he said uncertainly, but there was a definite lift in his shoulders that wasn't there three seconds ago. He squeezed my hand with a smile.

We strolled down the walkway to his car, swinging our arms as we walked. It was unusually warm—at least, I think it was. I didn't know what was usual for this time of year in Prescott, but it was definitely warmer than the last week and a half. It was, in fact, the perfect day for a picnic. Though, there was no way I'd say that to Asher. He might have already acted on his threat to have the word removed from the dictionary.

Asher turned us on the sidewalk, away from his car and started up the hill. I glanced over my shoulder and then remembered that Asher's grandparents live near my grandma.

"How close is their house?"

He pointed with his free hand, then turned us up a gravel walkway. "Right here."

They were literally one house away.

"Oh." I stopped abruptly, my hand slipping away from Asher's. I knew this house. Asher waited while I took a couple quick steps to catch up. "I've met your grandparents! Grandma sent me over with some banana bread a few days after we moved here. They are so nice."

I wasn't just being polite, either. It was the legit truth.

"They are the best. I bet Grams sent you home with a ton of food, right?"

"She did!" I laughed. "I brought her one measly loaf of banana bread, and I left with two loaves of homemade wheat bread, a jar of jam, and some butter she made with her grandkids." Oh, did she make that with Asher? "You?"

He shook his head. "My uncle Ryan and Aunt Hanne live here too. Not here-here; in Prescott Valley. They have five little kids. The oldest is, like, nine. She probably made the butter with them."

Asher stopped at the front door and rang the bell.

He didn't just walk in?

"They tell me to walk in all the time, but I feel weird doing it. It's their house, you know? I don't want to catch them off guard."

Which was really, very thoughtful of him.

Asher's grandma answered the door with a big smile and a hug for both of us. She smelled homey and caramel-y.

"Asher and Holland are here, Linus. Where are you?" she called as she led us through the house to the kitchen.

Ah-ha, we found the cause of the caramel smell. Two trays of caramel pecan sticky buns sat on cooling racks. The smell made my mouth water instantly.

"Linus!"

"I'm coming, I'm coming." A slow thump made its way down the hall.

Asher leaned over. "Don't mention his boot. He's super sensitive about it."

I didn't get a chance to ask what that meant by *boot*, but when his grandpa turned the corner, it became very obvious. The lower half of his leg was covered in a thick black boot. The kind people wear when they have a broken bone.

Despite Asher's warning, I now had an almost uncontrollable urge to ask what happened. I bit my tongue to keep that old fiend, Curiosity, reined in.

"Asher, my boy." Grandpa leaned in for a big old hug. He paused as he stood back up and looked at me under bushy gray eyebrows. "Who's this? You're not one of my grandkids!"

It was obvious he was teasing, so I laughed. "I'm Holland."

"Holland?" He squinted at me, then elbowed Asher. "Marry this girl. You should always marry the females with interesting names. Write that down; those are words of wisdom from your grandfather."

Grandma blew out a loud breath of air that made Asher bust up laughing. "You know you married a lady named Ann, right?"

"Ann is an interesting name." Grandpa held up both hands like he was under arrest. There might not have been police officers swarming him, but there was no denying he was in trouble. "It's my favorite name. Now, Holland, you call me Linus and her Ann, alright? None of this Mrs. and Mr. garbage. I'm too young for that. Give me a good handshake and say 'deal' so I know you were paying good attention."

I extended my hand. "Deal."

We gave a hearty shake, as did Asher, except his was with his head. "Grandpa, what kind of painkillers do they have you on? We might want to check the prescription."

Ann brought a plate of sticky buns to the table and gestured for us to all sit. "There's nothing in a pill bottle that will fix what your grandpa's got. He's just a plain goof to the soul."

Linus swatted her bottom as she passed on her way to the fridge.

With a groan, Asher dropped his head to his hand. "I'm sorry, Holland. This was the worst idea. I'm sorry you had to see that and, while I'm at it, I'm sorry for everything else my grandparents do and say while you are in their house."

Ann set a gallon of milk on the table, pausing to rest her elbow on Linus' shoulder. "Whatever do you mean by that, Asher? Your grandfather and I are delightful."

"That's one word for it."

She shook her finger at him as she went to a cupboard for drinking glasses.

Asher didn't need to worry about me. The only trouble I had at the moment was I needed to laugh my head off, but I thought it would be incredibly rude to do it to their faces. Seriously, his grandparents were adorable. In fact, they reminded me a lot of how my Grandma and Gramps acted before he passed away.

Ann sat in the chair next to Linus and handed out napkins. "Asher tells us you wanted to talk to Linus about Runway Careers."

Asher took his napkin with a relieved look. "Thank you. Yeah, she's in the club to get funding for it this year. Actually, she started the club that's trying to get funding for it."

"No," I shook my head. "Tenley did that. I just gave her the idea."

"In my experience, vast as it is," Linus winked, "I find that it's a lot of little ideas that make something move, like all the little pieces in a car engine. Everything plays an important part in getting the thing to work. So, don't you discount what you've done."

I smoothed my napkin out in front of me, trying to find a place for Shyness. I didn't see it that often and never quite knew what to do with it when it showed up.

Linus went on, "Anyway, what would you like to know?"

Asher put a sticky bun on my napkin. "Do you want milk?"

I nodded. "Thanks," I said, then turned to Linus. "Actually, I've met a lot of people who love Runway Careers so much; it really helped them figure out their passion. So, I—well, we were wondering if you would be willing to come and introduce the event this year."

Linus stopped chewing and pursed his lips, then he swallowed. "What do you mean by introduce? I don't recall that part of the new program."

I glanced at Asher. Even though he wasn't there when Tenley and I hashed this out, I needed a boost of confidence right now. He didn't disappoint. His eyes were fixed on me with the most encouraging look I'd ever seen. It was like I could hear the words, "Go on. You got this. You can do it," coming out of his eyes.

I took a deep breath. "Yeah, so, Asher told me the program got pretty wild for a few years, way over the top—"

Linus snorted.

"And I started thinking, because I've met so many people who were profoundly affected by your Runway Careers and because I'm not sure what I want to do as my career either, I'd really love to see the event the way it was when you started it. Maybe modernize a few things, but go back to the real reason you started it. So, I guess what I'm asking is, will you tell me your reasons? And then, will you share them with everyone else the night of the program?"

Linus set his sticky bun down and stuck his thumb in his mouth. His eyes roamed to Ann, who's smile was so sweet it gave me a tingle in the back of my neck.

"Well, how about that?" Linus murmured.

Ann turned to me. "Holland, this man of mine has been saying for years that he'd like to see Runway Careers become what it used to be. It's just lovely that you're going to make it happen. I'm thrilled, really thrilled."

Heat crept up my neck. "Oh, good."

Asher reached over and took my hand under the table where his grandparents couldn't see. His fingers were a little sticky but gloriously warm.

I smiled at him.

"How about it, Grandpa?" Asher said.

"Absolutely." Linus smacked the table lightly. With his grin firmly in place, he described Runway Career's first year, the year he started it. My eyes went out of focus as I was taken back in time. Images swirled and twirled around the room. I loved everything I was hearing.

Linus stopped talking, bringing me back to the room in a rush. His eyes twinkled. "If you can make it what it was, it would be my pleasure to announce Runway Careers. I got my old tux in the closet upstairs; there are only a few moth holes. My top hat and cane are somewhere around here. I could do a little dance number, whip out the old gumshoes."

Ann groaned and shook her head.

I didn't know what to say to that. I mean, it wasn't what I expected, but I guess that could work.

"Sounds great!" I smiled.

Linus placed a hand on Asher's shoulder. "I was joking before, now I'm serious. Marry this girl. Marry her yesterday."

Asher pushed Linus's arm away. "You know we're barely seventeen, right? That's not even legal."

"Oh posh," Linus waved his hand. "I'll give you adult permission right now. In fact, I'll go study up on the Internet. I heard you can watch a tube video thing and get certified as a marriage person in an hour. By the time you finish your movie, I can take care of everything."

"Grandpa, seriously?" Asher's ears were bright red. His hand under the table was starting to get a little sweaty. I squeezed it so he'd know I wasn't offended or, you know, freaked out.

"Let them be, Linus. You're such a tease," Ann said. "Why don't you two take these buns into the family room to watch your movie. We'll stay out of your way, won't we, Linus?"

He nodded solemnly. "Take your buns and go. I won't stop you."

Asher's hand slid away from mine so he could reach for the plate of treats. He shot a warning look at his grandpa before we left the kitchen.

I could hear Linus laughing all the way down the hall.

Asher didn't look at me until we were seated next to each other on the couch. When he did, his smile was painful. "I am so sorry about that. I thought he'd be better behaved. I don't know what I was thinking."

"He's adorable," I said. "I love his guts."

Asher laughed. "Yeah, me too. It's the rest of him that's hard to swallow sometimes." He fiddled with the remote in his hands. "Did you get the information you wanted?"

"Oh, yeah, no, I'm good." I pushed my hair behind my ear. "That was perfect, so, yay!"

"Yay." Asher continued to twirl the remote around and around.

"You okay?"

"Just... Yeah, I'm good. I'm just curious." He turned slightly so he was facing me more fully. "You said you're looking for a career. I thought you wanted to be a nurse."

"Oh." His question caught me off guard. I wasn't expecting him to pick up on that. "Yeah, I had a conversation with my best friend in Durango."

"Alicia?"

"Yeah." I gave him an incredulous look. I didn't even remember telling him about her, much less her name. It was astounding that he knew that. "Yeah, and she asked me some hard questions, and I guess I realized I decided to be a nurse because she did and," I shrugged, "I'm not sure that's really what I want to do."

"Why not? If I remember right, you're pretty handy with a band-aid." He held up his hand with the jagged scab across his palm.

I ducked my head with a smile. "Yes, but I'm not so good with the rest of it. I realized that I didn't ask Grandma a single thing about her broken bone or surgery; the thought makes my stomach churn. Alicia would have wanted every detail. I hate seeing Grandma in pain. Maybe my band-aid skills are a better fit for a kindergarten teacher or a mom."

Asher laughed. "I think you'd be great at either one of those things. You'd be great at anything you do."

It was incredibly sweet of him to say so. "Thank you."

"If you want to talk out options or anything, I'm here, and you can talk to me." He sighed. "That came out stupid. You know what I mean." He lifted the remote towards the TV and pushed a button. The screen lit up bright blue. "I hope this is alright, hanging out with my grandparents. Not the coolest date destination, but we'd get no peace at my house. It's always a zoo, and Chandler's there." Asher's shoulders tensed.

I looped my arm through his and rested my head on his shoulder. "This is perfect."

In the time it took to find the old *A Tale of Two Cities* on Amazon and get it started, he finally relaxed, his body melting into my side. His head rested on mine, and his breath was so steady he could have been asleep.

This is what I was saying before. Being with Asher was so...comfortable.

Tenley was thrilled that Linus agreed to introduce Runway Careers, but then she immediately changed the subject to something random. When I called her out on it, she said she refused to discuss details with me until I'd sorted everything out with the twins.

Only one more week and three more dates to go.

Chandler already set up our date earlier in the week. He said he'd come by Saturday in the late afternoon, and the date plan was up to me. I couldn't decide if that was a cop-out or super sweet. Once I decided that it was thoughtful to let the girl choose a date, that gave me all of Saturday morning to figure out what we were going to do.

By the time Chandler rang the doorbell at three thirty, I was ready with my plan.

And I had already banished my brothers to their bedroom with bribery. I would do the dishes for them all next week if they stayed away until Chandler was gone.

I should have known better.

Brett thundered down the stairs and rushed by, knocking me off balance so that I grabbed the wall instead of answering the door. He swung the door open, pinning me between the wall and the door with the doorknob jabbing into my back. I couldn't even protest with my face smooshed into the wall the way it was.

"Hey! I'm Brett. Are you the other twin that doesn't look like a twin?"

There was a long pause. "Yeah. Uh, is Holland here?"

Brett deflated enough for me to squeeze away from the door tourniquet. I brushed my hair out of my face and hip-checked Brett so he was now the one stumbling for balance.

"Sorry about that, Chandler. Brett is supposed to be in his room." I leaned over to accentuate the words, giving Brett my own version of Tenley's hairy eyeball. "I guess Rhett is my favorite brother."

"What?" Brett stomped his foot. "That's messed up. Rhett's eavesdropping right in there." He jabbed his finger toward the coat closet.

I gave him a look and casually opened the door.

Rhett fell out on my feet. "Hey, Holland. What's up?"

"Oh my gosh, you guys! You are the worst! Get up to your room now or I am not doing the dishes for you, ever."

They both ignored me. Rhett stood next to Brett, their faces in identical inspection mode. They looked Chandler all over, while Chandler looked at his phone.

"What are you doing on your phone?" Rhett finally asked.

"Big man stuff," Chandler grinned, not looking up.

Brett scoffed. "What does that even mean?"

"You'll understand when you're older." Chandler glanced over just enough to pat Brett on the head.

Brett swatted his hand away. "How old do you think we are? Five? We'll be thirteen next Tuesday, bruh!"

Chandler didn't answer; his thumbs flew across the phone screen. Rhett looked at Brett, who looked back at Brett, then they both looked at me.

"He's nothing like the other twin," they said like they were announcing his doom, and then they turned and trouped back upstairs.

"I'm so not doing the dishes for you!" I called after them. "Sorry about that, Chandler. Are you ready to go?"

"Born ready." He tucked his phone away with a grimace.

"Yeah?" I put a hand on my hip. "You look upset. Is everything okay?"

"Yeah, no. It's just some bad news."

"I'm sorry." I made a face. "Do you want to do this another time?"

Chandler's shoulders sagged. "Could we? I'm sorry; this was the worst day ever. I just want to go chill. I'll call you later, okay?"

And then he was gone.

Chapter Twenty

"There are dark shadows on the earth, but its lights are stronger in the contrast."
The Village Coquettes

In hindsight, it was a very good thing Chandler left. If he hadn't, I would have been out with Chandler when my mom called.

"Holland, honey, is Dad around?"

"I'll check. Are you okay?" Mom sounded close to tears, and that never happened. My mom didn't even cry at Hallmark movies. "What's going on?"

"I need your dad," she choked.

I ran to his office door and knocked, then opened the door.

"What in the world?"

"Mom's on the phone. It sounds bad." I shoved it into his hands and then left so I could give them privacy while I paced in front of the door. #listeningnotlistening.

The door flew open and Dad tried to hand me my phone back but dropped it on the carpet instead. "I need to go to the hospital. Can you take care of the boys?"

I followed him, jogging to keep up. "Yeah, of course, but what's going on?"

"There's a complication with Grandma's check up. I need to go, Holland. I'll call you, okay?" He kissed the top of my head and flung the garage door open.

"Yeah, but, is everything okay?"

My voice got lost in the roar of the engine. I watched Dad back carefully down the windy driveway, then roar out of sight.

Worry did not like this one bit.

I shut the garage door and went to find the twins. They were laying on their stomachs playing a video game upstairs.

"Hey, guys?" I couldn't go any further.

"What's wrong?" Rhett dropped his controller. "What's going on?"

Brett scooted closer to me, and I dropped to the floor, reaching out my arms so they would cuddle me like they used to when they were little.

"Is everything okay?" Brett asked, his voice tinged with worry.

I shook my head. "Something happened to Grandma." I had to stop to gather myself. "It's not good, but I don't know what it is."

"I already said a prayer," Rhett said. "So, we don't have to worry, okay?"

"Me too," Brett whispered.

The doorbell rang before the waterworks began.

"Is that Dad?" Rhett asked.

"He probably wouldn't use the doorbell."

"Then who is it?"

"Let's go find out." Brett stood and reached out his hand for me. I took it and held onto it all the way down the stairs to the front door.

It was Tenley.

"Hey, is everything okay?"

My chin wobbled.

She stepped inside and wrapped me up in her arms.

It's so strange how an act of kindness totally breaks the dam. Tears ran down my cheeks and flooded Tenley's shoulder. The twins each still clung to one of my hands. I was surrounded, and it felt incredible.

After a few minutes, the knot in my chest started to loosen, and I could take a deep breath without feeling it hitch. I pulled back and wiped at Tenley's coat.

"Oh, don't worry about it." She waved a hand. "This was Benny's ex-girlfriend's jacket. She left it at the house, and he still hasn't returned it."

I smiled despite everything.

"You don't have to tell me what's going on. Really. I was at Asher's grandparents' house dropping stuff off and saw someone zoom out of your driveway. At first I thought it was you, but then I got a closer look, and you do not have a beard. I just wanted to make sure you're okay. Are you?"

"No," I said. I explained quickly what was going on so I wouldn't start crying again.

"Holland, I'm so sorry. That's... Have you guys had dinner?"

I shook my head as I wiped a few stray tears from my cheeks.

"Okay, good. You sit tight. I'll be right back."

"What?"

She was gone before I could finish the question. I closed the door and looked at my brothers. "That was weird, right?"

They nodded.

"Okay, good. I thought maybe it was just me. What do you guys want to do?"

"Make cookies," Rhett said immediately. "There's chocolate chips in the freezer, behind the vegetables."

"Nuh-uh?" I gave him a skeptical look but headed to the freezer to check anyway.

He was totally right.

"How did you find out about these?" I asked, cradling the bag like it was precious.

Because it was.

Nothing sounded better than ooey, gooey chocolate chip cookies with real white flour and cane sugar.

"Grandma."

"Grandma also has cookies and stuff hidden behind the dish thingy," Brett pointed. "She gave me some marshmallows the other day, and they were amazing."

Hearing the word *Grandma* made my heart clench. "Alright, let's do this. We're making chocolate chip cookies."

"Correction," Brett said, taking the bag out of my hands. "*We're* making cookies. You're not allowed to touch anything unless we tell you to."

I checked my phone incessantly while the boys mixed the batter. Rhett pulled the first round of cookies out of the oven right when Dad called.

I put him on speaker.

"Dad, what's going on?"

His voice was heavy enough to hang in the air like the scent of chocolate and sugar. "There was a complication with your grandma's surgery that they didn't find until her check-up today. It's a long story. They admitted her to the hospital to try and fix it."

"She's not coming home?" Brett yelled. He always yelled when someone was on speaker, like he was afraid they wouldn't be able to hear him. But I also think he yelled this time to relieve his feelings. Tension was having a party up in here.

"Not tonight." Dad sounded tired. "Listen, will you kids be okay if your mom and I stay at the hospital? I already checked with the Whittakers a couple doors down. They are on call if you need anything. They even offered for you to spend the night there, but I thought you'd want to be home."

"Yes." I nodded even though he couldn't see me. "Yes to all of it. We'll be fine, and we want to be here when you guys get home. Any idea when that will be?"

"I'm sorry, sweetie. I need to go talk to the doctor. I'll keep you posted, okay?"

I said okay, but he was already gone.

Rhett picked a cookie off the sheet and flipped it between his hands for a minute. I guess to cool it off? I'd never seen anyone do that before, though it seemed to work. He pulled the cookie apart so the chocolate dripped between the two halves.

He gave one to me and one to Brett.

"I'll get the milk," Brett said.

I brought the cookie to my nose and inhaled. It smelled like my childhood when Mom used to bake all the time, before she got so scared about chemicals, additives and calories. I instantly felt better.

"Know what?"

"What?" Brett looked up with chocolate lining his mouth. He was just going for it.

"I think we should have a campout in the family room tonight. We'll eat cookies and make popcorn and watch movies until we fall asleep. Yeah?"

They looked at each other and then cheered. "Awesome!"

I took the first, amazing bite of my cookie and savored the sugar and butter on my tongue. "Oh, holy hand grenade, guys. This is amazing!"

Rhett ducked his head and Brett rolled his eyes. "Thank you, Captain Obvious."

"It was a compliment. You should say thank you."

"Thank you," he said in a high squeaky voice.

Now I rolled my eyes. "Keep that up, and I'll come touch the oven. The cookies will spontaneously combust, and then where will you be?"

Brett laughed but reached across the counter to scoop four cookies into his hands.

Just in case.

The doorbell rang in the middle of Rhett making him put them back.

I nibbled the last of my cookie as I walked to the door. When I opened it, the last bite fell through my fingers and onto the welcome mat.

That's because, standing on our front porch, was Tenley flanked by Dara, Ethan, Bryan, and Asher. Ryker was missing, but he did so many sports that wasn't really a surprise.

They were like the miracle of the five wisemen. Each one of them carried something amazing. Tenley had a huge salad. Dara was wearing her Ariel costume and carrying a vegetable tray. Bryan had four cartons of ice cream piled in his arms so I couldn't see his face. Ethan carried a couple of long hoagie sandwiches, and Asher had a plate with fruit on it and a couple cans of whipped cream nestled in the crook of his arms.

"You guys!"

"We brought you dinner!" Tenley raised the soda in the air. "Yay!"

Bryan cheered, then added, "Now let us in before I drop ice cream all over the ground."

I stepped aside and pulled the door open. There were no words to describe how I felt as I watched each one of them file into the kitchen. Asher was last. He waited for me to shut the door and then asked if I was really okay.

"If you'd asked me a few minutes ago, I would have said no." I gave him a wavery smile. "But now, I think I might be."

"Your grandma is the greatest." Asher smiled. "I'm rooting for her."

"Thank you." Tears welled up again, so I quickly jumped to a different subject. "I was worried about you guys too. Chandler canceled our date this afternoon and seemed really upset. I thought maybe something happened?"

Asher looked up for a minute, then his face dawned with realization. "He's fine."

That's it?

"Yeah?"

Asher shook his head. "You know how you told me I'm not allowed to say anything snarky or disrespectful about my brother?"

I nodded.

"Then don't ask me to elaborate. I'm sure he'll tell you about it when you guys go on your date."

Oh yeah, the dates. I didn't even want to think about that right now. Asher's eyes darted around my face, then he shook his head. "You know what? Let's put all that on hold until your grandma is better. You let us know when you're ready to start back up again, okay?"

I smiled with relief. That is exactly what I needed, to not worry about something that now seemed so stupid and silly when my grandma was in peril. "Thank you."

"Where the heck are you guys?" Tenley bellowed. "I'm starving!"

I made sure the front door was locked and then followed Asher into the kitchen.

The next twenty-four hours were not my favorite, so I'm just going to skim over them really quick. My friends, minus Ryker who had a track meet, ate dinner and watched movies with us until almost midnight. By the time they left, Rhett was in love with Dara, and Brett thought Tenley was bomb diggity. His words, not mine.

Dad came home the next morning to shower and check on us. We got more information then. Apparently something went wrong with Grandma's blood clotting, and Grandma almost died. It took them three days to get her stable and then fix whatever happened.

Three days that I might not have survived if it wasn't for my friends. They brought food over after school, sat with me and let me cry and let me yell, and entertained my brothers when they started going stir crazy.

Best. Friends. Ever.

Grandma came home the fourth day, tired and way too pale. Mom instantly went into organization mode and emerged with a schedule to help take care of Grandma. She wasn't supposed to put weight on her foot for at least two weeks.

And then we fell into a routine.

I took the twins to school so Mom could take the morning shift. Dad took the noon and early afternoon shift while I was at school and Mom was at the gym. Then I took the late afternoon shift and some evenings. There wasn't room in my mind for anything else besides the schedule and keeping Grandma alive. It was a good thing Asher had already suggested we pause the dates because I couldn't even with that right now.

One afternoon in February, I hurried home from school to take my turn with Grandma. Mom and I passed in the hall, and she filled me in on the morning so far. Things were looking up physically, but Grandma wasn't doing awesome emotionally.

I stopped outside the bedroom door to think about that. If I were stuck in bed, weak and weary, what would I want more than anything? When I get the stomach flu or a super bad cold, I never felt like reading or even watching movies. I just wanted someone to talk to.

That was easy. Over the last few weeks, I'd told Grandma all about Runway Careers and the changes we were making. She loved it and was so excited to go to it—except her excitement was overshadowed with fear. I could see it when I talked to her. I think she was afraid she wouldn't feel up to going, or maybe even that she wouldn't be here anymore by then.

What Grandma needed was an escape. Something fun and happy that would take her away from the heaviness she'd been through.

Grandma needed a story.

I started towards my bedroom to pick a book to read to her, then I stopped. Something inside pushed the pause button. A wavery memory flickered to the front of my mind. When I was little, I used to write Grandma and Grandpa every week with stories I made up for fun. Then when we would visit, they sat me down with cookies and milk and listened to my stories. Grandpa, when he was sick, called me one day and asked for a story.

I turned back around and walked into Grandma's room. "Hey, lady! How are you?"

"Hi, dear." Grandma's face was gray, but her smile was lovely. "How was school today?"

I sat in the fluffy chair Dad had moved to Grandma's bedside. "Oh, you know, pretty much normal. The usual. Same old. Homework, classes, teenage angst, just like always. Except..."

Grandma had been nodding along absently. When my voice rose climatically on the last word, her eyes darted to me.

"At lunch time, I was sitting in the library trying to come up with an idea for my creative writing assignment: magic in the real world. I was supposed to write about something ordinary that turned extraordinary in a fantastical way. Now, I don't know about you, Grandma, but I have tons of experience with the ordinary part. Extraordinary is something else, and fantastical is a whole different level.

"I decided to pick up a book of fairy tales to help me think. That section of the library was right near where I sat, so I reached over and tugged a red book off the shelf. Except, it wouldn't budge! The book stuck there like it wanted to stay forever. I took both hands and pulled so hard that I fell backwards when it came off the shelf."

"Oh my, were you okay?"

I nodded and brushed imaginary dust off my shoulders. "I set the book on the table and tried to open it, but it was as if someone stuck the pages together with gorilla glue. I was afraid I'd rip the cover right off. There were some other people at the table next to me; they just stared at me like I was nuts. In their defense, I guess it's weird to see someone standing over a book, leveraging themselves with their leg on a chair while trying to open it—and failing.

"I slapped the book with my hand and fell back into the chair. The longer I stared at it, the more ridiculous this whole thing was. I just needed a story for creative writing; I didn't have to read this book, specifically. I went back to the shelf for a different fairy tale compilation, and what did my eyes see? The red book on the table flew open by itself, the pages fluttering like butterfly wings."

Grandma smiled. "You don't say?"

"I was equal parts relieved and wigged out. I've never had a book open by itself, have you?"

Grandma shook her head.

"Right? Super weird. I wanted to ask the kids at the other table if they saw what I saw, but they were gone. I wasn't sure if they left because the book freaked them out or if they left before that happened. Either way, I figured I had only a short time with the book before another weird thing happened, so I started reading on the page that was open.

"'Holland,' it said, 'you have been chosen for your outstanding kindness and freakish good-looks to receive a fairy gift. If you accept, turn to page one hundred.'"

"That is a very honest book." Grandma layered her hands over one another and relaxed into the headboard. "I concur."

"Aw shucks, you have to say that." I ducked my head.

"I have to do no such thing. It is simply the truth. Now tell me, did you turn to page one hundred?"

"Of course!" I lifted my hands. "How could I not? This was obviously meant for me. I don't know anyone else named Holland, and books don't usually talk to countries, soooooo it made sense. I flipped the pages—they were so soft they felt like fresh-spun silk—and on page one hundred, there was an illustration of a fairy. She was adorable, blonde with big blue eyes and wings that carried every color of the rainbow. In one hand, she held a purse, and in the other, a coin. Words appeared like a thought bubble above her head. 'Holland,' it said, 'you must choose: a wishing coin or a purse of mystery.'"

"Such choices!" Grandma's eyes lit up.

"I know! What would you choose?"

Grandma's face wrinkled in concentration. "A wish is always nice, but those generally have limitations on them. Can't make people fall in love, can't change the past, and so on. I think I'd be just curious enough to pick the purse."

"Even if it was empty? Or full of spiders? Or..." I couldn't think of anything worse than those two things.

Grandma nodded. "Curiosity is a powerful thing. What did you choose?"

I loved that she said *did* like all this had really happened. "Well, Grandma, I don't deny the pull of curiosity; however, I had a particular thing in mind that I was sure a wish would fix."

"Yes?" She leaned forward slightly.

"Yes." I took her hand. "You see, I know this lady who is amazing and wonderful, and everyone loves her. She's having a hard time right now, some challenges that are making her feel less than she is. If it were just about me, I think I would have chosen the bag to satisfy that noisy curiosity, but a wish would guarantee that I could help this lady, who I love so much, feel better in some small way. So that's what I did. I pointed to the coin, and the fairy reached through the pages to set it on the table in front of me. I've read enough to know you have to be careful with wishes, so I was ready. I held the coin tightly and whispered, 'I wish Grandma would know, deep in her soul, how much we love her and how much we need her around.'"

Grandma's mouth worked side to side, her eyes welling up with tears. "Oh, Holland."

"Yeah? Did it work?"

She reached out her hands as far as she could. I leaned forward so they could wrap around me and pull me into her side. "You sweet, sweet girl. How did you know I needed to hear that today?"

"What are you talking about?" I kissed her cheek. "I'm just telling you about my freaky experience in the library." I sat up and brushed her hair out of her eyes. "Did it work?"

"More than you know." A tear slid down her cheek. "You have a gift for storytelling. You're so creative. You know, I always thought you'd be a writer."

Her words washed over me like a wave, then dissipated into the air. That is, until I laid in bed that night, thinking over the day. That's when they swelled and stayed in the back of my mind, crashing over each other like waves until I fell asleep.

·❤·❤·❤·❤·❤·

When I headed down the hall to grab breakfast the next morning, Grandma called me into her room. She took my hand as soon as I got near enough and looked at me with her warm brown eyes. "I'm going to talk to your Tenley today and see what I can do to help you with Runway Careers. I can't be out and about, but I can certainly make calls and organize. I don't want you kids to worry one second more about it. There are so many people in this town who would love to help."

"Grandma, thank you!" I squeezed her hand tight. Tenley kept assuring me everything was fine, but I knew she was doing a lot, and it had to be stressful. Anything to alleviate her burden sounded fabulous to me.

"There's more." She took a deep breath. "I'm going to be there. I'm going to go to Runway Careers with you this year. I'm going to be better."

Chapter Twenty-One

•❤•❤•❤•❤•❤•

"I can never close my lips where I have opened my heart."
Master Humphrey's Clock

Two weeks later, I was leaning against the wall at lunch time, listening to Ryker and Bryan argue about dragons, when I totally fell asleep. I don't know how long I was out, but it was long enough for Asher to scoot over next to me and for me to drool on his shoulder.

"Oh, gross! I'm sorry!" I wiped at the puddle on his shirt. All signs of sleepiness completely disappeared. Shame pulled me close and wouldn't let go.

Cause nothing says 'date me' like drooling.

"It's not a big deal. It will dry. Come here." Asher put his arm around me and pressed lightly so I would move closer.

"But, isn't the bell about to ring?" I'd been too caught up in the drool dilemma to notice what else was going on around me. Now, it was very clear that things were not normal. For example, Asher and I were the only people in sight. "The bell already rang, didn't it?"

"Yeah," Asher shrugged like it was not a big deal. "I mean, I think so. I couldn't really hear it over your snoring."

"No!" Now Shame started wiggling between us. "Are you serious?"

Asher laughed, deep and manly. "Yes, but it was cute. Don't feel bad."

"Too late!" I groaned and flopped my head back on his shoulder.

Asher rested his head over mine. "It was seriously cute."

"I can't believe I fell asleep and snored at school. I think I might be one of those people who should never go out in public. Like, maybe I should homeschool."

"Don't do that." Asher's fingers entwined with mine, weaving in and out.

My breath caught in my throat. "Why not?"

"I like seeing you every day. I would miss you."

A warm feeling crept over me, like someone draped a Minky blanket over my body. I nuzzled Asher's shoulder with my cheek and finally let myself relax.

He let out a sigh full of contentment that felt almost as good as a hug. My thoughts went hazy. I think I was drifting off to sleep again when I heard Chandler's voice. The muscles against my cheek tensed up, and I was suddenly wide awake.

"What the heck are you doing, Asher?"

"Shhhh," he answered. "Don't wake her up. She's had it rough for weeks."

"Rough weeks. Yeah, nice excuse. You're just trying to one-up. It's not even your turn for a date; it's mine."

"We put that on hold, Chandler, remember? Until her grandma is better. This isn't a date. She fell asleep leaning against the wall, and I didn't want her to get a neck crick or fall over or something."

"So thoughtful." His voice dropped sarcasm like a torrential rain storm.

Asher sighed, not content this time. "Can we talk about this later? Let's just let her sleep and hash out our issues at home, okay?"

"How about you move your butt, and I'll be her pillow."

"Are you serious right now? That would wake her up. This isn't about a stupid dating competition, Chandler. This is about Holland's grandma almost dying. Holland has spent every extra minute taking care of her. She's exhausted. Can you pull your head out of your own crap for two seconds and take a look at that? Everything is not about you, you know?"

"Whatever, Asher; you're not in my head. You know you're just trying to get her to like you more than me. It might work for now, but watch your back 'cause I got some big stuff planned."

"Chandler," Asher's voice sounded tired, "I don't care if she likes you more than me. I care that she's having a hard time. If you wake her up, I will shave your head while you're sleeping, and I'm not even joking."

Chandler scoffed, and I heard some footsteps fade away. I didn't dare peek my eyes open to check if Chandler was still there. I wasn't quite ready for Asher to know that I'd heard everything they said.

I needed to think.

Something was stirring inside me. Something important. Chandler and Asher swirled around and around. That time Chandler helped me open my locker. Asher inviting me to sit with his friends. Chandler holding my hand at the movie. Asher's picnic date at the country club. Chandler canceling our date. Asher coming over to stay with me while my parents were at the hospital.

Wow.

I've been really stupid.

I opened my eyes and lifted my head, completely forgetting the part where I should have pretended like I was just waking up. Asher looked at me, his expression confused.

"Holland—"

I didn't let him finish. Before I could lose my nerve, I placed my hand on the back of his neck, moving his face closer to mine. He let out a light exhale, tickling my bottom lip. With a whole symphony orchestra conducting my emotions, I pressed my lips against his, trying to put everything I was feeling into that touch.

Asher didn't respond for a really long time. He might possibly have been in shock. I started to pull back, wondering if I'd made a huge mistake, when his other arm came around me, moving me impossibly close to his chest. His heart pounded against mine until our beats synced.

My thoughts stilled for once in my life. There was nothing in my head except a delicious buzzing. It didn't matter that I've never kissed a guy before or that I didn't really know what I was doing. I could have stayed in that moment for the rest of my life with Asher's lips moving on mine and his heartbeat in my ears.

Suddenly, Asher froze.

He untangled himself, grabbed my hand, and yanked me to my feet. He took off running, dragging me behind him like a child's pull toy. I was so disoriented that it was all I could do to put one foot in front of the other.

Asher led us through the office door. He paused, breathing heavily, in front of Mrs. Goddard's desk. "Good morning, Mrs. Goddard. Can I show Holland how to use the copy machine in the teacher's lounge?"

Mrs. Goddard didn't even look up from her keyboard. "Sure, Asher."

His grip tightened on my hand. "Thanks."

We turned a couple corners and opened a door marked Teacher's Lounge.

No one was inside.

Asher let go of my hand to shut the door. With his back to me, he rested his forehead on the door. "What just happened?"

"I was...going to ask you the same thing." I said, trying to catch my breath. My heart raced like I'd just done a hundred-yard dash.

He still didn't turn around. "Someone was coming. I didn't want you to get suspended for making out in the hall during fifth period." He took a shuddery breath. "Were we just making out in the hall during fifth period?"

With his back still turned to me, Asher didn't get to see the slow smile that spread across my face. For months I'd been in a state of constant confusion, and now I could see everything so clearly.

I knew exactly what I wanted.

Asher slowly turned, leaning his back against the door. His face was completely blank, but his eyes shone like blue flashlights. "Why did you kiss me?"

I pressed my lips together. "Why did you kiss me back?"

Asher's eyes slowly lowered to my mouth.

The space between us was seriously offending me. I closed the distance, throwing my arms around his neck. His arms wrapped around my waist, squeezing me like an anaconda so that I couldn't get a full breath.

I didn't kiss him this time, and he didn't kiss me. We just hung on like we were trying to say all the things without speaking any words.

After a couple minutes, Asher's arms slackened enough that I could lean back and see his face. I ran my fingers through the hair at the nape of his neck. I'd wanted to do that since the first time I saw him.

"Asher?"

His eyes were partly closed. "Hm?"

"I am seriously in something with you."

He looked at me, a smile curling his lips. "Something?"

"Yeah," I nodded, seriously. "It's not 'like'. It's more than that, and I don't know if it's love yet either. I've never been in love before. Have you?"

Asher shook his head.

"What about that girl, the other one everyone talks about that you and Chandler fought over?"

Asher took a long time to answer. His hands slid up and down my back in a very distracting way. "Monica. I liked her, but it was different than this. This is different."

"Are you in something with me, too?" I asked, teasing him.

Asher bent and kissed me lightly, like butterfly wings on my lips. "Correct answer: yes."

I leaned my cheek into his chest and squeezed as tight as I could. And that's when I remembered Chandler. Really, I probably should have remembered him sooner.

I stepped back, pulling myself out of Asher's arms. I couldn't think straight with him so close, and I definitely needed to straighten something out. "What about Chandler?"

A cloud went across Asher's face. "You're in something with him too."

It wasn't a question.

"No," I shook my head. "That's not it at all. I meant, what do we tell him? There's supposed to be more dates and a round table discussion, remember?"

Asher blinked. "You don't like Chandler?"

"Sure, I like him."

"I mean, you don't... You don't want to... You don't like him like..."

I took Asher's hand and held it in the space between us. "I think Chandler is a great guy and I was kind of swept away by him, but you are what I want, Asher. Just you."

It took a moment, then a smile spread across Asher's face. "Really?"

"Really, really."

Asher let out a heavy breath and leaned his head against the door. "I seriously can't believe it."

"Why not?"

"Chandler wins everything," he said to the ceiling. "Always. I've been preparing myself to not care when you told me you wanted to date Chandler instead of me. Even after you kissed me just now, I sort of expected that I'd have to share you with him."

I wrinkled my nose. "I'm not really a multiple guy kind of girl."

"You really…"

I squeezed his hand. "Believe it, buster."

"Even after that stupid date at the country club?" He closed his eyes for a long moment, then stared at me. "You can't seriously want to be with me after that."

I put my free hand on my hip. "If you can't believe it, how about you just *pretend* I'm crazy in love with you, okay? Like, fake it until you make it, you know? Pretend until it sinks in that I choose you over Chandler." I sighed as my hand dropped to my side. "Until then, I really need us to figure out what we're going to tell Chandler because I don't want to hurt him. But I also don't want to date him ever again."

Asher pressed his lips together. "Crazy in love, huh?"

"It could happen. You're pretty awesome."

He shook his head. "You really think that? It's so weird that you really think that, and it's even weirder that I'm starting to believe that it's true."

"Good. Now, what do we do?"

Asher sighed. "I really don't want to talk about Chandler right now."

"Come on, you big baby," I shoved him lightly. "This is the last time we ever have to talk about him, and then it can just be about us forever."

"Us." Asher savored the word.

I let go of his hand so I could pace and think while Asher had his moment. Chandler cared a lot about appearances. His man card was important. He was way competitive.

"Hey! How about this?" I stopped walking and lifted my hands. "How about we think of a way to make Chandler dump me? Like, he decides *he* doesn't like *me* anymore."

Asher thought for a moment, then grinned. "That is brilliant."

I loved the enthusiasm. "Would it work, though?"

"If we push all his buttons, I totally think we can make this work."

"Yeah? What can I do that he would hate the most? Here, I'll make a list." I found my phone and opened the notes app.

Asher pulled the phone out of my hand and set it on a table. "Let's talk about that in a minute."

He wrapped his arms around me, his fingers playing with the ends of my hair.

I sighed and melted into him.

We didn't talk again for way longer than a minute.

Chapter Twenty-Two

"We forge the chains we wear in life."
A Christmas Carol

For the next few days, every time Chandler had the phone, he texted me constantly. Pictures of himself working out, testimonials from other girls he's dated, questions and inquiries. 'What's your favorite color' came up multiple times. Chandler really was a nice guy; I could tell he was trying hard. He just had a major flaw.

He wasn't Asher.

We set up a date for the night before Runway Careers. I asked Chandler if I could plan it, and I was more than ready when he showed up.

"Hey, Holland. Whoa!" Chandler stepped back, his eyes huge.

I smiled like everything was normal. It's totally normal to borrow Dara's eighties throwback costume for a date. I donned a bright, neon pink mesh shirt over a white tee with a matching pink skirt and knee-high socks. Oh, and a side ponytail.

"Are you ready?"

"Are you?" His face slowly morphed into that look people get when they are trying not to throw up.

Perfect.

"Yeah, why?" I flounced by him towards the car.

He followed at a much slower, less-than-enthusiastic pace.

I opened my own door; he seemed to have forgotten that he usually did that for me. That's okay. This night was going to be a little overwhelming for him. I could cut him all kinds of slack. As soon as he was settled in the driver's seat, I announced the plan.

"There's a great Indie bookstore doing amateur poetry readings in fifteen minutes! Doesn't that sound fun? After that, I thought we could check out some other local bookstores. I'm trying to find a copy of *The History of the Kings of Britain*."

"Why?" His lip curled dramatically.

"Because it's hard to find, silly! It will be like a treasure hunt! Then we can do dinner, but I won't tell you where. I want that to be a surprise."

"Super," Chandler said.

I smiled.

It was, wasn't it?

The bookstore was surprisingly packed when we arrived. There was only standing room in the back, which went well with my purposes, but also made me wonder if the poetry reading was actually really good and this was going to backfire on me.

I had nothing to worry about.

Really.

About thirty minutes into it, I almost fell asleep standing up—something I didn't think was possible until that moment. Chandler let out a tortured sigh so often that it was like he didn't realize he was doing it anymore.

When they paused for an intermission, I had my smile all ready. "Wasn't that amazing! I just love amateur poetry. That one that compared *Star Wars* to daily life was so brilliant."

Chandler's smile was painful. Like, broken bone levels. "Uh-huh."

"We can stay for the second half, or we can start our book search. What do you want to do?"

"Book search," Chandler said quickly.

I think this was the first and last time in his entire life that he uttered those words in reference to something he wanted to do.

I gave him directions to the bookstore, a cute little one near the grocery store. Without even trying, I can generally spend at least an hour exploring a new bookstore. With Chandler slowly dying beside me, I pushed it to ninety minutes. And then on to the next. And the next. And the next.

Was it mean that the book we were looking for was obscure and also out of print?

It was definitely mean that I kept making him smell the books. I was almost sorry. Or, at least, I would have been if the look on his face wasn't so hilarious. He would probably rather go to a root canal appointment than be on this date.

"Gosh, I'm just so bummed none of these bookstores have the book I'm looking for. Do you think we should try the next one or go out to eat?"

"Eat," Chandler said. "Let's go eat. I'm starving."

Oh goodie.

I directed him to this restaurant my mom has been dying to try. Organic, vegan, gluten free, sugar free...

Chandler was going to love it.

And by that, I meant hate it with a fiery passion.

"I've never been here." he said as we pulled into the parking lot. "What is this place?"

"My mom found it," I said as I opened the car door. "It's supposed to be really good."

For you. As in, healthy. I was discovering that the key to being a little teeny tiny bit manipulative was to choose words carefully. Say as little as possible. Leave key things unsaid.

Chandler got the door to the restaurant for me, which was very nice of him considering what I was putting him through. A chalkboard sign told us to sit wherever we wanted. I chose a seat in the exact center of the eating area because the chances of people bumping into us as they squeezed around were much higher there.

A waiter joined us just a few moments later. His hair was in dreadlocks, and a tattoo of a tree went all the way up his arm.

Chandler couldn't stop looking at it.

The waiter dropped menus on the table and asked for our drink requests.

"I'll have water," I said with a smile and then held my breath.

"Do you have Diet Coke?" Chandler asked.

The waiter looked offended. "No."

"Pepsi?"

He put his hand with the pad of paper on his hip. "We don't participate in the sale of additive-packed beverages."

Chandler blinked. "What are the drink options?"

The waiter heaved a great sigh. "Water, carrot juice, wheatgrass juice, beet juice…"

Chandler held up a hand to get him to stop. "I'll take water. Water is fine."

When the waiter huffed off, Chandler picked up his menu like it was a dead thing. I heard a lot of muttering from behind the laminated paper. When Chandler put it down again, I greeted him with a toothy grin.

"Find something good?"

"The turkey wrap doesn't sound terrible."

That's because he didn't realize it said *tofurkey*.

"Cool," I said in an unintentional mimic of his favorite word. "I'm getting the vegetable babaganoush wrap."

"What the heck is babaganoush?"

The waiter set our waters in front of us and then took our orders with rolling eyes. My foot jiggled from the anticipation. When Chandler saw his dinner, he was either going to dump me on the spot or toss his cookies. Either way, it was going to be something big.

Conversation was stilted while we waited. I expected Chandler to lose all patience and explode, but he was deeply contemplative as he swirled his straw around the glass. My phone vibrated in my back pocket. I pulled it out discreetly to check.

An email from Asher. We stopped texting so Chandler wouldn't accidentally, or on purpose, read any of our texts when it was his phone day. I really wanted to read it, but I put my phone back without opening anything. I wasn't an actress like Dara; I wouldn't be able to keep it together if he said something humorous about this date night of horrors.

Our waiter dropped plates on the table and walked away without a word. I didn't even look at mine; I was so curious to see how Chandler would react.

At first, he stared. Then he poked it with his finger, his nose wrinkling. Finally, he got the courage to bend over and sniff.

He reeled back, almost knocking over the hipster group of college kids trying to get around him. Pretty much every one of them gave him a dirty look.

"What is this?" Chandler said in a horrible voice. "It smells like something died on my plate."

I picked up the ends of my wrap and took a bite like nothing was amiss. It wasn't awesome. Sure, the eggplant was bitter and it could use a round of salt, but I'd developed immunity to weird foods after living with my mom. I could pretty much eat anything without gagging.

Chandler watched me eat as if I had bats for ears. When I didn't die a gregarious death, he picked up his wrap super fast and took a bite.

"Ugh!" His tongue came out, along with half the food in his mouth. He reached for a napkin to wipe his tongue. "What is this?"

"Tofurkey wrap," I said calmly, taking another bite.

"I ordered the turkey." He looked ready to call the waiter over and pull out his dreads.

"No," I shook my head. "You ordered tofurkey. They don't have turkey; this place is vegan."

"Bless you."

I laughed. "Vegan means no meat, actually no animal products at all. You've heard that word before."

He just stared at me. "So, there's no meat? No meat in this whole place?"

I nodded. "Correct answer: yes."

"Then, this is... What did you call it?"

"Tofurkey. Tofu turkey."

"Tofu?"

I swear he turned green.

"It's not terrible." I tried hard to hide a smile. "Tofu is versatile. It just takes the flavor of whatever you put it with."

He opened his gluten free wrap to see what it was with. "What is this stuff?" He poked the paste under the tofurkey.

My best guess was some kind of bean paste. Maybe kidney bean based on the color. When I shared this opinion with him, Chandler swore under his breath. He pushed his food away, then stared at the table while I finished eating.

Our waiter brought the check, with a haughty glance at Chandler's untouched plate. "Was there something wrong with the tofurkey wrap?"

Chandler's glare might possibly have the power to give the waiter male pattern baldness at some future time. We wouldn't know for a few years, but I was pretty sure it was powerful enough to make it happen. Poor guy; he would really miss those dreads.

Chandler didn't say a word while he paid for our meal, when we got in the car, or when he drove me home. I had other things planned for our date, but it looked like Chandler had reached the very frayed end of his rope.

"See you at Runway Careers tomorrow," I said brightly when he pulled up into my driveway.

He grunted.

Once I was out of the car, he sped away. The tires actually squealed. No joke. It was thrilling. I'd never seen tires peel out like that in real life. When Chandler was out of sight, I opened my phone and read Asher's very sassy email. It was a good thing I hadn't read it sooner. I would have broken character for sure.

Before I went inside, I hit him back with a response.

Mission Accomplished

Asher emailed me first thing in the morning to let me know Chandler was super moody.

Then he asked me what career I chose.

I didn't answer right away. Nervous was making me second guess myself.

The phone rang while I was trying to decide what to say.

"Hey, Asher."

"Hey, baby," he said in a deep voice that was probably supposed to be sexy but was just super ridiculous.

I laughed.

"Come on, spill your guts, woman. What are you going to wear for your career?"

"You are such a girl!" I stalled. "Asking me what I'm wearing today. Do you want to coordinate outfits? Because I was thinking of a swimsuit, jeans, and three-inch heels."

"I'd like to see that sometime."

"Oh, boy." I rolled my eyes. "How about you tell me what you're going to wear."

"Correct answer: a button-up shirt and slacks."

"Slacks?" The only person I ever heard say that word was my grandma.

"Stop it." Asher's voice was fake stern. "I want to be like Mr. Derkins when I grow up."

"You want to yell at kids who run in the hall?"

"No, Hols. I want to teach high school history. Now, you."

How was that so easy for him to say? I want to teach history, no big deal. Mine felt like a big deal. The words kept getting stuck in my throat. I thought of Grandma's face when she told me how much she loved my stories.

"I want to be a writer." I took a deep breath to slow down my racing heart.

"No way."

"Yes." I nodded, trying on the feeling it gave me to admit that out loud. "That's what I want to do for a career."

"That's awesome, Hols! That is really, super cool. Have you written anything I can read?"

I hesitated. "Yes and no. I mean, I've written some things; I've been messing around a little, but I don't think I'm ready for anyone to read my writing yet."

"Well, when you are ready, I'm ready. More than ready. I'm totally prepared to be your biggest fan."

I laughed like he was silly, but something bubbled inside me. I was going to do this. I was going to figure out how to make writing a career. Nursing never made me feel this way. I was finally on the exact right track. "Asher, you are the best!"

"So true, though I notice you didn't say anything about my other qualities, like how hot I am. I really think that was an oversight you should take care of. Right now."

"Oh, my gosh, you weirdo. I'm going. I'll see you soon." I laughed around the words.

Seriously, Asher was the worst.

And, okay, the best too.

Mostly the best.

I hung up after Asher said good-bye and went to check on my family. Grandma was having a fabulous day, but I knew she would have come with us even if she wasn't. She wanted to be there, and I wanted her to see all the people she rallied to the cause. Plus, she'd enjoy watching my dad, her only son, walk the runway. Really, how many moms got to see that?

We all showed up a little early so I could help Tenley with last-minute chaos. I helped Grandma get settled and then went backstage.

Which was surprisingly chaos free.

I was expecting the tornado de Tenley like at the carnival, but she was wearing her power suit, chatting easily with an adult dressed up in doctor scrubs. When she saw me, she waved me over.

"Hey, Holland! This is my dad, Dr. Frost."

I shook his hand. "So nice to meet you."

"You as well."

Tenley said, "Did Asher find you?"

"I haven't seen him."

And there was the hairy eyeball. "And what is going on with you two? Don't tell me nothing because I know there's something. Asher is way too happy for nothing."

"You should have dressed up as a detective instead of a super, high-power executive," I teased.

"President." She sniffed. "Come on, tell me!"

I couldn't keep the grin from spreading. "I can't say anything until later."

"Later when?"

Basically after Chandler dumped me. Hopefully that was coming soon.

"I can't say that either."

"But," she waved her hand around in circles, "you guys worked everything out, yes?"

I grinned.

"That's a yes. Okay, find your boy toy and then go get your dad. We'll do prep about twenty minutes before go time. Also, tell your Grandma thank you for me. Because of her, this thing practically planned itself. There is literally nothing for us to do except wait."

"Awesome, I will!" I waved to her and her dad, then went looking for Asher. When I walked by an open door, a hand darted out and grabbed my arm. I didn't even have time to shriek as Asher pulled me into a storage closet and shut the door.

He cupped my face and kissed me until my lips began to tingle. "I missed you."

"You saw me yesterday."

"Too long," he breathed and kissed me again.

I kissed him back, then leaned my ear against his chest to enjoy the moment before we had to go.

Because we did have to go.

I couldn't think of a single workable scenario that played out with the two of us snuggling in the closet for the rest of the night.

"You smell so good." His nose nuzzled against my neck.

It seriously tickled.

And was beyond adorable.

"We need to go," I sighed.

"I know," he sighed back.

We both sighed again, then pulled apart. Asher squeezed my hand before he let it go, then he opened the door just a crack.

"The coast is clear. You go first. I'll count to ten and follow."

"This is so cloak and dagger." I slipped through the opening. "See you in a bit."

"Hey," he whispered, "if you get nervous up there, find me, okay? My family is sitting behind yours. You got this."

That's when I remembered neither of his parents were participating in the model runway. Part of me was disappointed; it would be nice to have him backstage, but the other part was glad that I could see him when I was out there. It helped, actually.

"Thanks, Asher."

There was a slight pause, and then he said, "Hey, Holland?"

"Yeah?"

"I think I'm falling in love with you."

Did he just say he was in love with me? I couldn't have heard that right. Wait, did I?

I whipped around. "What?"

Asher had already disappeared back into the closet. The only answer I got was a blank white door.

I stared at it for a moment, then smiled.

"I think I'm falling in love with you too," I whispered, then went to find my dad.

While we were waiting backstage for Runway Careers to start, I took the opportunity to examine all the 'models'. There were so many. People in scrubs and business suits, a few construction workers, waitresses and waiters, someone in paint-splattered clothes.

This was so stinking cool!

Marilyn Monroe linked her arm through mine. "Are you nervous?"

"Dara!" I leaned back to see her better. "Oh, my gosh. You look amazing!"

She fluffed her hair in a quasi humble way and smiled. "My mom."

A tall woman with Dara's cute nose held out a hand. "Holland, right? I'm so happy to meet you!"

"Me too!" I took in her long, flowy dress and apron with sewing scissors and measuring tape. "I mean, I'm happy to meet you too!"

She laughed. "This is a great thing you kids did. Thank you so much."

"It was really Tenley—" I started.

Dara squeezed my arm. "And your Grandma. We all worked really hard. Tenley just held the whip."

My dad walked in then, and headed right for us. I introduced him to Dara and Dara's mom. We were soon joined by Ethan, who wore a suit and carried an American flag, and his dad, who was in full army uniform; Ryker, who was in a basketball jersey, and his mom, who wore black pants and a polo with the name of a hotel on it; and Bryan, who wore a robe and bunny slippers, with his mom donning yoga pants and his dad in a police uniform.

"What's with the slippers?" Dara asked, her eyebrows raised. "Do you want to live in your parent's basement and play video games, for real?"

"No!" Bryan huffed. "I want to work from home as a coder."

I glanced at my dad, who shook his head indulgently. "Yeah, we should talk, son."

The noise on the other side of the curtain slowly faded. We all naturally hushed. The atmosphere had shifted enough that I could sense something was about to happen. Dara grabbed my hand.

"This is it!"

My stomach curdled.

"Deep breaths," Dara whispered. "And whatever you do, do not imagine the audience in their underwear. It's really not helpful at all."

I nodded and hoped she wasn't grossed out by how sweaty my palm was. Applause rang through the rafters, and then a voice.

"Welcome, ladies and gentlemen, students and families, to Runway Careers." Linus paused to let more applause run its course. "It is my pleasure to welcome you to this experience. Runway Careers isn't new to any of us, is it? I don't know if you noticed, but it's evolved over the years. What, with the professional DJ's and MC's and whatnot. That's all well and good, but every so often, it's nice to step back and figure out why we're doing things. It gives perspective.

"I've been asked to take you back to the roots of Runway Careers. When I was a junior in high school in the seventies, there wasn't a lot of talk of what we would do post schooling. You can imagine, there was a lot of living in the moment. When the war broke out in Vietnam, it was a hard slap for a lot of us. It made us look at life differently. With the help of many, many wonderful people in this community—including my dear wife, Ann—we put together Runway Careers to give purpose and hope to our generation. I don't know about the rest of you, but I never thought it would catch on the way it did. It seems there's not many people around here who haven't been touched by this event.

"I am deeply humbled and thankful to all of you for continuing this tradition year after year, for showing up, and for contributing. It's my hope that it will continue to bless the lives of high school students for many, many years in the future. Before I turn the mic over to these kids,

I want you to give a monstrous round of applause to the newly formed Extracurricular Club at Prescott High School for their efforts to bring us back to our roots with this event, and for Shawna Morriss for reminding us all what's important."

I gasped, and my eyes stung. I didn't know Linus was going to give Grandma a shout-out! That was seriously the sweetest thing. I wish I could see her face right now.

"Thank you all. Let the Runway Careers commence!"

There was more clapping and then Tenley's voice. "Thank you! I'd like to introduce my dad, Doctor…"

Her words faded as I went over what I planned to say about my dad. I was so nervous that the words jumbled all over my mind. Then I heard Asher's voice like he was standing right next to me.

You got this.

I got this.

I had this.

I could do this.

That little burst of a memory brought Confidence with it, and Confidence carried me through the curtain and to the microphone. I clutched it in my sweaty hand and looked over the crowd for Asher. He wasn't hard to find; his bright blue eyes were fixed on me.

And guess what?

He was falling in love with me.

I smiled. "My dad, Peter Morriss, is a computer coder. All you that like to shop on the Internet, you can thank my dad." I paused to let people finish laughing. "Without his coding genius, things would not go so smoothly online. He spends hours meticulously setting up and maintaining the codes he writes. He might be working at home, but believe me when I say he's working! Coding isn't a fluff job at all." As I explained the satisfaction in the challenge of coding, I watched my dad wiggle his tush down the runway. At the end, he pulled his laptop out from under his arm, opened it, and spun a slow circle. Then he struck a pose that would probably stay in my mind forever and strutted back toward me.

Who knew he was such a goof?

The applause after his performance was accented with a bunch of cat-calls.

And we were done.

Dad gave me a huge hug behind the curtain, then we took the brief transition to sneak back to our seats in the audience. I asked him ahead of time if that was okay; I really wanted to see the show as part of the audience.

I took the empty chair right in front of Asher. Chandler was probably nearby, so I didn't look at Asher or talk to him, but I knew he was there, and that was enough. A few minutes into Dara's introduction, he leaned forward. There wasn't much of a gap between the auditorium seats, so his exhale warmed the back of my neck.

Ryker, Bryan, and Ethan each took their turns. Tenley wanted the club to go first to sort of set the tone. Then a bunch of people I didn't know introduced their friend's or family member's career to the rest of us. Some were super nervous; others really hammed it up. I just sat there and loved every minute of it.

Then a boy with round glasses took the microphone, and something in me zinged. "Hey! This is my mom, Carmela Dewitt. But that's not her real name; that's her pen name."

A woman stepped out with her hair in a messy bun, carrying a stack of books under her arm. I was mesmerized as the boy described her day-to-day job of writing books for teenagers. The joys and the struggles, the triumphs and the failures.

The world around me faded for those short moments. It was like I was the only person in the audience. When Carmela turned and glanced down, she was looking at me.

This was it.

This was the moment everyone had been talking about. Maybe I was dabbling with the thought before, maybe I was maybe-ing. But now I knew. I had just found my career at Runway Careers.

I was such a statistic!

"Wow," Asher breathed against my hair.

Had he felt it too? I wanted to turn around and ask him, see what he thought, talk it all out. Maybe do all of that while sitting in his lap, running my hands through his perfect hair.

Instead, I sat through the rest of the show with my leg jiggling. I had to find Mrs. Dewitt and talk to her. I wanted to know everything about what she did.

Tenley thanked everyone for coming, announced that the career models would be in the foyer with the refreshments to answer questions, and then the lights came up. As much as I wanted to throw myself in Asher's arms and drag him to the foyer, I made myself focus on other things. It was going to take a minute to get Grandma moving, and I wanted to stick with her too.

"Holland?"

I looked up. "Chandler, hi."

Was it weird I'd forgotten all about him?

He looked me up and down. "What are you supposed to be?"

I guess my career wasn't as obvious as the full fireman getup he wore. "An author." I felt shy saying it, but also empowered.

This was what I wanted.

He put his hands on his hip and sighed heavily. "Yeah, I thought it was something like that."

Luckily, my brain wasn't completely mush from my transformative experience earlier. I caught Chandler's tone and felt a tingle in my pinkie finger. This was it; he was going to break up with me.

"Look, you're a hottie and everything, but I don't think this is going to work."

I widened my eyes as much as I could, trying to look innocent. "What's not going to work?"

His hand flickered between the two of us. "This, you and me. It's not going to work. We are obviously going in completely different directions."

"What do you mean?" I added a squeak to the last word.

"Don't make a scene, okay? Be cool. There's a lot of people here."

Which was pretty much the same thing as begging me to make a scene.

"Are you saying you don't want to date me anymore?" I raised my voice gradually so the last part was practically a shout.

"Holland."

"Chandler, you can't do this to me." I grabbed his hand and hung on like a spider monkey. "You can't leave me like this."

His eyes darted to the right and to the left. We were accumulating a pretty good-sized crowd. "Holland," he hissed.

"Please reconsider, Chandler. I'll change. I'll be cooler. I'll be whatever you want me to be. You can't quit on me now!" I was practically wailing, flinging my arms. I even got a few tears to squeeze out of the corner of my eyes. Laugh tears, but he didn't need to know that.

Tears were tears.

He pulled his hand away from mine, or he tried. I was holding on so tight that he had to use those big muscles to yank himself free, and then he almost smacked a passing man in the face. Chandler's neck was bright red.

"It's over. Don't call me." And then he pushed his way into the crowd, trying as hard as he could to get away from me.

I lifted both arms to his retreating back and cried, "Chandler, no! I can't live without you. Don't leave me. Chandlerrrrrrrrrrrrrrrrrrrrrrrrrrrrrrrrrrrrrrrrrrrrrrr."

He didn't turn around.

Which was really nice because I doubled over laughing, unable to contain it anymore. Asher took my hand and kissed it. "That was amazing. No, really. I filmed it. I'm going to play it when Chandler's acting like a butt."

That just made me laugh harder.

"Holland," Dara appeared at my side, her eyes bright, "I think you chose the wrong career."

I appreciated the compliment, especially because Dara knows her stuff, but I was sure I hadn't chosen wrong. I chose the perfect career for me, and I also chose the perfect guy for me. I might not be sure of a lot of things, but I was positive about that.

The crowd made its way to the foyer. As the aisle cleared, the twins helped Grandma into her wheelchair. Dad pushed it while the rest of us trailed behind like a mini parade.

"Holland, just a sec." Asher pulled me back a little, letting the others go ahead. I looked up at him, wondering what he was doing. He bent his head low so he didn't have to talk very loud. "I know you want to talk to Carmela super bad, but I have to know something."

I did want to talk to Carmela, but I also wanted to know what he was going to say. The look on his face gave my arms goosebumps.

"Did you mean it," he paused, his eyes searching my face, "when you said you're falling in love me?"

"You heard that?"

He nodded. "Did you mean it?"

Silly boy, was he *still* questioning? He should know by now that the *something* I thought I was falling into had now formed a very distinct shape.

A slow smile spread from one side of my face to the other.

"Correct answer: yes."

Acknowledgements

First of all, I have to thank Kaleb and Megan for naming their daughter Holland because it is seriously my new favorite name and this story wouldn't have been the same without it!

Shakespeare said a rose by any other name would smell as sweet but I'm positive this MC by any other name would not be nearly as adorable!

This book also wouldn't have been as adorable without my darling daughters and their willingness to brainstorm while they play Minecraft or watch cheesy romcoms. Multi-tasking, yay! They are just that good! You girls are my bestest friends. You make my story sooooooo much better. (Yes, that has a double meaning!)

Thank you, Publishing Team - Staci, Holli, Jason, and Bridget. You're like awesome fairy god-peoples who make my dreams come true over and over again with each book. There are no words to tell you how much I love you guys!

I'm so grateful for alpha readers, friends, and family members who keep me writing with their interest, feedback, encouragement and overall awesomeness. Thank you for being THERE.

And, of course, the biggest thank you to my very last crush. How much do I love you, Chad? Correct answer: twenty forty-three!

About the Author

Cori Cooper always knew she wanted to be an author, (though she still would have ADORED something like Runway Careers anyway), but it still took a lot of years to get the courage to give that a whirl. She doesn't believe in trying to change the past, so instead, she'll tell you this for free: Don't be afraid to try. You CAN do it. And never never NEVER give up! This applies to everything and anything you want to do.

Cori lives with her family in the magical Arizona Mountains, which she's pretty convinced is the setting for all the fairy tales.

Besides writing stories, she adores hanging out with her family, playing board games as long as she doesn't have to read the instructions, watching Jane Austen remakes unless they are too modern, baking without recipes which means frequent kitchen fails and collecting fuzzy knees socks that don't match.

Connect with Cori

Instagram, Bookbub, Goodreads, Pinterest, Facebook and her website, www.coristories.com

If you like this book - be sure to check out the others!

The Bake Believe Trilogy:
Bake Believe, Bake Off, Bake Happy

Senior Year at Cromer High books:
Sage Advice
The Importance of Being Roxie
The Perfect Girl for Kai
Gavin to the Rescue

Ways to Improve Bailey
One Quarter Villain
Tears into Gold
A Tale of Two Crushes
Darby's Cafe
Drama, Drama, Drama
Merry's Christmas

9 781953 491862